Curiosities of Olden Times

S. Baring-Gould

Curiosities of Olden Times

ISBN: 978-1-64799-602-4

PREFACE

An antiquary lights on many a curiosity whilst overhauling the dusty tomes of ancient writers. This little book is a small museum in which I have preserved some of the quaintest relics which have attracted my notice during my labours. The majority of the articles were published in 1869. I have now added some others.

Lew Trenchard,
September 1895

CONTENTS

THE MEANING OF MOURNING

A strip of black cloth an inch and a half in width stitched round the sleeve—that is the final, or perhaps penultimate expression (for it may dwindle further to a black thread) of the usage of wearing mourning on the decease of a relative.

The usage is one that commends itself to us as an outward and visible sign of the inward sentiment of bereavement, and not one in ten thousand who adopt mourning has any idea that it ever possessed a signification of another sort. And yet the correlations of general custom—of mourning fashions, lead us to the inexorable conclusion that in its inception the practice had quite a different signification from that now attributed to it, nay more, that it is solely because its primitive meaning has been absolutely forgotten, and an entirely novel significance given to it, that mourning is still employed after a death.

Look back through the telescope of anthropology at our primitive ancestors in their naked savagery, and we see them daub themselves with soot mingled with tallow. When the savage assumed clothes and became a civilised man, he replaced the fat and lampblack with black cloth, and this black cloth has descended to us in the nineteenth century as the customary and intelligible trappings of woe.

The Chinaman when in a condition of bereavement assumes white garments, and we may be pretty certain that his barbarous ancestor, like the Andaman Islander of the present day, pipeclayed his naked body after the decease and funeral of a relative. In Egypt yellow was the symbol of sorrow for a death, and that points back to the ancestral nude Egyptian having smeared himself with yellow ochre.

Black was not the universal hue of mourning in Europe. In Castile white obtained on the death of its princes. Herrera states that the last time white was thus employed was in 1498, on the death of Prince John. This use of white in Castile indicates chalk or pipeclay as the daub affected by the ancestors of the house of Castile in primeval time as a badge of bereavement.

Various explanations have been offered to account for the variance of colour. White has been supposed to denote purity; and to this day white gloves and hat-bands and scarves are employed at the funeral of a young girl, as in the old ballad of "The Bride's Burial":—

1

A garland fresh and fair
Of lilies there was made,
In signs of her virginity,
And on her coffin laid.
Six pretty maidens, all in white,
Did bear her to the ground,
The bells did ring in solemn swing
And made a doleful sound.

Yellow has been supposed to symbolise that death is the end of human hopes, because falling leaves are sere; black is taken as the privation of light; and purple or violet also affected as a blending of joy with sorrow. Christian moralists have declaimed against black as heathen, as denoting an aspect of death devoid of hope, and gradually purple is taking its place in the trappings of the hearse, if not of the mourners, and the pall is now very generally violet.

But these explanations are afterthoughts, and an attempt to give reason for the divergence of usage which might satisfy, but these are really no explanations at all. The usage goes back to a period when there were no such refinements of thought. If violet or purple has been traditional, it is so merely because the ancestral Briton stained himself with woad on the death of a relative.

The pipeclay, lampblack, yellow ochre, and woad of the primeval mourners must be brought into range with a whole series of other mourning usages, and then the result is something of an "eye-opener." It reveals a condition of mind and an aspect of death that causes not a little surprise and amusement. It is one of the most astonishing, and, perhaps, shocking traits of barbarous life, that death revolutionises completely the feelings of the survivors towards their deceased husbands, wives, parents, and other relatives.

A married couple may have been sincerely attached to each other so long as the vital spark was twinkling, but the moment it is extinguished the dead partner becomes, not a sadly sweet reminiscence, but an object of the liveliest terror to the survivor. He or she does everything that ingenuity can suggest to get him or herself out of all association in body and spirit with the late lamented. Death is held to be thoroughly demoralising to the deceased. However exemplary a person he or she may have been in life, after death the ghost is little less than a plaguing, spiteful spirit.

There is in the savage no tender clinging to the remembrance of the loved one, he is translated into a terrible bugbear, who must be evaded and avoided by every contrivance conceivable. This is due, doubtless, mainly to the inability of the uncultivated mind to

2

discriminate between what is seen waking from what presents itself in phantasy to the dreaming head. After a funeral, it is natural enough for the mourners to dream of the dead, and they at once conclude that they have been visited by his revenant. After a funeral feast, a great gorging of pork or beef, it is very natural that the sense of oppression and pain felt should be associated with the dear departed, and should translate itself into the idea that he has come from his grave to sit on the chests of those who have bewailed him.

Moreover, the savage associates the idea of desolation, death, discomfort, with the condition of the soul after death, and believes that the ghosts do all they can to return to their former haunts and associates for the sake of the warmth and food, the shelter of the huts, and the entertainment of the society of their fellows. But the living men and women are not at all eager to receive the ghosts into the family circle, and they accordingly adopt all kinds of "dodges," expedients to prevent the departed from making these irksome and undesired visits.

The Venerable Bede tells us that Laurence, Archbishop of Canterbury, resolved on flying from England because he was hopeless of effecting any good under the successor of Ethelbert, king of Kent. The night before he fled he slept on the floor of the church, and dreamed that St. Peter cudgelled him soundly for resolving to abandon his sacred charge. In the morning he awoke stiff and full of aches and pains. Turned into modern language, we should say that Archbishop Laurence was attacked with rheumatism on account of his having slept on the cold stones of the church. His mind had been troubled before he went to sleep with doubts whether he were doing right in abandoning his duty, and very naturally this trouble of conscience coloured his dream, and gave to his rheumatic twinges the complexion it assumed.

Now Archbishop Laurence regarded the Prince of the Apostles in precisely the light in which a savage views his deceased relatives and ancestors. He associates his maladies, his pains, with theirs, if he should happen to dream of them. If, however, when in pain, he dreams of a living person, then he holds that this living person has cast a magical spell over him.

Among nature's men, before they have gone through the mill of civilisation, plenty to eat and to drink, and some one to talk to, are the essentials of happiness. They see that the dead have none of these requisites, they consider that they are miserable without them. The writer remembers how, when he was a boy, and attended a funeral of a relative in November, he could not sleep all night—a bitter, frosty night—with the thought how cold it must be to the dead in the vault, without blankets, hot bottle, or fire. It was in vain

3

for him to reason against the feeling; the feeling was so strong on him that he was conscious of an uncomfortable expectation of the dead coming to claim a share of the blanket, fire, or hot bottle. Now the savage never reasons against such a feeling, and he assumes that the dead will return, as a matter of course, for what he cannot have in the grave.

The ghost is very anxious to assert its former rights. A widow has to get rid of the ghost of her first husband before she can marry again. In Parma a widow about to be remarried is pelted with sticks and stones, not in the least because the Parmans object to remarriage, but in order to scare away the ghost of No. 1, who is hanging about his wife, and who will resent his displacement in her affections by No. 2.

To the present day, in some of the villages of the ancient Duchy of Teck, in Würtemberg, it is customary when a corpse is being conveyed to the cemetery, for relatives and friends to surround the dead, and in turn talk to it—assure it what a blessed rest it is going to, how anxious the kinsfolk are that it may be comfortable, how handsome will be the cross set over the grave, how much all desire that it may sleep soundly and not by any means leave the grave and come haunting old scenes and friends, how unreasonable such conduct as the latter hinted at would be, how it would alter the regard entertained for the deceased, how disrespectful to the Almighty who gives rest to the good, and how it would be regarded as an admission of an uneasy conscience. Lively comparisons are drawn between the joys of Paradise and the vale of tears that has been quitted, so as to take away from the deceased all desire to return.

This is a survival of primitive usage and mode of thought, and has its analogies in many places and among diverse races.

The Dacotah Indians address the ghost of the dead in the same "soft solder," to induce it to take the road to the world of spirits and not to come sauntering back to its wigwam. In Siam and in China it is much the same; persuasion, flattery, threats are employed.

Unhappily all ghosts are not open to persuasion, and see through the designs of the mourners, and with them severer measures have to be resorted to. Among the Sclavs of the Danube and the Czechs, the bereaved, after the funeral, on going home turn themselves about after every few steps and throw sticks, stones, mud, even hot coals in the direction of the churchyard, so as to frighten the spirit back to the grave so considerately provided for it. A Finnish tribe has not even the decency to wait till the corpse is covered with soil; they fire pistols and guns after it as it goes to its grave, and lies in it.

In Hamlet, at the funeral of Ophelia, the priest says—

> For charitable prayers,
> Shards, flints, and pebbles should be thrown on her.

Unquestionably it must have been customary in England thus to pelt a ghost that was suspected of the intention to wander. The stake driven through the suicide's body was a summary and complete way of ensuring that the ghost would not be troublesome.

Those Finns who fired guns after a dead man had another expedient for holding him fast, and that was to nail him down in his coffin. The Arabs tie his legs together. The Wallacks drive a long nail through the skull; and this usage explains the many skulls that have been exhumed in Germany thus perforated. The Icelanders, when a ghost proved troublesome, opened the grave, cut off the dead man's head, and made the body sit on it. That, they concluded, would effectually puzzle it how to get about. The Californian Indians were wont to break the spine of the corpse so as to paralyse his lower limbs, and make "walking" impossible. Spirit and body to the unreasoning mind are intimately associated. A hurt done to the body wounds the soul. Mrs. Crowe, in her Night Side of Nature, tells a story reversing this. A gentleman in Germany was dying—he expressed great desire to see his son, who was a ne'er-do-well, and was squandering his money in Paris. At that same time the young man was sitting on a bench in the Bois de Boulogne, with a switch in his hand. Suddenly he saw his old father before him. Convinced that he saw a phantom, he raised his switch, and cut the apparition once, twice, and thrice across the face; and it vanished. At that moment the dying father uttered a scream, and held his hands to his face— "My boy! my boy! He is striking me again—again!" and he died. The Algonquin Indians beat the walls of the death-chamber to drive out the ghost; in Sumatra, a priest is employed with a broom to sweep the ghost out. In Scotland, and in North Germany, the chairs on which a coffin has rested are reversed, lest the dead man should take the fancy to sit on them instead of going to his grave. In ancient Mexico, certain professional ghost ejectors were employed, who, after a funeral, were invited to visit and thoroughly explore the house whence the dead had been removed, and if they found the ghost lurking about, in corners, in cupboards, under beds— anywhere, to kick it out. In Siberia, after forty days' "law" given to the ghost, if it be still found loafing about, the Schaman is sent for, who drums it out. He extorts brandy, which he professes to require, as he has to conduct the deceased personally to the land of spirits, where he will make it and the other guests so fuddled that they will forget the way back to earth.

In North Germany a troublesome ghost is bagged, and the bag emptied in some lone spot, or in the garden of a neighbour against whom a grudge is entertained.

Another mode of getting rid of the spirit of the dear departed is to confuse it as to its way home. This is done in various ways. Sometimes the road by which it has been carried to its resting-place is swept to efface the footprints, and a false track is made into a wood or on to a moor, so that the ghost may take the wrong road. Sometimes ashes are strewn on the road to hide the footprints. Sometimes the dead is carried rapidly three or four times round the house so as to make him giddy, and not know in which direction he is carried. The universal practice of closing the eyes of the dead may be thought to have originated in the desire that he might be prevented from seeing his way.

In many places it was, and is, customary for the dead body to be taken out of the house, not through the door, but by a hole knocked in the wall for the purpose, and backwards. In Iceland in the historic period this custom was reserved for such as died in their seats and not in their beds. One or two instances occur in the Sagas. In Corea, blinders made of black silk are put on the dead man's eyes, to prevent him from finding his way home.

Many savage nations entirely abandon a hut or a camp in which a death has occurred for precisely the same reason—of throwing out the dead man's spirit.

It was a common practice in England till quite recently for the room in which a death had occurred to be closed for some time, and this is merely a survival of the custom of abandoning the place where a spirit has left the body. The Esquimaux take out their dying relatives to huts constructed of blocks of ice or snow, and leave them there to expire, for ghosts are as stupid as they are troublesome, they have no more wits than a peacock, they can only find their way to the place where they died.

Other usages are to divert a stream and bring the corpse in the river-bed, or lay it beyond running water, which according to ghost-lore it cannot pass. Or again, fires are lighted across its path, and it shrinks from passing through flames. As for water, ghosts loathe it. Among the Matamba negroes a widow is flung into the water and dipped repeatedly so as to wash off the ghost of the dead husband, which is supposed to be clinging to her. In New Zealand, among the Maoris, all who have followed the corpse dive into water so as to

6

throw off the ghost which is sneaking home after them. In Tahiti, all who have assisted at a burial run as hard as they can to the sea and take headers into it for the same object. It is the same in New Guinea. We see the same idea reduced to a mere form in ancient Rome, where in place of the dive through water, a vessel of water was carried twice round those who had followed the corpse, and they were sprinkled. The custom of washing and purification after a funeral practised by the Jews is a reminiscence of the usage, with a novel explanation given to it.

In the South Pacific, in the Hervey Islands, after a death men turn out to pummel and fight the returning spirit, and give it a good drubbing in the air.

Now, perhaps, the reader may have been brought to understand what the sundry mourning costumes originally meant. They were disguises whereby to deceive the ghosts, so that they might not recognise and pester with their undesired attentions the relatives who live. Indians who are wont to paint themselves habitually, go after a funeral totally unbedecked with colour. On the other hand, other savages daub themselves fantastically with various colours, making themselves as unlike what they were previously as is possible. The Coreans when in mourning assume hats with low rims that conceal their features.

The Papuans conceal themselves under extinguishers made of banana leaves. Elsewhere in New Guinea they envelop themselves in a wickerwork frame in which they can hardly walk. Among the Mpongues of Western Africa, those who on ordinary occasions wear garments walk in complete nudity when suffering bereavement. Valerius Maximus tells us that among the Lycians it was customary in mourning for the men to disguise themselves in women's garments.

The custom of cutting the hair short, and of scratching and disfiguring the face, and of rending the garments, all originated from the same thought—to make the survivors irrecognisable by the ghost of the deceased. Plutarch asserts that the Sacæ, after a death, went down into pits and hid themselves for days from the light of the sun. Australian widows near the north-west bend of the Murray shave their heads and plaster them with pipeclay, which, when dry, forms a close-fitting skull-cap. The spirit of the late lamented on returning to his better half either does not recognise his spouse, or is so disgusted with her appearance that he leaves her for ever.

There is almost no end to the expedients adopted for getting rid of the dead. Piles of stones are heaped over them, they are buried deep in the earth, they are walled up in natural caves, they are enclosed in megalithic structures, they are burned, they are sunk in the sea. They are threatened, they are cajoled, they are hoodwinked. Every sort of trickery is had recourse to, to throw them off the scent of home and of their living relations.

The wives, horses, dogs slain and buried with them, the copious supplies of food and drink laid on their graves, are bribes to induce them to be content with their situation. Nay, further—in very many places no food may be eaten in the house of mourning for many days after an interment. The object of course is to disappoint the returning spirit, which comes seeking a meal, finds none, comes again next day, finds none again, and after a while desists from returning out of sheer disgust.

A vast amount of misdirected ingenuity is expended in bamboozling and bullying the unhappy ghosts; but the feature most striking in these proceedings is the unanimous agreement in considering these ghosts as such imbeciles. When they put off their outward husk, they divest themselves of all that cunning which is the form that intelligence takes in the savage. Not only so, but although they remember and crave after home comforts, they absolutely forget the tricks they had themselves played on the souls of the dead in their own lifetime; they walk and blunder into the traps which they had themselves laid for other ghosts in the days of their flesh.

Perhaps the lowest abyss of dunder-headedness they have been supposed to reach is when made to mistake their own identity. Recently near Mentone a series of prehistoric interments in caves have been exposed. They reveal the dead men as having had their heads daubed over with red oxide of iron. Still extant races of savages paint, plaster, and disfigure their dead. The prehistoric Greeks masked them. The Aztecs masked their deceased kings, and the Siamese do so still. We cannot say with absolute certainty what the object is—but we are probably not far out when we conjecture the purpose to be to make the dead forget who they are when they look at their reflection in the water. There was a favourite song sung some sixty years ago relative to a little old woman who got "muzzy." Whilst in this condition some naughty boys cut her skirts at her knees. When she woke up and saw her condition, "Lawk!" said the little old woman, "this never is me!" And certain ancient peoples treated their dead in something the same way; they disguised and disfigured them so that each ghost waking up might exclaim, "Lawk! this never is me!" And so having lost its identity, did not consider it had a right to revisit its old home and molest its old acquaintances.

CURIOSITIES OF CYPHER

In 1680, when M. de Louvois was French Minister of War, he summoned before him one day a gentleman named Chamilly, and gave him the following instructions:

"Start this evening for Basle, in Switzerland; you will reach it in three days; on the fourth, punctually at two o'clock, station yourself on the bridge over the Rhine, with a portfolio, ink, and a pen. Watch all that takes place, and make a memorandum of every particular. Continue doing so for two hours; have a carriage and post-horses awaiting you;, and at four precisely mount, and travel night and day till you reach Paris. On the instant of your arrival, hasten to me with your notes."

De Chamilly obeyed; he reached Basle, and on the day and at the hour appointed, stationed himself, pen in hand, on the bridge. Presently a market-cart drives by; then an old woman with a basket of fruit passes; anon, a little urchin trundles his hoop by; next an old gentleman in blue top-coat jogs past on his gray mare. Three o'clock chimes from the cathedral tower. Just at the last stroke, a tall fellow in yellow waistcoat and breeches saunters up, goes to the middle of the bridge, lounges over, and looks at the water; then he takes a step back and strikes three hearty blows on the footway with his staff. Down goes every detail in De Chamilly's book. At last the hour of release sounds, and he jumps into his carriage. Shortly before midnight, after two days of ceaseless travelling, De Chamilly presented himself before the minister, feeling rather ashamed at having such trifles to record. M. de Louvois took the portfolio with eagerness, and glanced over the notes. As his eye caught the mention of the yellow-breeched man, a gleam of joy flashed across his countenance. He rushed to the king, roused him from sleep, spoke in private with him for a few moments, and then four couriers who had been held in readiness since five on the preceding evening were despatched with haste. Eight days after, the town of Strasbourg was entirely surrounded by French troops, and summoned to surrender: it capitulated and threw open its gates on the 30th of September 1681. Evidently the three strokes of the stick given by the fellow in yellow costume, at an appointed hour, were the signal of the success of an intrigue concerted between M. de Louvois and the magistrates of Strasbourg, and the man who executed this mission was as ignorant of the motive as was M. de Chamilly of the motive of his.

Now this is a specimen of the safest of all secret

9

communications, but it can only be resorted to on certain rare occasions. When a lengthy despatch is required to be forwarded, and when such means as those given above are out of the question, some other method must be employed. Herodotus gives us a story to the point: it is found also, with variations, in Aulus Gellius.

"Histiæus, when he was anxious to give Aristagoras orders to revolt, could find but one safe way, as the roads were guarded, of making his wishes known: which was by taking the trustiest of his slaves, shaving all the hair from off his head, and then pricking letters upon the skin, and waiting till the hair grew again. This accordingly he did; and as soon as ever the hair was grown, he despatched the man to Miletus, giving him no other message than this: 'When thou art come to Miletus, bid Aristagoras shave thy head, and look thereon.' Now the marks on the head were a command to revolt."—Bk. v. 35.

In this case no cypher was employed; we shall come, now, to the use of cyphers.

When a despatch or communication runs great risk of falling into the hands of an enemy, it is necessary that its contents should be so veiled, that the possession of the document may afford him no information whatever. Julius Cæsar and Augustus used cyphers, but they were of the utmost simplicity, as they consisted merely in placing D in the place of A; E in that of B, and so on; or else in writing B for A, C for B, etc.

Secret characters were used at the Council of Nicæa; and Rabanus Maurus, Abbot of Fulda and Archbishop of Mayence in the ninth century, has left us an example of two cyphers, the key to which was discovered by the Benedictines. It is only a wonder that any one could have failed to unravel them at the first glance. This is a specimen of the first:

.Nc.p.t v:rs:··s B::n.f:c.. :rch. gl::r.::s.q:.:: m:rt.r.s

The secret of this is that the vowels have been suppressed and their places filled by dots,—one for i, two for a, three for e, four for o, and five for u. In the second example, the same sentence would run—Knckpkt vfrsxs Bpnkfbckk, etc., the vowel-places being filled by the consonants—b, f, k, p, x. By changing every letter in the alphabet, we make a vast improvement on this last; thus, for instance, supplying the place of a with z, b with x, c with v, and so on. This is the system employed by an advertiser in a provincial paper which I took up the other day in the waiting-room of a station, where it had been left by a farmer. As I had some minutes to spare, before the train was due, I spent them in deciphering the following:

Jp Sjddjzb rza rzdd ci sijmr, Bziw rzdd xr ndzt:

and in ten minutes I read: "If William can call or write, Mary will be glad."

A correspondence was carried on in the Times during May 1862 in cypher. I give it along with the explanation.

Wws.—Zy Efpdolj T dpye l wpeepc ez mjcyp qzc jzf—xlj T daply qfwwj zy lww xleepcd le esp tyepcgtph? Te xlj oz rzzo. Ecfde ez xj wzgp—T lx xtdpclmwp. Hspy xlj T rz ez Nlyepcmfcj tq zywj ez wzzv le jzf.—May 8.

This means—"On Tuesday I sent a letter to Byrne for you. May I speak fully on all matters at the interview? It may do good. Trust to my love. I am miserable. When may I go to Canterbury if only to look at you?"

A couple of days later Byrne advertises, slightly varying the cypher:

Wws.—Sxhrdktg hdbtewxcv "Tmwxqxixdc axzt" udg pcdewtg psktgexhtbtce ... QNGCT. "Discover something Exhibition-like for another advertisement. Byrne."

This gentleman is rather mysterious: I must leave my readers to conjecture what he means by "Exhibition-like." On Wednesday came two advertisements, one from the lady—one from the lover. WWS. herself seems rather sensible—

Tydeplo zq rztyr ez nlyepcmfcj, T estyv jzf slo xfns mpeepc delj le szxp lyo xtyo jzfc mfdtypdd.—WWS., May 10.

"Instead of going to Canterbury, I think you had much better stay at home and mind your business."

Excellent advice; but how far likely to be taken by the eager wooer, who advertises thus?—

Wws.—Fyetw jzfc qlespc lydhpcd T hzye ldv jzf ez aczgp jzf wzgp xp. Efpdol ytrse le zyp znwznv slpp I dectyr qczx esp htyozh qzc wpeepcd. Tq jzt lcp yze lmwp le zyp T htww hlte. Rzo nzxqzce jzf xj olcwtyr htqp.

"Until your father answers I won't ask you to prove you love me. Tuesday night at one o'clock have a string from the window for letters. If you are not able at one I will wait. God comfort you, my darling wife."

Only a very simple Romeo and Juliet could expect to secure secrecy by so slight a displacement of the alphabet.

When the Chevalier de Rohan was in the Bastille, his friends wanted to convey to him the intelligence that his accomplice was dead without having confessed. They did so by passing the following words into his dungeon, written on a shirt: "Mg dulhxcclgu ghj yxuj; lm ct ulgc alj." In vain did he puzzle over the cypher, to which he had not the clue. It was too short: for the shorter a cypher letter, the more difficult it is to make out. The light faded, and he tossed on his

11

hard bed, sleeplessly revolving the mystic letters in his brain, but he could make nothing out of them. Day dawned, and, with its first gleam, he was poring over them: still in vain. He pleaded guilty, for he could not decipher "Le prisonnier est mort; il n'a rien dit."

Another method of veiling a communication is that of employing numbers or arbitrary signs in the place of letters, and this admits of many refinements. Here is an example to test the reader's sagacity:

§ †431 45 2+9 +§51 4= 8732+ 287 45 2+9 †¶=+

I just give the hint that it is a proverb.

The following is much more ingenious, and difficult of detection.

	A	B	C	D	E	F	G	H
A	a	d	g	k	n	q	t	x
B	b	e	h	l	o	r	u	y
C	c	f	i	m	p	s	w	z

Now suppose that I want to write England; I look among the small letters in the foregoing table for e, and find that it is in a horizontal line with B, and vertical line with B, so I write down BB; n is in line with A and E, so I put AE; continue this, and England will be represented by Bbaeacbdaaaeab. Two letters to represent one is not over-tedious: but the scheme devised by Lord Bacon is clumsy enough. He represented every letter by permutations of a and b; for instance,

A was written *aaaaa*, B was written *aaaab*

C   "   "   *aaaba*, D   "   "   *aabaa*

and so through the alphabet. Paris would thus be transformed into abbba, aaaaa, baaaa, abaaa, baaab. Conceive the labour of composing a whole despatch like this, and the great likelihood of making blunders in writing it!

A much simpler method is the following. The sender and receiver of the communication must be agreed upon a certain book of a specified edition. The despatch begins with a number; this indicates the page to which the reader is to turn. He must then count the letters from the top of the page, and give them their value numerically according to the order in which they come; omitting those which are repeated. By these numbers he reads his despatch. As an example, let us take the beginning of this article: then, I = 1, n = 2, w = 3, h = 4, e = 5, m = 6, d = 7, l = 8, o = 9, u = 10, v = 11, omitting to count the letters which are repeated. In the middle of the communication the page may be varied, and consequently the numerical significance of each letter altered. Even this could be read with a little trouble; and the word "impossible" can hardly be said to apply to the deciphering of cryptographs.

A curious instance of this occurred at the close of the sixteenth century, when the Spaniards were endeavouring to establish relations between the scattered branches of their vast monarchy, which at that period embraced a large portion of Italy, the Low Countries, the Philippines, and enormous districts in the New World. They accordingly invented a cypher, which they varied from time to time, in order to disconcert those who might attempt to pry into the mysteries of their correspondence. The cypher, composed of fifty signs, was of great value to them through all the troubles of the "Ligue," and the wars then desolating Europe. Some of their despatches having been intercepted, Henry IV. handed them over to a clever mathematician, Viete, with the request that he would find the clue. He did so, and was able also to follow it as it varied, and France profited for two years by his discovery. The court of Spain, disconcerted at this, accused Viete before the Roman court as a sorcerer and in league with the devil. This proceeding only gave rise to laughter and ridicule.

A still more remarkable instance is that of a German professor, Hermann, who boasted, in 1752, that he had discovered a cryptograph absolutely incapable of being deciphered, without the clue being given by him; and he defied all the savants and learned societies of Europe to discover the key. However, a French refugee, named Beguelin, managed after eight days' study to read it. This cypher—though we have the rules upon which it is formed before us—is to us perfectly unintelligible. It is grounded on some changes of numbers and symbols; numbers vary, being at one time multiplied, at another added, and become so complicated that the letter e, which occurs nine times in the paragraph, is represented in eight different ways; n is used eight times, and has seven various signs. Indeed the same letter is scarcely ever represented by the same figure; but this is not all: the character which appears in the place of i takes that of n shortly after; another symbol for n stands also for t. How any man could have solved the mystery of this cypher is astonishing.

Now let me recommend a far simpler system, and one which is very difficult of detection. It consists of a combination of numbers and letters. Both parties must be agreed on an arrangement such as that in the second line below, for on it all depends.

1   2   3   4   5   6   7   8   9   10

13

Now in turning a sentence such as "The army must retire" into cypher, you count the letters which make the sentence, and find that T is the first, H the second, E the third, A the fourth, R the fifth, and so on. Then look at the table. T is the first letter; 4 answers to 1; therefore write the fourth letter in the place of T; that is A instead of T. For h the second, put the seventh, which is y; for E, take the second, h. The sentence will stand "Ayh utsr emma yhutsr." It is all but impossible to discover this cypher.

All these cryptographs consist in the exchange of numbers or characters for the real letters; but there are other methods quite as intricate, which dispense with them.

The mysterious cards of the Count de Vergennes are an instance. De Vergennes was Minister of Foreign Affairs under Louis XVI., and he made use of cards of a peculiar nature in his relations with the diplomatic agents of France. These cards were used in letters of recommendation or passports which were given to strangers about to enter France; they were intended to furnish information without the knowledge of the bearers. This was the system. The card given to a man contained only a few words, such as:

ALPHONSE D'ANGEHA

Recommandé à Monsieur
le Comte de Vergennes, par le Marquis de Puysegur,
Ambassadeur de France à la Cour de Lisbonne.

The card told more tales than the words written on it. Its colour indicated the nation of the stranger. Yellow showed him to be English; red, Spanish; white, Portuguese; green, Dutch; red and white, Italian; red and green, Swiss; green and white, Russian; etc. The person's age was expressed by the shape of the card. If it were circular, he was under 25; oval, between 25 and 30; octagonal, between 30 and 45; hexagonal, between 45 and 50; square, between 50 and 60; and oblong showed that he was over 60. Two lines placed below the name of the bearer indicated his build. If he were tall and lean, the lines were waving and parallel; tall and stout, they converged; and so on. The expression of his face was shown by a flower in the border. A rose designated an open and amiable countenance, whilst a tulip marked a pensive and aristocratic appearance. A fillet round the border, according to its length, told whether the man was bachelor, married, or widower. Dots gave information as to his position and fortune. A full stop after his name showed that he was a Catholic; a semicolon, that he was a Lutheran; a comma, that he was a Calvinist; a dash, that he was a Jew; no stop indicated him as an Atheist. So also his morals and character were pointed out by a pattern in the angles of the card, such as one of these:

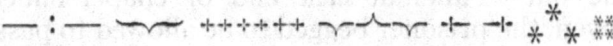

Consequently, at one glance the minister could tell all about his man, whether he were a gamester or a duellist; what was his purpose in visiting France; whether in search of a wife or to claim a legacy; what was his profession—that of physician, lawyer, or man of letters; whether he were to be put under surveillance or allowed to go his way unmolested.

We come now to a class of cypher which requires a certain amount of literary dexterity to conceal the clue.

During the Great Rebellion, Sir John Trevanion, a distinguished Cavalier, was made prisoner, and locked up in Colchester Castle. Sir Charles Lucas and Sir George Lisle had just been made examples of, as a warning to "malignants": and Trevanion has every reason for expecting a similar bloody end. As he awaits his doom, indulging in a hearty curse in round Cavalier terms at the canting, crop-eared scoundrels who hold him in durance vile, and muttering a wish that he had fallen, sword in hand, facing the foe, he is startled by the entrance of the gaoler who hands him a letter:

"May't do thee good," growls the fellow; "it has been well looked to before it was permitted to come to thee."

Sir John takes the letter, and the gaoler leaves him his lamp by which to read it:

Worthie Sir John—Hope, that is ye beste comfort of ye afflictyd, cannot much, I fear me, help you now. That I wolde saye to you, is this only: if ever I may be able to requite that I do owe you, stand not upon asking of me. 'Tis not much I can do: but what I can do, bee you verie sure I wille. I knowe that, if dethe comes, if ordinary men fear it, it frights not you, accounting it for a high honour, to have such a rewarde of your loyalty. Pray yet that you may be spared this soe bitter, cup. I fear not that you will grudge any sufferings: only if bie submission you can turn them away, 'tis the part of a wise man. Tell me, an if you can, to

15

do for you any thinge that you wolde have done. The general goes back on Wednesday. Restinge your servant to command.

R. T.

Now this letter was written according to a preconcerted cypher. Every third letter after a stop was to tell. In this way Sir John made out—"Panel at east end of chapel slides." On the following even, the prisoner begged to be allowed to pass an hour of private devotion in the chapel. By means of a bribe, this was accomplished. Before the hour had expired, the chapel was empty— the bird had flown.

An excellent plan of indicating the telling letter or word is through the heading of the letter. "Sir," would signify that every third letter was to be taken; "Dear sir," that every seventh; "My dear sir," that every ninth was to be selected. A system, very early adopted, was that of having pierced cards, through the holes of which the communication was written. The card was then removed, and the blank spaces filled up. As for example:

> My dear X.—[The lines I now send you are forwarded by the kindness of the [Bearer, who is a friend. [Is not the message delivered yet [to my Brother? [Be quick about it, for I have all along [trusted that you would act with discretion and despatch.—Yours ever,
>
> Z.

Put your card over the note, and through the piercings you will read: "The Bearer is not to be trusted."

The following letter will give two totally distinct meanings, according as it is read, straight through, or only by alternate lines:—

> Mademoiselle,—
>
> Je m'empresse de vous écrire pour vous déclarer que vous vous trompez beaucoup si vous croyez que vous êtes celle pour qui je soupire. Il est bien vrai que pour vous éprouver, Je vous ai fait mille aveux. Après quoi vous êtes devenue l'objet de ma raillerie. Ainsi ne doutez plus de ce que vous dit ici celui qui n'a eu que de l'aversion pour vous, et qui aimerait mieux mourir que de se voir obligé de vous épouser, et de changer le dessein qu'il a formé de vous haïr toute sa vie, bien loin de vous aimer, comme il vous l'a déclaré. Soyez donc désabusée, croyez-moi; et si vous êtes encore constante et persuadée que vous êtes aimée vous serez encore plus exposée à la risée de tout le monde, et

particulièrement de celui qui n'a jamais été et ne sera jamais

Votre ser'teur M. N.

We must not omit to mention Chronograms. These are verses which contain within them the date of the composition. In 1885 I built a boathouse by a lake in my grounds. A friend wrote the following chronogram for it, which I had painted, and affixed to the house:

> Thy breaD upon the Waters Cast
> In CertaIn trust to fInd.
> sInCe Well thou know'st God's eye doth Mark,
> Where fIshes' eyes are bLind.

This gives the date.

$$D = 500 + W = 510 + C = 610 + I = 611$$
$$+ C = 711 + I = 712 + I = 713 + I = 714$$
$$+ C = 814 + W = 824 + M = 1824$$
$$+ W = 1834 + I = 1835 + L = 1885.$$

The W represents two V's, i.e. 10.

A very curious one was written by Charles de Bovelle: we adapt and explain it:—

The heads of a mouse and five cats	M.CCCCC
Add also the tail of a bull	L
Item, the four legs of a rat	IIII
And you have my date in full	M.CCCCCL.IIII
	(1554.)

It is now high time that we show the reader how to find the clue to a cypher. And as illustration is always better than precept, we shall exemplify from our own experience. With permission, too, we shall drop the plural for the singular.

Well! My friend Matthew Fletcher came into a property some years ago, bequeathed to him by a great-uncle. The old gentleman had been notorious for his parsimonious habits, and he was known through the county by the nickname of Miser Tom. Of course every one believed that he was vastly rich, and that Mat Fletcher would come in for a mint of money. But, somehow, my friend did not find the stores of coin on which he had calculated, hidden in worsted stockings or cracked pots; and the savings of the old man which he did light upon consisted of but trifling sums. Fletcher became firmly persuaded that the money was hidden somewhere; where he could

17

not tell, and he often came to consult me on the best expedient for discovering it. It is all through my intervention that he did not pull down the whole house about his ears, tear up every floor, and root up every flower or tree throughout the garden, in his search after the precious hoard. One day he burst into my room with radiant face.

"My dear fellow!" he gasped forth, "I have found it!"

"Found what?—the treasure?"

"No—but I want your help now," and he flung a discoloured slip of paper on my table.

I took it up, and saw that it was covered with writing in cypher.

"I routed it out of a secret drawer in Uncle Tom's bureau!" he exclaimed. "I have no doubt of its purport. It indicates the spot where all his savings are secreted."

"You have not deciphered it yet, have you?"

"No. I want your help; I can make neither heads nor tails of the scrawl, though I sat up all night studying it."

"Come along," said I, "I wish you joy of your treasure. I'll read the cypher if you give me time." So we sat down together at my desk, with the slip of paper before us. Here is the inscription:—

$$
\begin{array}{c}
\text{D}\\
+\ \lambda282\S9\beta9\beta2\lambda\chi879 +)789(9(88\P7 \div)8\!-\!2\S + 9 \times \S2\S\\
\text{A}\\
-29\S\!-\!)^{*}\overline{8228}\chi7\lambda\theta82\lambda^{*}9\chi79 + \times\S\!-\!7\!-\!\beta^{*}\gamma\chi9\!-\!\P\\
\text{B}\\
\beta\!-\!\chi8)\lambda \times 8\|\S8\!-\!= \overline{8\chi2\S8\chi82\S}\!-\! + \S8\chi8\!\!\rightarrow\!\!\S8\chi82\S82\\
8\chi7\beta\lambda(2\S8 + 8\|\chi\lambda = \lambda\P9\beta\|\lambda7 = -\! +\! \div\!-\!\chi881\lambda\chi^{*}92\\
-\! + 2.
\end{array}
$$

"Now," said I, "the order of precedence among the letters, according to the frequency of their recurrence, is this, e a o i t d h n r s u y c f g l m w b k p q x z. This, however, is their order, according to the number of words begun by each respectively, s c p a d i f b l b t, etc. The most frequent compounds are th, ng, ee, ll, mm, tt, dd, nn. Pray, Matthew, do you see any one sign repeated oftener than the others in this cryptograph?"

"Yes, 8; it is repeated twenty-three times," said Fletcher, after a pause.

"Then you may be perfectly satisfied that it stands for e, which is used far oftener than any other letter in English. Next, look along the lines and see what letters most frequently accompany it."

18

"2 § undoubtedly; it follows 8 in several places, and precedes it in others. In the third line we have 2 § 8—82 §—§ 8—8 § 8 and then 2 § 8 again."

"Then we may fairly assume that 2 § 8 stands for the."

"The, to be sure," burst forth Fletcher. "Now the next word will be money. No! it can't be, the e will not suit; perhaps it is treasure, gold, hoard, store."

"Wait a little bit," I interposed. "Now look what letters are doubled."

"88 and 22," said my friend Mat.

"And please observe," I continued, "that where I draw a line and write A you have e, then double t, then e again. Probably this is the middle of a word, and as we have already supposed 2 to stand for t, we have—ette—, a very likely combination. We may be sure of the t now. Near the end of the third line, there is a remarkable passage, in which the three letters we know recur continually. Let us write it out, leaving blanks for the letters we do not know, and placing the ascertained letters instead of their symbols. Then it stands—eχtheχeth—heχeheχ ethe—. Now here I have a χ repeated four times, and from its position it must be a consonant. I will put in its place one consonant after another. You see r is the only one which turns the letters into words.—erthereth—here . here the— surely some of these should stand out distinctly separated—er there th— here . here the. Look! I can see at once what letters are wanting; th— between there and here must be than, and then ✠ here is, must be, where. So now I have found these letters,

8 = e, r = t, § = h, χ = r, — = a, + = n, ✠ = w,

and I can confirm the χ as r by taking the portion marked A— etter. Here we get an end of an adjective in the comparative degree; I think it must be better."

"Let us next take a group of cyphers higher up; I will pencil over it D. I take this group because it contains some of the letters which we have settled —eathn. Eath must be the end of a word, for none begins with athn, thn, or hn. Now what letter will suit eath? Possibly h, probably d."

"Yes," exclaimed Fletcher, "Death, to be sure. I can guess it all: 'Death is approaching, and I feel that a solemn duty devolves upon me, namely, that of acquainting Matthew Fletcher, my heir, with the spot where I have hidden my savings.' Go on, go on."

"All in good time, friend," I laughed. "You observe we can confirm our guess as to the sign) being used for d, by comparing the passage—29§—)*8228χ, which we now read, t. had better. But t. had better is awkward; you cannot make 9 into o; 'to had,' would be no sense."

19

"Of course not," burst forth Fletcher. "Don't you see it all? I had better let my excellent nephew know where I have deposited—"

"Wait a bit," interrupted I; "you are right, I believe. I is the signification of 9. Let us begin the whole cryptograph now:— N.tethi.i.t.re.ind.e."

"Remind me!" cried Fletcher.

"You have it again," said I. "Now we obtain an additional letter besides m, for t. remind me is certainly to remind me. We must begin again:—Note thi.i. to remind me."

"This is," called out my excited friend, whose eyes were sparkling with delight and expectation. "Go on; you are a trump!"

"These, then, are our additional letters:—) = d, 7 = m, β = s, 9 = i, λ = o. To remind me i.i. ee. m. death ni.h; for m. death, I read my death, and i.i. ee., I guess to be, if I feel. So it stands thus:— 'Note.—This is to remind me, if I feel my death nigh, that I had better——'"

I worked on now in silence; Fletcher, leaning his chin on his hands, sat opposite, staring into my face with breathless anxiety. Presently I exclaimed:

"Halves, Mat! I think you said halves!"

"I—I—I—I—my very dear fellow, I——"

"A very excellent man was your uncle; a most exemplary——"

"All right, I know that," said Fletcher, cutting me short. "Do read the paper; I have a spade and pick on my library table, all ready for work the moment I know where to begin."

"But, really, he was a man in a thousand, a man of such discretion, such foresight, so much——"

Down came Fletcher's hand on the desk.

"Do go on!" he cried; and I could see that he was swearing internally; he would have sworn ore rotundo, only that it would have been uncivil, and decidedly improper.

"Very well; you are prepared to hear all?"

"All! by Jove! by Jingo! prepared for everything."

"Then this is what I read," said I, taking up my own transcript:—

"Note.—This is to remind me, if I feel my death nigh, that I had better move to Birmingham, as burials are done cheaper there than here, where the terms of the Necropolis Company are exorbitant."

Fletcher bounded from his seat. "The old skinflint! miser! screw!"

"A very estimable and thrifty man, your great-uncle."

"Confounded old stingy—," and he slammed the door upon himself and the substantive which designated his uncle.

20

And now, the very best advice I can give to my readers, is to set to work at once on the simple cypher given near the commencement of this paper, and to find it out.

STRANGE WILLS

Of course we ought to begin with Adam's will, the father of all wills; and if we could produce that patriarchal document, we should undoubtedly find in it the germs of all the merits, faults, and eccentricities of wills to come. But, unfortunately, though a testament of Adam does exist, it is a forgery; and nothing will convince us to the contrary,—not even the Mussulman tradition, which asserts that on the occasion of our great forefather beginning to make his bequests, seventy legions of angels brought him sheets of paper and quill pens, nicely nibbed, all the way from Paradise; and that the Archangel Gabriel set-to his seal as witness. What! four hundred and twenty thousand sheets of paper!—surely a needless consumption of material, when there was nothing to be bequeathed but a view over the hedge of an impracticable garden.

If we pass to Noah's testament, we are again among the apocrypha. In it, Noah portions his landed property, the globe, into three shares, one for each son: America is not included in the division for obvious reasons. It was left for "manners" sake, and manners has never got it.

The testament of the twelve Patriarchs must be glanced at, which is received as semi-canonical by the Armenian Church, though it is unquestionably apocryphal. Reuben speaks of sleep as having been in Paradise, only a sweet ecstasy; whereas, after the Fall, it has become a continually recurring image of death. Simeon bewails his former hostility to Joseph; and relates, that his brother's bones were preserved in the Royal treasury of Egypt. Levi is oracular; Judah rejoices in the sceptre left to his race; Issachar unfolds the future of the Jews; Zebulun relates that the brethren supplied themselves with shoes from the money which they got by the sale of Joseph. There seems to be some allusion to this tradition in the Prophet Amos (ii. 6; viii. 6). Dan recommends his posterity to practise humility; Naphtali sees visions; Gad is contrite; Asher prophesies the coming of the Messiah; Joseph, the incarnation; Benjamin, the destruction of the Temple.

21

There exists a very curious and ancient testament of Job, which was discovered and published by Cardinal Maï, in 1839; it relates many details which we may look for in vain in the Canonical Book. In it Job's faithful wife, when reduced to the utmost poverty, sells the hair of her head to procure bread for her husband.

What a remarkable document a will is! It is the voice of a man now dead, coming back in the hush of a darkened house—from the vault, low and hoarse as an echo. It speaks, and people hearken; it commands, and people obey; law supports and enforces its wishes; no power on earth can alter it. We expect to hear the voice calm, earnest, and speaking true judgment; terrible indeed if it breaks out with a snarl of hate—more terrible still if it gibbers and laughs a hollow, ghost-like laugh. For, surely, the most solemn moment of a life is that when the will is written: that will, which is to speak for man when the voice is passed as a dream; when the heart which devises it has ceased to throb; the head which frames it has done with thinking—under the fresh mould; the hand which pens it has been pressed, thin and white, against a cold shroud, to moulder with it; surely he who, at such a moment, can write words of hate must have a black heart, but he who ventures then to gibe and jest must have no heart at all.

There is some truth in the old ghost-creed; man can return after death; he does so in his will. He comes to some, as Jupiter came to Danaë, in a shower of gold; to others, as a blighting spectre, whose promised treasures turn to dust. What excitement the reading of a will causes in a family! and what interest does the world at large take in the bequests of a person of position! The last words of great men seem always to have possessed a peculiar value in the eyes of the people.

"Live, Brutus, live!" shouts the Roman mob in Julius Cæsar; but on hearing what Cæsar's will promises, how

> To every Roman citizen he gives,—
> To every several man,—seventy-five drachmas.
> His private arbours, and new-planted orchards,
> On this side Tiber: he hath left them you,
> And to your heirs for ever;——

then the mob changes note, and with one voice shouts, "To Brutus, to Cassius;—burn all!"

Testamenta hominum speculum esse morum vulgo creditur.—Plin. jun., 8 Ess. 18.

So they are! They are the last touch of the brush in the great picture of civilisation, manners, and customs, lightening it up.

Would that space permitted me to enter into the history of wills: a few curious particulars alone can we admit.

To die without having made a will was formerly regarded with horror. A very common custom in the Middle Ages was that of leaving considerable benefactions to the Church. This was well enough, but the clergy were not satisfied until it was made compulsory.

Ducange says that neglect of leaving to the Church indicated a profanity which deserved punishment by a refusal of the rites of the last sacraments and burial. The clergy of Brittany, in the fourteenth century, claimed a third of the household goods; the death-bed became ecclesiastical property in the diocese of Auxerre; and Clement V. settled the claims of the Church by deciding that the parish priest might take as his perquisite a ninth of all the movables in the house of the dead man, after the debts of the deceased had been paid off.

A sufficiency of historical notes. I will proceed at once—perhaps somewhat strangely—to give the reader a specimen of a will coming decidedly under the heading of this article. It is that of a Pig. The will is ancient enough. S. Jerome, in his "Prœmium on Isaiah," speaks of it, saying, that in his time (fourth century) children were wont to sing it at school, amidst shouts of laughter. Alexander Brassicanus, who died in 1539, was the first to publish it; he found it in a MS. at Mayence. Later, G. Fabricius gave a corrected edition of it from another MS. found at Memel, and, since then, it has been in the hands of the learned. The original is in Latin; I translate, modifying slightly one expression and omitting one bequest:

> I, M. Grunnius Corocotta Porcellus, have made my testament, which, as I can't write myself, I have dictated.
>
> Says Magirus, the cook: "Come along, thou who turnest the house topsy-turvy, spoiler of the pavement, O fugitive Porcellus! I am resolved to slaughter thee to-day."
>
> Says Corocotta Porcellus: "If ever I have done thee any wrong, if I have sinned in any way, if I have smashed any wee pots with my feet; O Master Cook, grant pardon to thy suppliant!"
>
> Says the cook Magirus: "Halloo, boy! go, bring me a carving-knife out of the kitchen, that I may make a bloody Porcellus of him."
>
> Porcellus is caught by the servants, and brought out to execution on the xvi. before the Lucernine Kalends,

23

just when young colewortsprouts are in plenty, Clybaratus and Piperatus being Consuls.

Now when he saw that he was about to die, he begged hard of the cook an hour's grace, just to write his will. He called together his relations, that he might leave to them some of his victuals; and he said:

I will and bequeath to my papa, Verrinus Lardinus, 30 bush. of acorns.

I will and bequeath to my mamma, Veturina Scrofa, 40 bush. of Laconian corn.

I will and bequeath to my sister, Quirona, at whose nuptials I may not be present, 30 bush. of barley.

Of my mortal remains, I will and bequeath my bristles to the cobblers, my teeth to squabblers, my ears to the deaf, my tongue to lawyers and chatterboxes, my entrails to tripemen, my hams to gluttons, my stomach to little boys, my tail to little girls, my muscles to effeminate parties, my heels to runners and hunters, my claws to thieves; and, to a certain cook, whom I won't mention by name, I bequeath the cord and stick which I brought with me from my oak-grove to the sty, in hopes that he may take the cord and hang himself with it.

I will that a monument be erected to me, inscribed with this, in golden letters:

M. Grunnius Corocotta Porcellus, who lived 999 years,—six months more, and he would have been 1000 years old.

Friends dear to me whilst I lived, I pray you to have a kindness towards my body, and embalm it well with good condiments, such as almonds, pepper, and honey, that my name may be named through ages to come.

O my masters and my comrades, who have assisted at the drawing up of this testament, order it to be signed.

(Signed) Lucanicus.	Celsanus.
Pergillus.	Lardio.
Mystialicus.	Offellicus.

Cymatus.

Whilst on this subject we might say a word about the epitaph on the mule of P. Crassus; or about that written by Rapin on the ass, which, poor fellow, was eaten whilst in the flower of his age, during the siege of Paris, in 1590; or about Joachim du Bellay, who composed an epitaph on his cat; or about Justus Lipsius, who erected mausoleums for his three cats—Mopsus, Saphisus, and Mopsulus; but we are not writing on epitaphs or gravestones.

We proceed to give a few instances of animals which have received legacies.

If it is a keen trial for a husband to leave his wife, for a young man to be taken from his pleasures, or a commercial man from his business, can we wonder at old ladies feeling the wrench sharp which tears them from the society of their dear cats—the companions of their spinsterhood or widowhood; or at old bachelors being distressed at having to part with their faithful dogs?—to part with them for ever, too, unless we believe in the suggestion of Bishop Butler and Theodore Parker, that there is a future for beasts, and enjoy the confidence of Mr. Sewell of Exeter College, who dedicated one of his published poems "To my Pony in Heaven."

The Count de la Mirandole, who died in 1825, left a legacy to his favourite carp, which he had nourished for twenty years in an antique fountain standing in his hall. In low life we find the same love for an animal displayed by a peasant of Toulouse, in 1781, who doted on his old chestnut horse, and left the following will:

> I declare that I institute my chestnut horse sole legatee, and I wish him to belong to my nephew N.

This testament was attacked, but, curiously enough, it received legal confirmation.

The following clause from a will was in the English papers for March 1828:

> I leave to my monkey, my dear, amusing Jackoo, the sum of 10l. sterling, to be enjoyed by him during his life; it is to be expended solely in his keep. I leave to my faithful dog, Shock, and to my beloved cat, Tib, 5l. sterling a-piece, as yearly pension. In the event of the death of one of the aforesaid legatees, the sum due to him shall pass to the two survivors, and on the death of one of these two, to the last, be he who he may. After the decease of all parties, the sum left them shall belong to my daughter G——, to whom I show this preference, above all my children, because she has a large family and finds a difficulty in filling their mouths and educating them.

But a more curious case still is that of Mr. Berkley of Knightsbridge, who died 5th May 1805. He left a pension of £25 per annum to his four dogs. This singular individual had spent the latter part of his life wrapped in the society of his curs, on whom he lavished every mark of affection. When any one ventured to remonstrate with him for expending so much money on their

25

maintenance, or suggested that the poor were more deserving of sympathy than those mongrel pups, he would reply: "Men assailed my life: dogs preserved it." This was a fact, for Mr. B. had been attacked by brigands in Italy, and had been rescued by his dog, whose descendants the four pets were. When he felt his end approaching, he had his four dogs placed on couches by the sides of his bed. He received their last caresses, extended to them his faltering hand, and breathed his last between their paws. According to his desire, the busts of these favoured brutes were sculptured at the corners of his tomb.

In 1677, died Madame Dupuis, who, under her maiden name of Mademoiselle Jeanne Felix, had been known as a great musician. Her will was so extraordinary and malicious that it was nullified. To it was attached a memorandum, which is still more extraordinary. We shall not quote the passages wherein she vilifies her son-in-law, imputing to him every vice she can think of, but translate the final clause:

> I pray Mademoiselle Bluteau, my sister, and Madame Calogne, my niece, to take care of my cats. Whilst these two live, they shall have thirty sous a month, that they may be well fed. They must have, twice a day, meat soup of the quality usually served on table; but they must be given it separately, each having his own saucer. The bread must not be crumbled in the soup, but cut up into pieces about the size of hazel-nuts, or they cannot eat it. When boiled beef is put into the pot with the soaked bread, some thin slices of raw meat must be put in as well, and the whole stewed till it is fit for eating. When only one cat lives, half the money will suffice. Nicole Pigeon shall take care of the cats, and cherish them. Madame Calogne may go and see them.

Certainly people show their love in different ways. Councillor Winslow of Copenhagen (d. 24th June 1811) ordered by will that his carriage horses should be shot, to prevent their falling into the hands of cruel masters.

We need only mention the "cat and dog" money, which is yearly given to six poor weavers' widows of the names of Fabry or Ovington, at Christ Church, Spitalfields, and which, according to tradition, was left in the first instance for the support of cats and dogs; and remind our readers of the cow and bull benefactions in several English parishes, where money has been left to the parish to provide cattle whose milk may go to the poor. The poor have been often remembered by testators, as our numerous almshouses, benefactions, and doles prove.

It were difficult to choose a better sample of a charitable bequest, which could properly come under our title, than the following simple and touching will of a French priest, Jean Certain, curé of a little parish in the Côte d'Or, who died in 1740, worth some £1200:

> I brought with me nothing into my parish but my cassock and breviary,—these I leave to my heirs: the rest I bequeath to the poor of my parish.

Wives, poor bodies! do not come off well, for a crabbed husband will sometimes control and torment his good woman after he is dead and buried, or even play a bitter jest, as did one man, who left his wife 500 guineas, but with the stipulation that she was not to enjoy it till after her death, when the sum was to be expended on her funeral. Or, as the author of the following:

> Since I have had the misfortune of having had to wife Elizabeth M——, who, since our marriage, has tormented me in a thousand ways; and since, not content with showing her contempt for my advice, she has done everything that lay in her power to render my life a burden to me; so that Heaven seems only to have sent her into the world for the purpose of getting me out of it the sooner; and since the strength of Samson, the genius of Homer, the prudence of Augustus, the skill of Pyrrhus, the patience of Job, the subtlety of Hannibal, the vigilance of Hermogenes, would not suffice to tame the perversity of her character; and since nothing can change her, though we have lived separated for eight years, without my having gained anything by it but the loss of my son, whom she has spoiled, and whom she has persuaded to abandon me altogether; weighing carefully and attentively all these considerations, I have bequeathed, and do bequeath, to the aforesaid Elizabeth M——, my wife, one shilling.

The clause in Shakespeare's will must not be forgotten:

> I gyve unto my wief, my second-best bed, with the furniture, and nothing else.

We hope that this was not intended as a spiteful jest; but men are irritable, and women are so trying! The best bed would not have been a bad gift, as the grand four-poster was an expensive article in Elizabethan days; but the second-best seems rather a paltry legacy. However, as we are perfectly sure to have the noble army of

Shakespearean commentators down upon us if we venture to impute other than the highest and purest of motives to their idol, for the sake of peace we are perfectly willing to believe the bed to have been the most valuable gift that could have been made,—that sovereigns, roses, and angels were stitched into the coverlets and stuffed into the pillows; just as the miser Tolam bequeathed:

> To my sister-in-law, four old stockings which are under my bed, on the right.
> *Item:* To my nephew, Tarles, two more old stockings.
> *Item*: To Lieut. John Stone, a blue stocking, and my red cloak.
> *Item*: To my cousin, an old boot, and a red flannel pocket.
> *Item*: To Hammick, my jug without a handle.

Imagine the disgust of the legatees, till Hammick kicking the jug, smashed it, and out rolled a quantity of sovereigns. The stockings, boot, and flannel pocket were soon seized now, and found to be as auriferous as the old pot. Now why should not the second-best bed left to Mrs. Shakespeare have been as valuable a bequest?

Whilst talking about beds, let us not forget a very odd story. In the earlier part of this century, there lived in the neighbourhood of Caen, in Normandy, a Juge de Paix, M. Halloin, a great lover of tranquillity and ease; so much so indeed, that, as bed is the article of furniture most adapted to repose, he rarely quitted it, but made his bed-chamber a hall of audience, in which he exercised his functions of Justice of Peace, pronouncing sentence, with his head resting on a pillow, and his body languidly extended on the softest of feather-beds. However, his services were dispensed with, and he devoted himself for the remaining six years of his life to still greater ease. Feeling his end approach, M. Halloin determined on remaining constant to his principle, and showing to the world to what an extent he carried his passion for bed. Consequently, his last will contained a clause expressing his desire to be buried at night, in his bed, comfortably tucked in, with pillows and coverlets as he had died. As no opposition was raised against the execution of this clause, a huge pit was sunk, and the defunct was lowered into his last resting-place, without any alteration having been made in the position in which death had overtaken him.

Boards were laid over the bed, that the falling earth might not disturb this imperturbable quietist.

Many testators leave directions for the treatment of their bodies: some are over-solicitous for their preservation, whilst others choose to show their contempt for that body, which, after all, will rise again. Dr. Ellerby, the Quaker, for instance, bequeathed his lungs to one friend and his brains to another, with a threat that he would haunt them if they refused to accept the legacy. Others, from motives of humility, act somewhat similarly. The Emperor Maximilian I. willed that his hair should be shorn, and his teeth brayed in a mortar and then burned publicly in his chapel; also that his body should be buried in a sack with quicklime, beneath the foot-pace of the altar of S. George at Neustadt, so that his heart might be beneath the celebrant's feet. His intentions were carried out at the time; but afterwards his remains were translated to Inspruck, and they now lie under that goodly monument raised by Ferdinand I., his deeds graven tenderly in white marble about him, and eight-and-twenty mighty bronze paladins and princes standing guard about the choir wherein he sleeps.

If some folk leave injunctions about their bodies, others are as particular about their names. Henry Green, for instance, by will dated 22nd December 1679, gave to his sister, Catharine Green, during her life, all his lands in Melbourne, Derby, and after her decease to others in trust, upon condition that the said Catharine Green should give four green waistcoats to four poor women in a green old age, every year, such green waistcoats to be lined with green galloon lace, and to be delivered to the said poor women on or before 21st December, yearly, that they might be worn on Christmas Day.

That the good men do may live after them, at least on their tombstones, has induced some to leave money as bribes to the writers of their epitaphs. The Abbé de la Rivière, son of an appraiser of wood, who became Bishop-duke of Langres, devised 100 écus for that purpose. But La Monnoye wrote the following:

> Here lies a notable personage,
> Of family proud, of ancient lineage;
> His virtues unnumbered, his knowledge profound,
> Remarkably humble, remarkably wise;—
> Come, come! for twenty-five pound,
> I've told enough lies!

Another clause in the Abbé's will deserves to be recorded, from its pithiness:

> To my steward, I leave nothing; because he has been
> in my service for eighteen years.

This reminds one of an anecdote told of the Cardinal Dubois, whose servants came to him every New Year's Day to present their congratulations, and to receive a New Year's box. When the steward came in his turn, the Cardinal said to him:

Monsieur, I present you with all that you have stolen from me.

The pleasure of receiving a legacy must be generally mingled with pain, more or less intense, according to the nearness of relationship of the deceased, or the affection we have had for him: but, when a plump legacy drops into our laps from a totally unexpected quarter, and left by one for whom we did not care, or possibly whom we did not know,—the amount of pain must be very minute. Such a case was that of a lady who came in for a large fortune from an eccentric individual to whom she had never spoken, though she had seen him at the opera, or in the park. The wording of the will was:

> I supplicate Miss B—— to accept my whole fortune, too feeble an acknowledgment of the inexpressible sensations which the contemplation of her adorable nose has produced on me.

The following is as curious. A good citizen of Paris, who died about 1779, inserted this clause in his will:

> Item: I leave to M. l'Abbé Thirty-thousand-men, 1200 livres a year: I do not know him by any other name, but he is an excellent citizen, who certified me in the Luxembourg, that the English, that ferocious people which dethrones its monarchs, will soon be destroyed.

On opening the testament, the executors were sorely puzzled to know who this Abbé Thirty-thousand-men could possibly be. At last, several people deposed that this citizen, a sworn enemy of the English and a great politician, had been wont every day to march up and down the Allé des Larmes in the Luxembourg; there he used to meet with an Abbé who had as great an abhorrence of the English as himself, and who was perpetually urging:—"Those English rascals aren't worth a straw. 30,000 men only are wanted,—30,000 men raised,—30,000 embarked,—30,000 landed,—and London would be in the hands of 30,000 men. A mere trifle!"

This was verified, and the legacy was delivered over to the intrepid Abbé, who had little dreamed of the spoil his 30,000 men were to bring him.

There is a question which we have been asking ourselves repeatedly, and which we now put before the reader. Is it possible to classify these wills? We have tried to do so, and have failed in every attempt. First, we have distributed them according to the bequests contained in them;—legacies of money, goods, animals, persons. There is no reason which can justify such an arbitrary system. Then again, when we arrange them according to the motives of the testator, as, wills indited by a perverted moral sense, or those composed under the influence of an aberration of the intellect, then we are obliged to exclude that of Corocotta Porcellus, of Jean Certain, beside many others, which can hardly be forced into position under either of these heads. And it is because the mind of man is too intricate, his motives too involved, his feelings too transient, his principles too obscure, for us to divide and subdivide the actions springing from them, as we can settle the classes of molluscs, or determine the genera of butterflies,—that in this paper we have attempted nothing of the kind. For wills are, as has been shown, as diverse as the hearts of men, of which they are the transcripts. An anatomist may dissect the heart, may name and register every muscle and fibre,—but he can tell us nothing of the motives which impelled that heart to throb faster, or chilled it to a sudden stillness. The bitterness of hate has left no poison in its cavities, in it the fleeting passion has set no seal, emotion left no trace, pity relaxed no nerve. The impulses which brought forth so full a leafage of action are lost, as the sap from the bare tree.

So surely as the berry indicates the soundness of the root, the flower of the bulb, so does man's last will tell of the goodness or foulness of the heart which conceived it. The cankered root sends up only a sickly germ, which brings forth no fruit in due season; whilst the wine that maketh glad the heart of man, the oil which maketh him a cheerful countenance, and the bread that strengthens his heart, have burst from roots which mildew has never marred, nor worm fretted.

QUEER CULPRITS

According to Jewish law, "If an ox gore a man or a woman that they die, then the ox shall be surely stoned, and his flesh shall not be eaten: but the owner of the ox shall be quit." After giving this command, Moses proceeds to enforce the doctrine of the responsibility of the beast's owner, and to ensure his punishment, should he wittingly let a dangerous animal run loose; also to make provision for his security under some extenuating circumstances. These commands were carried into the laws of mediæval Europe; the jurists, at the same time, introducing refinements of their own, and enforcing them in numerous cases, which afford matter for curious inquiry, and are full of technicalities and peculiarities, at once amusing and instructive, as throwing light on the customs and habits of thought in those times.

Now take the case of a child injured by a sow, or a man killed by a bull: the trial was conducted in precisely the same manner as though sow and bull were morally criminal. They were apprehended, placed before the ordinary tribunal, and given over to execution.

Again: an inroad of locusts or snails takes place. Common law is helpless, it may pronounce judgment, but who is to execute its decrees? Temporal power being palpably unavailing, the spiritual tribunal steps in; the decision of the magistrates being useless, perhaps excommunication may suffice. This, then, was an established maxim. If the criminal could be reached, he was handed over to the ordinary courts of justice; if, however, the matter was beyond their control, he fell within the jurisdiction of Ecclesiastical Courts. Poor culprit, not a loophole left by which to escape!

Let us consider the manner of proceeding under the former circumstance. A bull has caused the death of a man. The brute is seized and incarcerated; a lawyer is appointed to plead for the delinquent; another is counsel for the prosecution. Witnesses are bound over, the case is heard, and sentence is given by the judge, declaring the bull guilty of deliberate and wilful murder; and, accordingly, that it must suffer the penalty of hanging or burning.

The following cases are taken from among numerous others, and will afford examples:

A.D. 1266. A pig burned at Fontenay-aux-Roses, near Paris, for having devoured a child.

1386. A judge at Falaise condemned a sow to be mutilated in its leg and head, and then to be hanged, for having lacerated and killed a child. It was executed in the square, dressed in man's clothes. The execution cost six sous, six deniers, and a new pair of gloves for the executioner, that he might come out of the job with clean hands.

1389. A horse tried at Dijon, on information given by the magistrates of Montbar, and condemned to death, for having killed a man.

1499. A bull was condemned to death at Cauroy, near Beauvais, for having in a fury "occis" a little boy of fourteen or fifteen years old.

A farmer of Moisy let a mad bull escape. The brute met and gored a man so severely that he only survived a few hours. Charles,

32

Count de Valois, having heard of the accident whilst at his château of Crépy, ordered the bull to be seized and committed for trial. This was accordingly done. The officers of the Count de Valois gathered all requisite information, received the affidavits of witnesses, established the guilt of the bull, condemned it to be hanged, and executed it on the gibbet of Moisy-le-Temple. The death of the beast thus expiated that of the man. But matters did not stop here. An appeal against the sentence of the Count's officers was lodged before the Candlemas parliament of 1314—drawn up in the name of the Procureur de l'Hôpital at Moisy, declaring the officers to have been incompetent judges, having no jurisdiction within the confines of Moisy, and as having attempted to establish a precedent. The parliament received and investigated the appeal, and decided that the condemnation of the bull was perfectly just, but found that the Count de Valois had no judicial rights within the territory of Moisy, and that his officers had acted illegally in taking part in the affair.

Here is a list of the expenses incurred on the occasion of a sow's execution for having eaten a child:—

To the expenditure made for her whilst in jail	6 sols
Item. To the executioner, who came from Paris to Meulan to put the criminal to death, by orders of the bailiff and the Procureur du Roi	54 sols
Item. To a conveyance for conducting her to execution	6 sols
Item. To cords to tie and bind her	2 sols 8 deniers
Item. To gloves	2 deniers

The charter of Eleanora, drawn up in 1395, and entitled "Carta de logu," containing the complete civil and criminal code for Sardinia, enjoins that oxen and cows, whether wild or domesticated, may be legally killed when they are taken marauding. Asses convicted of similar delinquencies—common enough, by the way— are treated more humanely. They are considered in the same light as thieves of a higher order in society. The first time that an ass is found in a cultivated field not belonging to its master, one of its ears is cropped. If it commits the same offence again, it loses the second ear; should the culprit be hardened in crime, and inveterate enough to trespass a third time, it is not hanged, does not even lose its tail, but is confiscated to the Crown and goes to swell the royal herd.

During the fourteenth and fifteenth centuries, the guilty animals suffered death on the gallows, and our sires considered that such a punishment must strike terror into the minds of all cattle-owners and jobbers, so as effectually to prevent them from suffering their beasts to stray at large over the country. Later on, however, these capital condemnations were done away with, the proprietor of the animal was condemned to pay damages, and the criminal was killed without trial.

One more specimen, and we shall pass to cases coming under Ecclesiastical Courts.

Country folk believe still that cocks lay eggs. This is an old superstition, people holding, formerly, that from these accursed eggs sprang basilisks, or horrible winged serpents.

Gross relates, in his Petite Chronique de Bâle, that in the month of August 1474, an abandoned and profligate cock of that town was accused of the crime of having laid one of these eggs, and was brought before the magistrates, tried, convicted, and condemned to death.

The court delivered over the culprit to the executioner, who burned it publicly, along with its egg, in a place called Kohlenberger, amidst a great concourse of citizens and peasants assembled to witness such a ludicrous execution.

The poor cock no doubt suffered on account of the belief prevalent at the period that it was in league with the devil. A cock was the offering made by witches at their sabbaths, and as these eggs were reputed to contain snakes—reptiles particularly grateful to devils—it was taken as a proof of the cock having been engaged in the practice of sorcery.

The annals of Ireland relate that in 1383 a cock was convicted of a similar offence in that island, and that it suffered at the stake; the heat of the flames burst the egg, and there issued forth a serpent-like creature, which, however, perished in the fire.

We shall pass now to the second part of our subject—namely, proceedings against snails, flies, mice, moles, ants, caterpillars, etc.

It has frequently happened, in all parts of the world, that an unusual number of vermin have made their appearance and destroyed the garden produce, or that flies have been so abundant as to drive the cattle mad from their bites. In such cases the sufferers had recourse to the Church, which hearkened to their complaints and fulminated her anathema against the culprits. The method of proceeding much resembled that already stated as being in vogue in the ordinary tribunals. The plaintiff appointed counsel, the court accorded a counsel to the defendants, and the ecclesiastical judge summed up and gave sentence.

All requisite forms of law were gone through with precision and minuteness. As a specimen we shall extract some details from a consultation on the subject, made by Bartholomew de Chasseneux, a noted lawyer of the sixteenth century.

After having spoken, in the opening, of the custom among the inhabitants of Beaume of asking the authorities of Autun to excommunicate certain insects larger than flies, vulgarly termed hureburs, a favour which was invariably accorded them, Chasseneux enters on the question whether such a proceeding be right. The subject is divided into five parts, in each of which he exhibits vast erudition.

The lawyer then consoles the inhabitants of Beaunois with the reflection that the scourge which vexes them devastates other countries. In India the hureburs are three feet long, their legs are armed with teeth, which the natives employ as saws. The remedy found most effectual is to make a female in the most dégagé costume conceivable perambulate the canton with bare feet. This method, however, is open to grave objections on the score of decency and public morality.

The advocate then discusses the legality of citing insects before a court of justice. He decides that such a summons is perfectly justifiable. He proceeds to inquire whether they should be expected to attend in person, and, in default of their so doing, whether the prosecution can lawfully be carried on. Chasseneux satisfies himself and us that this is in strict accordance with law.

The sort of tribunal before which the criminals should be cited forms the next subject of inquiry. He decides in favour of the Ecclesiastical Courts. The advocate proceeds to convince his readers, by twelve conclusive arguments, that excommunication of animals is justifiable; having done so, he brings forward a series of examples and precedents. He asserts that a priest once excommunicated an orchard, whither children resorted to eat apples, when—naughty chicks!—they ought to have been at church. The result was all that could have been desired, for the trees produced no fruit till, at the request of the Dowager Duchess of Burgundy, the inhibition was removed.

He mentions, as well, an excommunication fulminated by a bishop against sparrows, which, flying in and out of the church of S. Vincent, left their traces on the seats and desks, and in other ways disturbed the faithful. Saint Bernard, be it remembered, whilst preaching in the parish church of Foligny, was troubled by the incessant humming of the flies. The saint broke off his sermon to exclaim, "O flies! I denounce you!" The pavement was instantaneously littered with their dead bodies.

Saint Patrick, as every one knows, drove the serpents out of Ireland by his ban.

35

This is the form of excommunication as given by Chasseneux:—"O snails, caterpillars, and other obscene creatures, which destroy the food of our neighbours, depart hence! Leave these cantons which you are devastating, and take refuge in those localities where you can injure no one. I. N. P.," etc.

Chasseneux obtained such credit from this opinion that, in 1510, he was appointed by the authorities of Autun to be advocate for the rats, and to plead their cause in a trial which was to ensue on account of the devastation they committed in eating the harvest over a large portion of Burgundy.

In his defence, Chasseneux showed that the rats had not received formal notice; and, before proceeding with the case, he obtained a decision that all the priests of the afflicted parishes should announce an adjournment, and summon the defendants to appear on a fixed day.

At the adjourned trial, he complained that the delay accorded his clients had been too short to allow of their appearing, in consequence of the roads being infested with cats. Chasseneux made an able defence, and finally obtained a second adjournment. We believe that no verdict was given.

In a formulary of exorcisms, believed to have been drawn up by S. Gratus, Bishop of Aosta, in the ninth century, we find unclean beasts excommunicated as agents of Satan.

From such a superstition as this sprang the numerous legends of the Evil One having been exorcised into the form of a beast; as, for instance, by S. Taurinus of Evreux, and by S. Walther of Scotland, who died in 1214, and who charmed the devil into the shapes of a black dog, pig, wolf, rat, etc. The devil Rush, in the popular mediæval tale of Fryer Rush, was conjured into a horse, and made to carry enough lead on his back to roof a church.

Felix Malleolus relates that William, Bishop of Lausanne, pronounced sentence against the leeches which infested the Lake of Geneva and killed the fish, and that the said leeches retreated to a locality assigned them by the prelate. The same author relates at large the proceedings instituted against some mosquitoes in the thirteenth century in the Electorate of Mayence, when the judge before whom they were cited granted them, on account of the minuteness of their bodies and their extreme youth, a curator and counsel, who pleaded their cause and obtained for them a piece of land to which they were banished.

On the 17th of August 1487, snails were sentenced at Mâcon. In 1585, caterpillars suffered excommunication in Valence. In the sixteenth century, a Spanish bishop, from the summit of a rock, bade all rats and mice leave his diocese, and betake themselves to an island which he surrendered to them. The vermin obeyed, swimming in vast numbers across the strait to their domain.

In 1694, during the witch persecutions at Salem, in New England, under the Quakers Increase and Cotton Mather, a dog was strangely afflicted, and was found guilty of having been ridden by a warlock. The dog was hanged. Another dog was accused of afflicting others, who fell into fits the moment it looked upon them; it was also put to death. A Canadian bishop in the same century excommunicated the wood-pigeons; the same expedient was had recourse to against caterpillars by a grand vicar of Pont-du-Château, in Auvergne, as late as the eighteenth century.

The absurdity of these trials called forth several treatises during the middle ages. Philip de Beaumanoir in the thirteenth century, in his Customs of Beauvoisis, complained of their folly; and in 1606, Cardinal Duperron forbade any exorcism of animals, or the use, without license, of prayers in church for their extermination.

A book published in 1459, De Fascino, by a Spanish Benedictine monk, Leonard Vair, holds up the practice to ridicule. Eveillon, in his Traité des Excommunications, published in 1651, does the same.

One curious story more, and we shall give a detailed account of one of these trials.

We have taken this from Benoit's Histoire de l'Edit de Nantes (tom. v. p. 754), and give a translation of the writer's own words. "The Protestant chapel at La Rochelle was condemned to be demolished in 1685. The bell had a fate sufficiently droll: it was whipped, as a punishment for having assisted heretics; it was then buried, and disinterred, in order to represent its new birth in passing into the hands of Catholics.... It was catechised, and had to reply; it was compelled to recant, and promise never again to relapse into sin; it then made ample and honourable recompense. Lastly, it was reconciled, baptized, and given to the parish which bears the name of Saint Bartholomew. But the point of the story is, that when the governor, who had sold it to the parish, asked for payment, the answer made him was, that it had been Huguenot, that it had been newly converted, and that consequently it had a right to demand a delay of three years before paying its debts, according to the law passed by the king for the benefit of those recently converted!"

We propose now giving the particulars of a remarkable action brought against some ants, towards the commencement of the eighteenth century, for violation of the rights of property. It is related by P. Manoel Bernardes in his Nova Floresta (Lisbóa, 1728), and is quoted by M. Emile Agnel among his Curiosités Judiciaires et

37

Historiques; to whom and to the paper of M. Menabréa, entitled "Procès fait aux Animaux," in the twelfth volume of the Transactions of the Chambéry Society, we are indebted for much of our information.

> Action brought by the Friars Minor of the province of Pridade no Maranhao in Brazil, against the ants of the said territory.

"It happened, according to the account of a monk of the said order in that province, that the ants, which thereabouts are both numerous, large, and destructive, had, in order to enlarge the limits of their subterranean empire, undermined the cellars of the Brethren, burrowing beneath the foundations, and thus weakening the walls which daily threatened ruin. Over and above the said offence was another, they had burglariously entered the stores, and carried off the flour which was kept for the service of the community. Since the hostile multitudes were united and indefatigable night and day—

> Parvula, nam exemplo est, magni formica laboris
> Ore trahit quodcumque potest, atque addit acervo
> Quern struit ... (Horace, Sat. i.)—

the monks were brought into peril of famine, and were driven to seek a remedy for this intolerable nuisance: and since all the means to which they resorted were unavailing, the unanimity of the multitude being quite insurmountable, as a last resource, one of the friars, moved by a superior instinct (we can easily believe that), gave his advice that, returning to the spirit of humility and simplicity which had qualified their seraphic founder, who termed all creatures his brethren—brother Sun, brother Wolf, sister Swallow, etc.—they should bring an action against their sisters the Ants before the divine tribunal of Providence, and should name counsel for defendants and plaintiffs; also that the bishop should, in the name of supreme Justice, hear the case and give judgment.

"The plan was approved of; and after all arrangements had been made, an indictment was presented by the counsel for the plaintiffs, and as it was contested by the counsel for the defendants he produced his reasons, requiring protection for his clients. These latter lived on the alms which they received from the faithful, collecting offerings with much labour and personal inconvenience; whilst the ants, creatures whose morals and manner of life were clearly contrary to the Gospel precepts, and were regarded with horror on that account by S. Francis, the founder of the

38

confraternity, lived by fraud; and not content with acts of larceny, proceeded to open violence and endeavours to ruin the house. Consequently they were bound to show reason, or in default be concluded that they should all be put to death by some pestilence, or drowned by an inundation; at all events, should be exterminated from the district.

"The counsel for the little black folk, replying to these accusations, alleged with justice to his clients, in the first place: That, having received from their Maker the benefit of life, they were bound by a law of nature to preserve it by means of those instincts implanted in them. Item, That in the observance of these means they served Providence, by setting men an example of those virtues enjoined on them, viz. prudence—a cardinal virtue—in that they (the ants) used forethought, preparing for an evil day: 'Formicæ populus infirmus, qui præparat in messe cibum sibi' (Prov. xxx. 25); diligence, also, in amassing in this life merits for a life to come according to Jerome: 'Formica dicitur strenuus quisque et providus operarius, qui presenti vita, velut in æstate, fructus justitiæ, quos in æternum recipiet, sibi recondit' (S. Hieron., in Prov. vi.); thirdly, charity, in aiding each other, when their burden was beyond their strength, according to Abbat Absalon: 'Pacis et concordiæ vivum exemplum formica reliquit, quæ suum comparem, forte plus justo oneratum, naturali quadam charitate alleviat' (Absalon apud Picinellum, in Mundo symbolico, 8); lastly, of religion and piety, in giving sepulture to the dead of their kind, as writes Pliny, 'sepeliuntur inter se viventium solæ, præter hominem' (Plin., lib. xi. 36); an opinion borne also by the monk Malchus, who observes, 'Hæ luctu celebri corpora defuncta deportabant' (S. Hieron., in Vita Malchi).

"Item, That the toil these ants underwent far surpassed that of the plaintiffs, since their burdens were often larger than their bodies, and their courage greater than their strength.

"Item, That in the eyes of the Creator men are regarded as 'worms'; on account of their superior intelligence, perhaps superior to the defendants, but inferior to them morally, from having offended their Maker, by violating the laws of reason, though they observed those of nature. Wherefore they rendered themselves unworthy of being served or assisted by any creatures, since they (men) had committed greater crimes against heaven than had the clients of this learned counsel in stealing their flour.

"Item, That his clients were in possession of the spot in question before the appellants had established themselves there; consequently that the monks should be expelled from lands to which they had no other right than a seizure of them by main force.

"Finally, he concluded that the plaintiffs ought to defend their house and meal by human means which they (the defendants) would not oppose; whilst they (the defendants) continued their manner of life, obeying the law imposed on their nature, and rejoicing in the freedom of the earth; for the earth belongs not to the plaintiffs but to the Creator: 'Domini est terra et plenitudo ejus.'

"This answer was followed by replies and counter-replies, so that the counsel for the prosecution saw himself constrained to admit that the debate had very much altered his opinion of the criminality of the defendants. He had, the learned counsel for the defendants argued, admitted that the action was brought by brethren against sisters, brethren Monks against sister Ants. The sister Ants, conform to the law of nature imposed on them, continued the counsel for the insects; the brother Monks, claiming to be ruled by an additional law, that of reason, violate it, so that they place themselves only under the law of animal instinct, the same which regulates the ants. The latter are not raised to the level of man, but the friars have lowered themselves to that of brutes. Consequently, the action is not between man and beast, but between beast and beast. All arguments founded on the assumption of higher intelligence in man consequently break down.

"The judge revolved the matter carefully in his mind, and finally rendered judgment, that the Brethren should appoint a field in their neighbourhood, suitable for the habitation of the Ants, and that the latter should change their abode immediately under pain of major excommunication. By such an arrangement both parties would be content and be reconciled; for the Ants must consider that the Monks had come into the land to sow there the seed of the Gospel, and that they themselves could easily obtain a livelihood elsewhere, and at less cost. This sentence having been given, one of the friars was appointed to convey it to the insects, which he did, reading it aloud at the openings of their burrows.

"Wondrous event! 'It nigrum campis agmen,' one saw dense columns of the little creatures, in all haste, leaving their ant-hills, and betaking themselves direct to their appointed residence."

Manoel Bernardes adds, that this sentence was pronounced on the 17th of January 1713, and that he saw and examined the papers referring to this transaction, in the monastery of Saint Anthony, where they were deposited.

GHOSTS IN COURT

The following very curious story is from the Eyrbyggja Saga, one of the oldest and noblest of the Icelandic histories. As it results in an action unique in its way,—a lawsuit brought against a party of ghosts who haunted a house,—it well merits attention from all lovers of curiosities.

In the summer of 1000, the year in which Christianity was established in Iceland, a vessel came off the coast near Snæfellness, full of Irish and natives of the Hebrides, with a few Norsemen among them; the ship came from Dublin, and lay alongside of Rif, waiting a breeze which might waft her into the firth to Dögvertharness. Some people went off in boats from the ness to trade with the vessel. They found on board a Hebridean woman called Thorgunna, who, hinted the sailors, had treasures of female attire in her possession the like of which had never been seen in Iceland. Now when Thurida, the housewife at Frod river, heard this, she was all excitement to get a glimpse of these treasures, for she was a dashing, showy sort of a woman. She rowed out to the ship, and on meeting Thorgunna, asked her if she had really some first-rate ladies' dresses? Of course she had, was the answer; but she was not going to part with them to any one. Then might she see them? humbly asked Thurida. Yes, she might see them. So the boxes were opened, and the Iceland lady examined the foreign apparel. It was good, but not so very remarkable as she had anticipated; on the whole she was a bit disappointed, still she would like to purchase, and she made a bid. Thorgunna at once refused to sell. Thurida then invited the Hebridean lady home on a visit, and the stranger, only too glad to leave the vessel, accepted the invitation with alacrity.

On the arrival of the lady with her boxes at the farm, she asked to see her bed, and was shown a convenient closet in the lower part of the hall. There she unlocked her largest trunk, and drew forth a suit of bed-clothes of the most exquisite workmanship, and she spread over the bed English linen sheets and a silken coverlet. From the box she also extracted tapestry hangings and curtains to surround the couch; and the like of all these things had never been seen in the island before.

Thurida opened her eyes very wide, and asked her guest to share bed-clothes with her.

"Not for all the world," replied the strange lady, with sharpness; "I'm not going to pig it in the rushes, for you, ma'am!"

An answer which, the Saga writer assures us, did not particularly gratify the good woman of the house.

41

Thorgunna was stout and tall, disposed to become fat, with black eyebrows, a head of thick bushy brown hair, and soft eyes. She was not much of a talker, not very merry, and it was her wont to go to church every day before beginning her daily task. Many people took her to be about sixty years old. She worked at the loom every day except in haymaking time, and then she went forth into the fields and stacked the hay she had made. The summer that year was wet, and the hay had not been carried on account of the rain, so that at Frod river farm, by autumn, the crop was only half cut, and the rest was still standing.

One day appeared bright and cloudless, and the farmer, Thorodd, ordered the house to turn out for a general haymaking. The strange lady worked along with the rest, tossing hay till the hour of nones, when a black cloud crossed the sky from the north, and by the time that prayers had been said such a darkness had come on that it was almost impossible to see. The haymakers, at Thorodd's command, raked their hay together into cocks, but Thorgunna, for no assignable reason, left hers spread. It now became so dark that there was no seeing a hand held up before the face, and down came the rain in torrents. It did not last many minutes, and then the sky cleared, and the evening was as bright as had been the morning.

It was observed by the haymakers on their return to their work that it had rained blood, for all the grass was stained. They spread it, and it soon dried up; but Thorgunna tried in vain to dry hers, it had been so thoroughly saturated that the sun went down leaving it dripping blood, and all her clothes were discoloured. Thurida asked what could be the meaning of the portent, and Thorgunna answered that it boded ill to the house and its inmates. In the evening, late, the strange woman returned home, and went to her closet and stripped the stained clothes off her. She then lay down in her bed and began to sigh. It was soon ascertained that she was ill, and when food was brought her she would not swallow it.

Next morning the bonder came to her bedside to inquire how she felt, and to learn what turn the sickness was likely to take. The poor lady told him that she feared her end was approaching, and she earnestly besought him to attend to her directions as to the disposal of her property, not changing any particular, as such a change would entail misery on the family. Thorodd declared his readiness to carry out her wishes to the minutest detail.

"This, then," said she, "is my last request. I desire my body to be taken to Skalholt, if I die of this disease, for I have a presentiment that that place will shortly become the most sacred in the island, and that clerks will be there who will chant over me; and

42

do you reimburse yourself from my chattels for any outlay in carrying this into effect. Let your wife Thurida have my scarlet gown, lest she be put out at the further distribution of my effects, which I propose. My gold ring I bequeath to the Church; but my bed, with its curtains, tapestry, coverlet, and sheets, I desire to have burned, so that they go into nobody's possession. This I desire, not because I grudge the use of these handsome articles to anybody, but because I foresee that the possession of them would be the cause of innumerable quarrels and heart-burnings."

Thorodd promised solemnly to fulfil every particular to the letter.

The complaint now rapidly gained ground, and before many days Thorgunna was dead. The farmer put her corpse into a coffin; then took all the bed-furniture into the open air, and, raising a pile of wood, flung the clothes on top of it, and was about to fire the pile, when, with a face pale with dismay, forth rushed Thurida to know what in the name of wonder her husband was about to do with those treasures of needlework, the coverlet, sheets, and curtains of the strange lady's bed.

"Burn them! according to her dying request," replied Thorodd.

"Burn them?" echoed Thurida, casting up her hands and eyes; "what nonsense! Thorgunna only desired this to be done because she was full of envy lest others should enjoy these incomparable treasures."

"But she threatened all kinds of misfortunes unless I strictly obeyed her injunctions; and I promised to do what she bid," expostulated the worthy man.

"Oh, that is all fancy!" exclaimed the wife; "what misfortune can these articles possibly bring upon us?"

Thorodd still stood out; but in his house, as in many another, the gray mare was the better horse, and what with entreaties, embraces, and tears, he was forced to effect a compromise, and relinquish to his wife the hangings and the coverlet in order that he might secure immunity for burning the pillow and the sheets. Yet neither party was satisfied, says the historian.

Next day preparations were made for flitting the corpse to Skalholt, and trustworthy men were appointed to accompany it. The body was swathed in linen, but not stitched up; it was then put into the coffin and placed on horseback. So they started with it over the moor, and nothing particular happened till they reached Valbjarnar plain, where there are many pools and morasses, and the corpse had repeated falls into the mire. Well, after a bit they crossed the North river at Eyar ford, but the water was very deep, for there had been heavy rains.

At nightfall they reached Stafholt, and asked the farmer to take them in. He declined peremptorily, probably disliking the notion of housing a corpse, and he shut the door in their faces. They could go no farther that night, as the White river was before them, which was very deep and broad and could only be traversed in safety by day; so they took the coffin into an outhouse, and after some trouble persuaded the farmer to let them sleep in his hall; but he would not give them any food, so they went supperless to bed. Scarcely, however, was all quiet in the house before a strange clatter was heard in the shed serving as larder. One of the farm servants, thinking that thieves were breaking in, stole to the door, and on looking in, beheld a tall naked woman, with thick brown hair, busily engaged in preparing food. The poor fellow was so frightened that he fled back to his bed, quaking like an aspen leaf. In another moment the nude figure stalked into the hall, bearing victuals in both hands, and these she placed on the table. By the dim light the bearers recognised Thorgunna, and they understood now that she resented the churlishness of the host, and had left her coffin to provide food for them. The farmer and his wife were now speedily brought to terms, and leaving their beds they displayed the utmost alacrity in supplying the necessities of their guests. A fire was lighted; the wet clothes were taken off the travellers; curd and beer, and a stew of Iceland-moss were set before them.

Hist!—a little noise in the outhouse! It is only Thorgunna stepping back into her coffin.

Nothing transpired of any moment during the rest of the journey. The bearers had but to narrate the story of the preceding night's events, and they were sure of a ready welcome wherever they halted.

At Skalholt all went well; the clerks accepted the gold ring, and chanted over the body: they buried her deep, and put green turf over her. So, their errand accomplished, the servants of Thorodd returned home.

At Frod river there was a large hall, with a closed bedroom at one end of it. On each side of the hall were closets; in one of these closets dried fish were stacked up, and flour was kept in the other. Every evening, about meal-time, a great fire was lighted in the hall, and men used to sit before it ere they adjourned to supper. The same night that the funeral party returned the men were sitting chatting round the fire, when suddenly they perceived a phosphorescent half-moon grow into brilliancy on the wall of the apartment, and travel slowly round the hall against the sun. The

44

appearance continued all the while the men sat by the fire, and was visible every evening after. Thorodd asked Thorir Stumpleg, his bailiff, what this portended; and the man replied that it boded death to some one, but to whom he could not say.

One day a shepherd came in, gloomy, and muttering to himself in a strange manner. When addressed, he answered wildly, and they thought he must have lost his wits. The man remained in this state for some little while. One night he went to bed as usual, but in the morning when the men came to wake him, they found him lying dead in his place.

He was buried in the church.

A few nights after, strange sounds were heard outside the house; and one night when Thorir Stumpleg went outside the door, he saw the shepherd stride past him. Thorir attempted to slip indoors again, but the shepherd grasped him, and after a short tussle cast him in, so that he fell upon the hall floor bruised and severely injured. He succeeded in crawling to his bed, but he never rose from it again. His body was purple and swollen. After a few days he died, and was buried in the churchyard. Immediately after, his spectre was seen to walk in company with that of the shepherd.

A servant of Thorir now sickened, and after three days' illness died. Within a few days five more died. The fast preceding Christmas approached, though in those days the fashion of fasting was not introduced. In the closet containing dried fish, the stack was so big that the door could not be closed, and when fish were wanted, a ladder was placed against the pile and the top fish were taken away for use. In the evening, as men sat over the fire, the stack of dried fish was suddenly upset, and when people went to examine it, they could discover no cause. Just before Yule, also, Thorodd, the bonder, went out in a long boat with seven men to Ness, after some fish, and they were out all night. The same evening, the fires having been kindled in the hall at Frod river, a seal's head was seen to rise out of the floor of the apartment. A servant girl, who first saw it, rushed to the door, and catching up a bludgeon which lay beside it, struck at the seal's head. The blow made the head rise higher out of the floor, and it turned its eyes towards the bed-curtains of Thorgunna. A house-churl now took the stick and beat at the apparition, but he fared no better, for the head rose higher at each stroke till its forefins appeared, and the fellow was so frightened that he fainted away. Then up came Kiartan, the bonder's son, a lad of twelve, and snatching up a large iron mallet for beating the fish, he brought it down with a crash on the seal's head. He struck again and again, till he drove it into the floor, much as one might drive a pile; he then beat down the earth over it.

45

It was noticed by all that on every occasion the lad Kiartan was the only one who had any power over the apparitions.

Next morning it was ascertained that Thorodd and his men had been lost, for the boat was driven ashore near Enni; but the bodies were never recovered.

Thurida, and her son Kiartan, immediately invited all their kindred and neighbours to a funeral feast. They had brewed for Yule, and now they kept the banquet in commemoration of the dead. When all the company had arrived, and had taken their places—the seats of the dead men being, as customary, left vacant—the hall door was darkened, and the guests beheld Thorodd and his servants enter, dripping with water. All were gratified, for at that time it was considered a token of favourable acceptance with the goddess Ran if the dead men came to the wake; "and," says the Saga writer, "though we are Christian men, and baptized, we have faith in the same token still." The spectres walked through the hall without greeting any one, and sat down before the fire. The servants fled in all directions, and the dead men sat silently round the flames till the fire died out, then they left the house as they had entered it. This happened every evening as long as the feast continued, and some deemed that at the conclusion of the festivities the apparition would cease. The wake terminated, and the visitors dispersed. The fire was lighted as usual towards dusk, and in, as before, came Thorodd and his retinue, dripping with water; they sat down before the hearth, and began to wring out their clothes. Next came in the spectres of Thorir Stumpleg and the six who had died in bed after him, and had been buried; they were covered with mould, and they proceeded to shake the mould off their clothes upon Thorodd and his men.

The inmates of the house deserted the room, and remained without light and heat in another apartment. Next day the fire was not lighted in the hall but in the other room; the farm-people reckoning upon the ghosts keeping to the hall. But no! in came the spectral train, and upon the living men vacating their seats, the ghosts occupied them, and sat looking grimly into the red fire till it died out, whilst the terrified servants spent the evening in the hall.

On the third day two fires were kindled—one in the hall for the ghosts, and another in the small chamber for the living men; and so it had to be done throughout the whole of Yule.

Fresh disturbances now began in the fish closet, and it seemed as though a bull were among the fish, tossing them about; and this went on night and day. A man set the ladder against the stack and climbed to the top. He observed emerging from the pile of stockfish a tail like that of a cow which had been singed, but soft and covered with hair like that of a seal. The fellow caught the tail and pulled at it, calling lustily for help. Up ran men and women, and all dragged at the tail, but none of them could pull it out; it seemed stiff and dead, yet suddenly it was whisked out of their hands, and rasped the skin off their palms. The stack was now taken down, but no traces of the tail could be found, only it was discovered that the skin had been peeled off the fish, and at the bottom of the stack not a bit of flesh was left upon them.

Thorgrima, the widow of Thorir Stumpleg, fell ill shortly after this; on the evening of her burial she was seen in company with Thorir and his party. All those who had seen the tail were now attacked, and died—men and women. In the autumn there had been thirty household servants at Frod river, of these now eighteen were dead, the ghosts had frightened five away, and at the beginning of the month of May there remained but seven.

Things had come to such a pass as to render ruin imminent, unless some decisive measure were pursued to rid the house of the spectres that haunted it. Kiartan, accordingly, determined on consulting Snorri, the Lawman, his mother's brother, and one of the shrewdest men Iceland ever produced. Kiartan reached his uncle's house at Helgafell at the same time that a priest arrived from Gizor White, the apostle of Iceland. Snorri advised Kiartan to take the priest with him to Frod river, to burn all the bed-furniture of Thorgunna, to hold a court at his door, and bring a formal action at law against the spectres, and then to get the priest to sprinkle the house with holy water, and to shrive the survivors on the farm. Along with him Snorri sent his son Thord Kausi, with six men, that he might summons Kiartan's father, considering that there might be a little delicacy in the son bringing an action against the ghost of his own father.

So it was settled, and Kiartan rode home. On his way he called at neighbours' houses and asked help: so that by the time he reached Frod river his party was considerably swelled. It was Candlemas day, and they drew up at the farm door just after the fires had been lighted and the ghosts had assumed their customary places. Kiartan found his mother in bed, with all the premonitory symptoms of the same complaint which had carried off so many others in the house. The lad passed the spectres, and going up to the bed of Thorgunna, removed the quilt and curtains and every article which had belonged to her. Then he pushed boldly up to the fire past the ghosts, and took a brand from it.

In a few minutes he had made a pile of brushwood, and had thrown the bed-furniture on the top. The flames roared up around the luckless articles and consumed them. A court was next constituted at the door, according to proper legal forms, and Kiartan

47

summoned Thorir Stumpleg, whilst Thord Kausi summoned Thorodd for entering a gentleman's house without permission, and bringing mischief and death among his retainers.

Every spectre there present was summoned by name in due and legal form. The plaintiffs argued their case, and witnesses were called and examined. The defendants were asked what exceptions they had to plead, and upon their remaining silent, sentence was pronounced. Each case was taken separately, and the court sat long. The first action disposed of was that against Thorir. He was ordered to leave the house forthwith. Upon hearing this decree of the court, Stumpleg rose from his chair and said—

"I sat whilst sit I might," and hobbled out of the hall by the door opposite to that before which the court was held.

The case of the shepherd was next disposed of. On hearing the sentence he rose,—

"I go; better had I been dismissed before," he vanished through the door.

When Thorgrima was ordered to depart, she followed the others, saying,—

"I remained whilst to remain was lawful."

Each who left said a few words which evinced a disinclination to desert the fireside for the grave and sea depths.

The last to go was Thorodd, and he said,—

"There is now no peace for us here; we are flitting one by one."

After this Kiartan went in, and the priest took holy water and sprinkled the walls of the house; then he sang mass, and performed many ceremonies.

So the spectres haunted Frod river no more; Thurida got better rapidly, and the prospects of the farm mended.

STRANGE PAINS AND PENALTIES

Punishment is efficacious in deterring from crime only if it be certain and speedy. Severity is quite a minor point, and it will be found that the deterring effect of punishment is by no means proportionate to its cruelty.

The first requisite is certainty, for human nature is so constituted that if there be a chance of escape, ninety-nine out of a hundred will be found to run the risk. A slight punishment, if certain, is infinitely more likely to produce the required results than the most terrible exhibition of cruelty upon representative criminals. If certainty be a main requisite, speediness is also necessary; lasting and cruel punishments harden but do not reclaim.

Of this our forefathers in the middle ages were profoundly ignorant. With an inefficient police, it was not to be expected that one tithe of the malefactors, then so numerous, should fall into the hands of justice, and the authorities endeavoured to make up for this imperfection by exaggerated severity, and by grotesqueness in the punishments they inflicted.

I have said our forefathers in the middle ages, for the Anglo-Saxons and Danes were far too sensible to resort to cruel or absurd penalties, when milder and reasonable ones would answer their purpose.

Thus the laws of Canute direct that the correction of a criminal should be so regulated that it may appear seemly in the eyes of Him who said, "Forgive us our trespasses, as we forgive them that trespass against us," and they enjoin that the judge should not be unduly severe, but lean rather to a gentle punishment; and also that if it appeared likely that the criminal was fully penitent and inclined to amend, full mercy should be shown to him.

Indeed it was a feature characteristic of Saxon and Danish laws, that compensation should be aimed at and the reclamation of the criminal, rather than retribution. Capital punishments were sanctioned, but in all cases an opportunity was offered for the substitution of a fine. Thus, by the law of King Ina, if a thief were caught, he was sentenced to death, but his life could be redeemed by pecuniary satisfaction being made to the persons robbed. So the fine inflicted on a murderer was regulated according to the sum at which the life of the murdered party was valued; thus, if a man slew a freeman, he had to make compensation to the amount of one hundred shillings, but for the murder of a thrall a much less sum was demanded. If a freeman slew his thrall, he paid a nominal fine to the king for a breach of the peace; but if a slave killed his master, the doctrine of blood for blood was carried into effect, as the thrall had no personal property to pay in compensation for his crime.

Fines were imposed by the Anglo-Saxons for all kinds of personal injuries.

Thus by the laws of King Ethelbert, for breaking a man's front tooth the fine imposed was six shillings, but a molar was regarded as worth only one shilling, and a canine tooth was valued at six.

King Alfred however, revised these laws, and taking into consideration the fact that the molar is a double tooth, and that it is a very serviceable tooth besides, he raised its market value to fifteen shillings.

If a man struck out the eye of another and blinded him, he was obliged to make satisfaction with fifty shillings, and one who was in a troublesome mood and had plenty of loose cash to dispose of, might break a neighbour's rib for three shillings, and dislocate his shoulder for twenty. According to the decrees of the Witan, a fine of one shilling was enacted for crushing the finger-nail of a neighbour, but if the thumb-nail had suffered, three shillings was its value.

A testy Saxon might venture to pull the nose of his enemy if he had three shillings to spare, but then he had to be cautious, for if the pull were sufficiently violent to make the nose bleed, he had to pay six shillings. It was the almost universal custom throughout Europe that forgiveness should be judged according to the laws of their native country, and not according to the law of the land in which the offence was committed; and "thus," says Dr. Henry, "the nose of a Spaniard was perfectly safe in England, because it was valued at thirteen marks, but the nose of an Englishman ran a great risk in Spain, because it was valued at twelve shillings. An Englishman might have broken a Welshman's head for a mere trifle, but few Welshmen could afford to return the compliment."

Among the Anglo-Saxons the penalty inflicted on coiners was the loss of one hand; hardly a cruel sentence in comparison with that which was inflicted during the middle ages, up to the close of the sixteenth century, namely, boiling alive in oil or water.

An old German code of laws gives the following horrible directions: "Should a coiner be caught in the act, then let him be stewed in a pan, or in a caldron half an ell deep for the body, so that the man may be bound to a pole which shall be passed through the rings of the caldron, and which shall be tightly strapped and bound to upright posts on either side, and thus he shall be made to stew in oil and wine." A scene such as this was witnessed in Sweden in 1500, by Archbishop Olaus Magnus of Upsala, and instances without number might be cited from German and French city registers. Taking one town alone, Lübeck, we find that a poor fellow who gave himself out to be the dead king Frederick II., and who was probably an inoffensive madman, was thus put to death in 1287.

A second instance occurred in the year 1329, when the man was boiled in the market-place in the midst of a vast concourse of people. A similar sentence was pronounced in 1459, and again in 1471, but in this instance, at the last moment, in consideration of the

50

earnest entreaty of the bishop, the sentence was commuted to burning alive on a pile of faggots, at the Mühlenthor. This poor wretch was less fortunate than the coiner Jacob von Jülich, who, when crouching in the caldron, and shrieking with agony, obtained the mercy of having his head struck off.

In the sixteenth century, coiners were hanged instead of boiled: till lately, however, the caldron which was used for this horrible purpose was visible in the market-place of Osnabrück.

A punishment much in vogue during the middle ages for those who were guilty of stabbing with intent to wound, but without causing death, was sufficiently terrible. The hand which had dealt the blow was placed upon a table with the fingers spread out, and the weapon which had been used was struck violently into the back of the hand, pinning it to the table, and the criminal had to draw his hand away without removing the knife. This was statute law pretty nearly throughout Europe, and it continued in force till the middle of the seventeenth century, but the Frisian laws permitted the penalty to be remitted if the culprit chose to pay compensation to the amount of twenty-five gulden.

In 1638, Count Anthony Gunter of Oldenburg ordered a post to be erected before the church, or in the market, and the criminal to be fastened to it by a knife driven through his hand; and thus he was to stand for three hours. This law was not abrogated in Germany till 1661.

Mutilation was common enough in the middle ages. We find in the laws of William the Conqueror—

"We forbid that criminals of any sort should be killed or hanged, but let their eyes be plucked out, or let their hands and feet be chopped off, so that nothing may remain of the culprit but a living trunk, as a memorial of his crime." How different this from the tone of Saxon laws.

At Avignon, in 1245, false witnesses had their noses and upper lips cut away, and the same penalty was inflicted in Switzerland on blasphemers.

Eugène Sue suggested that capital punishment should be replaced by privation of sight. But if his system were carried into effect, those unhappy individuals who have either been born blind or have lost their sight by accident, would be compelled to carry about with them a certificate to the effect that they were honest men, as did the Arab grammarian Zamakuschari, who died in 1144. This writer, having had a foot frost-bitten in Kharism, carried ever about with him an attestation to the fact, signed by a number of persons of credit, so that no one would regard him as a criminal who had suffered mutilation.

51

Our own King John, according to Matthew Paris, invented a punishment of great cruelty. Geoffry, Archdeacon of Norwich, having offended him, he had him encased in a sheet of lead, which was folded round him and fitted to his shoulders like a cloak. The unhappy man died of the burden and of horror. "This," says an Anglo-Norman writer, "is the judgment of 'pain fort et dure'; to wit, the condemned shall be placed in a low chamber locked. And he shall lie naked on the ground without litter, bedding, or cloth, and without anything over him; and he shall lie on his back with his head to the west, and his feet to the east, and one arm shall be drawn to one quarter of the room by a rope, and the other arm in like manner to the other quarter, and in the same way shall his legs be extended, and upon his body shall be placed iron and stone, as much as he can bear; the first day he shall have three lumps of barley bread, but nothing to drink, and next day he shall drink thrice, as much as he wants, of water brought from near at hand to the prison, excepting that it be running water, and he shall have no bread, and this succession shall be followed till he dies."

Can it be believed that such a terrible death as this was inflicted in the reign of Queen Elizabeth, on the 25th of March 1586, and that the person who suffered was a woman, on the indictment "that she had harboured and maintained Jesuit and seminary priests, traitors to the Queen's Majesty and the laws; and that she had heard mass, and the like." The law of the land required that those who would not plead "guilty" or "not guilty," should be made to plead, "by being laid upon the back on the ground, and as much weight laid upon the accused as he or she can bear, and that the accused shall so continue for three days, and should he or she still refuse to plead, then to be pressed to death, the hands and feet tied to a post, and a sharp stone set under the back." The unfortunate woman,—her name was Margaret Clitheroe,—labouring under the idea that she was being martyred for her religion, whereas she was simply a victim to her own obstinacy in refusing to plead, endured this fearful death. Had she pleaded she would have escaped, for the evidence against her was of so slender a nature that she must have been acquitted. The judge, Clinch, who gave the sentence, did so with great reluctance, and only because, as the law stood, it was impossible for him to evade it.

In the reign of James I., we learn from Sir Walter Scott, a Highland chief in Ross, of the name of M'Donald, hearing that a poor widow had determined to go on foot to Edinburgh to see the king, and obtain from him justice against the chief, sent for her, and telling her that the way was long, and that she would require to be well shod for the journey, had a blacksmith brought, and made him nail her shoes to her feet, in the same way in which horses are shod. The widow, however, was a woman with a will of her own, and as soon as she had recovered, she betook herself on foot to Edinburgh, and casting herself at the feet of the king, besought of him punishment on the tyrannical chief. King James, indignant at her treatment, had M'Donald seized along with twelve of his accomplices, and had iron soles nailed to their feet. They were exposed in this condition to the public gaze, and were then decapitated.

When Richard Cœur de Lion was on his way to the Holy Land he drew up a code of criminal laws by which discipline was to be maintained among his troops. One of these contains the following article:—"If any one is convicted of theft, boiling pitch shall be poured over his head, and then a pillowful of feathers shall be shaken over it, so that the fellow may be certainly recognised. And he shall be abandoned on the first land where the vessel touches."

This reminds me of the trick played by certain wags on a poor nun in 1198. They covered her with honey, rolled her in feathers, mounted her on horseback, and paraded her about the town. Philip Augustus, hearing of this, had the unfortunate jokers seized and plunged into a vat of boiling water.

A curious ordinance in force at Dortmund, in Westphalia, A.D. 1348, required that, "if two women quarrel so as to come to blows, and at the same time use abusive language, they shall be required to carry, the whole length of the town along the High Street, two stones weighing together one hundred pounds, attached to chains. The first woman shall carry them from the east gate to the west gate, whilst the second goads her on with a needle fastened to the end of a stick," and both are directed to wear the lightest of all possible costumes. "The second is then to take the stones upon her shoulders and to carry them back to the east gate, the first applying the same stimulus." This punishment was common all over Germany. In Lübeck the stones were shaped like bottles, in other places they were rudely-carved heads of women with protruding tongues; and in some towns they were in the shape of cats. At Hamburg a procession of women sounding cows' horns was part of the programme, and at Worms a band of bell-ringers.

The old English cucking-stool for shrews is well known; it was common abroad also, with some customs peculiarly foreign. For instance, the unfortunate persons who had to do penance for their shrewish tongues were sometimes put into a large hamper, or a cage, and so suspended to a gallows, in the evening to be plunged, basket and all, into the nearest pond.

53

In the museum at Cahors the iron cage in which shrews were dipped is still shown.

Fools' caps have long served as punishment in village schools, but their use in them was probably derived from the legal practice of condemning certain delinquents to the use of peculiar caps. Thus in Germany some minor crimes were punished by the culprit being sentenced to sit all day on a post in the middle of a canal, with a tall scarlet steeple cap on his head. In Rome, bankrupts were condemned to wear in public black bonnets of a sugar-loaf form. At Lucca they wore them of an orange colour; and in Spain they bore in addition an iron collar.

The ancient Roman manner of punishing parricide, by casting the murderer into the water in a sack which contained as well a cock, an ape, and a serpent, was not unused in the middle ages, and we find it threatened in an ordinance of the Provost of Paris, published on 25th June 1493, in which all persons sick with smallpox are bidden leave Paris at a day's notice, or suffer the penalty above mentioned.

I might extract accounts of the most fearful of punishments which the cruelty of man could devise, from Oriental sources, but the barbarities practised by the Mussulmans are sickening through their excessive cruelty. Suffering enough has been undergone in our own quarter of the globe, and that too at no great distance of time from the age in which we live.

I will instance, in conclusion, the painful account of the execution of Balthazar Gerard, who assassinated William of Orange, on the 10th of July 1584, as given by Brantôme. "First he was racked with extraordinary cruelty, without his uttering a word, except that he persisted in his former assertion.

"Then, before he died, for eighteen days he was tortured with excessive cruelty. On the first day he was taken into the public square, where there was a caldron of boiling oil, into which was thrust the arm which had dealt the blow. On the morrow this arm was chopped off, and it fell at his feet. He calmly moved it with his foot, and pushed it before him down from the scaffold. On the third day his breast and the front of his arm were plucked with red-hot pincers; on the following day his back and the back of his arm, and legs, were treated in the same manner. This was continued for eighteen days, and after each torture he was conducted back to prison, he all the while enduring his sufferings with great constancy. The greatest torture of all that he endured, except death, was when he was bound naked in the middle of the square, and around him at a little distance waggon-loads of charcoal were set on fire, and thus he was wrapped in flame. The poor sufferer bore the roasting for a long while, and then at last he lost patience and cried out; whereupon he was removed. For the final torture he was broken on the wheel, but he did not die at once, for they had only broken his legs and arms, so as to make him linger. Thus he lived for six hours, imploring some one to bring him a drop of water, but no one had the courage to give it him. At length the officer was entreated to put an end to this scene, and to strangle him, lest he should die in despair, and so his soul perish. The executioner approached, and when close to him asked how he felt. The tortured man replied, 'As you left me.' But when the cord was produced to be put round his neck, he raised himself, as though fearing death, as he had not feared it before, and said to the executioner:—'Ah! pray leave me alone. Do not torture me any more! Pray let me die as I am!' So having been strangled, his life closed. Awful were the torments he endured!"

WHAT ARE WOMEN MADE OF?

In the palmy days of childhood we were taught in nursery jingle, and we implicitly believed, that little girls were made of

Sugar and spice
And all that's nice.

But, growing older, we learned to our disappointment that they were produced from Adam's rib; and when we asked why woman was made of that particular bone, we were told because it was the most crooked in Adam's body.

"Observe the result," preached Jean Raulin, in the beginning of the sixteenth century: "man, composed of clay, is silent and ponderous; but woman gives evidence of her osseous origin by the rattle she keeps up. Move a sack of earth and it makes no noise; touch a bag of bones and you are deafened with the clitter-clatter."

This observation did not fall to the ground; it was repeated by Gratian de Drusac in his Controversies des Sexes Masculin et Féminin, 1538. The learned in medieval times did not spare women. Jean Nevisan, professor of law at Turin, who died in 1540, is harder still on them in his Sylva Nuptialis. Therein he audaciously asserts that woman was formed by the Author of Good till the head had to be made, and that was a production of the great enemy of mankind. "Permisit Deus illud facere dæmonio."

But the Rabbis are equally unsparing. They assert that when Eve had to be drawn from the side of Adam she was not extracted by the head, lest she should be vain; nor by the eyes, lest they should be wanton; nor by the mouth, lest she should be given to tittle-tattle; nor by the ears, lest she should be inquisitive; nor by the hands, lest she should be meddlesome; nor by the feet, lest she should be a gadabout; nor by the heart, lest she should be jealous; but she was drawn forth by the side; yet, notwithstanding these precautions, she has every fault specially guarded against, because, being extracted sideways, she was perverse.

Another Rabbinical gloss on the text of Moses asserts that Adam was created double; that he and Eve were made back to back, united at the shoulders, and that they were severed with a hatchet. Eugubinus says that their bodies were united at the side.

Antoinette Bourignon, that extraordinary mystic of the seventeenth century, had some strange visions of the primeval man and the birth of Eve. The body of Adam, she says, was more pure, translucent, and transparent than crystal, light and buoyant as air. In it were vessels and streams of light, which entered and exuded through the pores. The vessels were charged with liquors of various colours of intense brilliancy and transparency; some of these fluids were water, milk, wine, fire, etc. Every motion of Adam's body produced ineffable harmonies. Every creature obeyed him; nothing could resist or injure him. He was taller than men of this time; his hair was short, curled, and approaching to black. He had a little down on his lower lip. In his stomach was a clear fluid, like water in a crystal bowl, in which tiny eggs developed themselves, like bubbles in wine, as he glowed with the ardour of Divine charity; and when he strongly desired that others should unite with him in the work of praise, he deposited one of these eggs, which hatched, and from it emerged his consort, Eve.

The inhabitants of Madagascar have a strange myth touching the origin of woman. They say that the first man was created of the dust of the earth, and was placed in a garden, where he was subject to none of the ills which now afflict mortality; he was also free from all bodily appetites, and though surrounded by delicious fruit and limpid streams, yet felt no desire to taste of the fruit or quaff the water. The Creator had, moreover, strictly forbidden him either to eat or to drink. The great enemy, however, came to him, and painted to him in glowing colours the sweetness of the apple, the lusciousness of the date, and the succulence of the orange. In vain:

56

the first man remembered the command laid upon him by his Maker. Then the fiend assumed the appearance of an effulgent spirit, and pretended to be a messenger from heaven commanding him to eat and drink. The man at once obeyed. Shortly after a pimple appeared on his leg; the spot enlarged into a tumour, which increased in size and caused him considerable annoyance. At the end of six months it burst, and there emerged from the limb a beautiful girl.

The father of all living turned her this way and that way, sorely perplexed, and uncertain whether to pitch her into the water or give her to the pigs, when a messenger from heaven appeared, and told him to let her run about the garden till she was of a marriageable age, and then to take her to himself as a wife. He obeyed. He called her Bahouna, and she became the mother of all races of men.

There seems to be some uncertainty as to the size of our great mother. The French orientalist, Henrion, member of the Academy, however, fixed it with a precision satisfactory, at least, to himself. He gives the following table of the relative heights of several eminent historical personages:—

Adam was precisely 123 feet 9 inches high

Eve	118 "	9.75 in.	"
Noah	103 "		"
Abraham	27 "		"
Moses	13 "		"
Hercules	10 "		"
Alexander	6 "		"
Julius Cæsar	5 "		"

It is interesting to have the height of Eve to the decimal of an inch. It must, however, be stated that the measures of the traditional tomb of Eve at Jedda give her a much greater stature. "On entering the great gate of the cemetery, one observes on the left a little wall three feet high, forming a square of ten to twelve feet. There lies the head of our first mother. In the middle of the cemetery is a sort of cupola, where reposes the middle of her body, and at the other extremity, near the door of egress, is another little wall, also three feet high, forming a lozenge-shaped enclosure: there are her feet. In this place is a large piece of cloth, whereon the faithful deposit their offerings, which serve for the maintenance of a constant burning of perfumes over the midst of her body. The distance between her head and feet is 400 feet. How we have shrunk since the creation!"—Lettre de H. A. D., Consul de France en Abyssinie, 1841.

But to return to the substance of which woman was made. This is a point on which the various cosmogonies of nations widely differ. Probably the discoverers of these cosmogonies were men, for they seldom give to woman a very distinguished origin. But then the poets make it up to her. Nature, the singer of the Land of Cakes tells us,

> Her 'prentice hand she tried on man,
> And then she made the lasses, O.

Guillaume de Salluste du Bastas (b. 1544; d. 1590) composed a lengthy poem on the Creation, in which he does ample justice to the ladies. His poem was translated into Latin by Dumonin, and into German, Spanish, Italian, and English.

A specimen will suffice:—

> The mother of mortals in herself doth combine
> The charms of an Adam, and graces all Divine.
> Her tint his surpasses, her brow is more fair,
> Her eye twinkles brighter, more lustrous her hair;
> Far sweeter her utterance, her chin is quite smooth,
> Dream of Beauty incarnate, a lover and a love!

Our own Milton has done poor Eve justice in lines which need no quotation.

Pygmalion, says the classic story, which is really a Phœnician myth of creation, made a woman of marble or ivory, and Aphrodite, in answer to his prayers, endowed the statue with life. We do not believe it. No woman was ever marble. She may seem hard and cold, but she only requires a sturdy male voice to bid her

> Descend, be stone no more!

to show that the marble appearance was put on, and that she is, and ever was, genuine palpitating flesh and blood.

"Often does Pygmalion apply his hands to the work. One while he addresses it in soft terms, at another he brings it presents that are agreeable to maidens, as shells, and smooth pebbles, and little birds, and flowers of a thousand hues, and lilies, and painted balls, and tears of the Heliades, that have distilled from the trees. He decks her limbs, too, with clothing, and puts a long necklace on her neck. Smooth pendants hang from her ears, and bows from her breast. All things are becoming to her."—Ovid, Metam. x. 254-266.

There is something tender and kindly in this myth; it represents woman as man would have her, pure as the ivory, modestly arrayed, simple, and delighted with small trifles, birds, and pebbles, and flowers—a thing of beauty and a joy for ever. But Hesiod gives a widely different account of the creation of woman. According to him, she was sent in mockery by Zeus to be a scourge to man:—

> The Sire who rules the earth and sways the pole
> Had spoken; laughter fill'd his secret soul:
> He bade the crippled god his hest obey,
> And mould with tempering water plastic clay;
> With human nerve and human voice invest
> The limbs elastic, and the breathing breast;
> Fair as the blooming goddesses above,
> A virgin's likeness with the looks of love.
> He bade Minerva teach the skill that sheds
> A thousand colours in the gliding threads;
> He call'd the magic of love's golden queen
> To breathe around a witchery of mien,
> And eager passion's never-sated flame,
> And cares of dress that prey upon the frame;
> Bade Hermes last endue, with craft refined
> Of treacherous manners, and a shameless mind.
>
> Hesiod, Erga, 61-79.

If such was the Greek theory of the creation of woman, it speaks ill for the Greek men; for woman is ever what man makes her. If he chooses her to be giddy and light and crafty, giddy, light, and crafty will she become; but if he demands of her to be what God made her, modest, and thrifty, and tender, such she will ever prove. This our grand old Northern forefathers knew, and they made her creation a sacred matter, and fashioned her from a nobler stock than man. He was of the ash, she of the elm; they called the first woman Embla, or Emla, which means a laborious female—from the root amr, aml, ambl, signifying "work." "One day as the sons of Bör were walking along the sea-beach, they found two stems of wood, out of which they shaped a man and a woman. The first, Odin, infused into them life and spirit; the second, Vili, endowed them with reason and the power of motion; the third, Ve, gave them speech and features, hearing and vision." This reminds one of the ancient Iranian myth of Ahoura Mazda creating the first pair,

Meschia and Meschiane, from the Beivas tree. But the Scandinavians also spoke of three primeval mothers: Edda (great-grandmother), Amma (grandmother), and Mother, from whom sprang the three classes of thrall, churl, and earl. It is noticeable that these primeval women are represented as good housewives in the venerable Rîgsmàl, which describes the wanderings of the god Heimdal, under the name of Rîg. The deity comes to the hut of Edda, and at once—

> From the ashes she took a loaf,
> Heavy and thick, with bran mixed;
> More beside she laid upon the board;
> There is set a bowl of broth on the table;
> There is a calf boiled, and cates the best.

Then he goes to the house of Amma, the wife of Afi.

> Afi's wife sat plying her rock
> With outspread arms, busked to weave.
> A hood on her head, a sark over her breast,
> A kerchief round her neck, and studs on her shoulders.

He next enters the hall of Mother.

> The housewife looked on her arms,
> Smoothed her veil, and fastened her sleeves,
> Her headgear adjusted. A clasp was on her bosom,
> Her robe was ample, her sark blue;
> Brighter her brow, fairer her breast,
> Whiter her neck than purest snowdrift.
> She took, did Mother, a figured cloth
> Of white linen, and the table decked.
> She then took cakes of snow-white wheat,
> On the table them she laid.
> She set forth salvers, silver adorned,
> Full of game, and pork, and roasted birds.
> In a can was wine, the cups were costly.

Not a word of disparagement of woman is found in those old cosmic lays. The sturdy Northerner knew her value, and he respected her, whilst the frivolous Greek despised her as a toy.

The Provençal troubadours caught the classic misappreciation of woman. Massillia was a Greek colony, and Greek manners, tastes, and habits of thought prevailed for long in the south-east of France. The troubadours idolised her, as an idol-puppet, but they knew not how to commend, and by commending develop in her those qualities which lie ready to germinate when called for by man—devotion, self-sacrifice, patience, gentleness, and all those homely yet inestimable treasures, the domestic virtues. Pierre de Saint Cloud, in the opening of his poem on Renard, has his fling at poor Eve. He says that Adam was possessed of a magic rod, with which he could create animals at pleasure, by striking the earth with it. One day he smote the ground, and there sprang forth the lamb. Eve caught the rod from his hand, and did as he had done; forthwith there bounded forth the wolf, which rent the creation of Adam. He struck, and the domestic fowls came forth. Eve did likewise, and gave being to the fox. He made the cattle, she the tiger; he the dog, she the jackal.

Turning to America, we encounter a host of myths relative to the first mother. The sacred book of the Quiches tells of the gods Gucumatz, Tepu, and Cuz-cah making man of earth, but when the rain came on he dissolved into mud. Then they made man and woman of wood, but the beings so made were too thick-headed to praise and sacrifice, wherefore they destroyed them with a flood; those who escaped up tall trees remain to this day, and are commonly called monkeys. The three gods having thus failed, consulted the Great White Boar and the Great White Porcupine, and with their assistance made man and woman of white and red maize. And men show by their headstrong character that the mighty boar had a finger in their creation, and women by their fretfulness indicate the great porcupine as having had the making of them.

The Minnatarees have a story that the first woman was made of such rich and fatty soil that she became a miracle of prolificness; she came out of the earth on the first day of the moon of buffaloes, and ere it waned, she had a child at her breast. Every month she bestowed upon her husband a son or a daughter, and these children were fertile equally with their mother. This was rather sharp work, and the Great Spirit, seeing that the world would be peopled in no time, at this rate, killed the first parents, and diminished the productiveness of their children.

The Nanticokes relate that their great ancestor was without a wife, and he wandered over the face of the earth in search of one: at last the king of the musk rats offered him his daughter, assuring him that she would make the best wife in the world, as she could keep a house tidy, was very shrewd, and neat in her person. The Nanticoke hesitated to accept the obliging offer, alleging that the wife was so very small, and had four legs. The Micabou of the musk rats now appeared, and undertook to remedy this defect. "Man of the Nanticokes," said the spirit, "rise, take thy bride and lead her to

61

the edge of the lake; bid her dip her feet in water, whilst thou, standing over her, shalt pronounce these words:

> "For the last time as musk rat,
> For the first time as woman.
> Go in beast, come out human!"

The spirit's directions were obeyed to the letter. The Nanticoke took his glossy little maiden musk rat by the paw, led her to the border of the lake, and whilst she dipped her feet in the water, he used the appointed formulary; thereupon a change took place in the little animal. Her body was observed to assume the posture of a human being, gradually erecting itself, as a sapling, which, having been bent to earth, resumes its upright position. When the little creature became erect, the skin began to fall from the head and neck, and gradually unveiling the body, exhibited the maiden, beautiful as a flowery meadow, or the blue summer sky, or the north lit up with the flush of the dancing lights, or the rainbow which follows the fertilising shower. Her hand was scarce larger than a hazel-leaf, and her foot not longer than that of the ringdove. Her arm was so slight that it seemed as though the breeze must break it. The Nanticoke gazed with delight on his beauteous bride, and his gratification was enhanced when he saw her stature increase to the proportions of a human being.

Other American Indian tribes assert that the Great Spirit, moved with compassion for man, who wasted in solitude on earth, sent a heavenly spirit to be his companion, and the mother of his children. And I believe they are about right. But the Kickapoos tell a very different tale.

There was a time throughout the great world, say they, when neither on land nor in the water was there a woman to be found. Of vain things there were plenty—there were the turkey, and the blue jay, the wood duck, and the wakon bird; and noisy, chattering creatures there were plenty—there were the jackdaw, the magpie, and the rook; and gadabouts there were plenty—there were the squirrel, the starling, and the mouse; but of women, vain, noisy, chattering, gadabout women, there were none. It was quite a still world to what it is now, and it was a peaceable world, too. Men were in plenty, made of clay, and sun-dried, and they were then so happy, oh, so happy! Wars were none then, quarrels were none. The Kickapoos ate their deer's flesh with the Potowatomies, hunted the otter with the Osages, and the beaver with the Hurons. Then the great fathers of Kickapoos scratched the backs of the savage Iroquois, and the truculent Iroquois returned the compliment.

Tribes which now seek one another's scalps then sat smiling benevolently in each other's faces, smoking the never-laid-aside calumet of peace.

These first men were not quite like the men now, for they had tails. Very handsome tails they were, covered with long silky hair; very convenient were these appendages in a country where flies were numerous and troublesome, tails being more sudden in their movements than hands, and more conveniently situated for whisking off the flies which alight on the back. It was a pleasant sight to see the ancestral men leisurely smoking, and waving their flexible tails at the doors of their wigwams in the golden autumn evenings, and within were no squalling children, no wrangling wives. The men doted on their tails, and they painted and adorned them; they platted the hair into beautiful tresses, and wove bright beads and shells and wampum with the hair. They attached bows and streamers of coloured ribbons to the extremities of their tails, and when men ran and pursued the elk or the moose, there was a flutter of colour behind them, and a tinkle of precious ornaments.

But the red men got proud; they were so happy, all went so well with them, that they forgot the Great Spirit. They no more offered the fattest and choicest of their game upon the memahoppa, or altar-stone, nor danced in his praise who dispersed the rains to cleanse the earth, and his lightnings to cool and purify the air. Wherefore he sent his chief Manitou to humble men by robbing them of what they most valued, and bestowing upon them a scourge and affliction adequate to their offence. The spirit obeyed his Master, and, coming on earth, reached the ground in the land of the Kickapoos. He looked about him, and soon ascertained that the red men valued their tails above every other possession. Summoning together all the Indians, he acquainted them with the will of the Wahconda, and demanded the instant sacrifice of the cherished member. It is impossible to describe the sorrow and compunction which filled their bosoms when they found that the forfeit for their oblivion of the Great Spirit was to be that beautiful and beloved appendage. Tail after tail was laid upon the block and amputated.

The mission of the spirit was, in part, performed. He now took the severed tails and converted them into vain, chattering, and frisky women. Upon these objects the Kickapoos at once lavished their admiration; they loaded them as before with beads, and wampum, and paint, and decorated them with tinkling ornaments and coloured ribbons. Yet the women had lost one essential quality which as tails they had possessed. The caudal appendage had brushed off man the worrying insects which sought to sting or suck his blood, whereas the new article was itself provided with a sharp

63

sting, called by us a tongue; and far from brushing annoyances off man, it became an instrument for accumulating them upon his back and shoulders. Pleasant and soothing to the primeval Kickapoo was the wagging to and fro of the member stroking and fanning his back, but the new one became a scourge to lacerate.

However, woman retains indications of her origin. She is still beloved as of yore; she is still beautiful, with flowing hair; still adapted to trinketry. Still she is frisky, vivacious, and slappy; and still, as of old, does she ever follow man, dangling after him, hanging at his heels, and never, of her own accord, separating from him.

The Kickapoos, divested of their tails, the legend goes on to relate, were tormented by the mosquitoes, till the Great Spirit, in compassion for their woes, mercifully withdrew the greater part of their insect tormentors. Overjoyed at their deliverance, the red men supplicated the Wahconda also to remove the other nuisances, the women; but he replied that the women were a necessary evil and must remain.[1]

This is worse treatment than that which the ladies received from Hesiod. We have all heard of a young and romantic lady who was so enraptured with the ideal of American Indian life as delineated by Fenimore Cooper, that she fled her home, and went to the savages in Canada. We hope she did not fall to the lot of a Kickapoo.

Poor woman! it is pleasanter to believe that she is made from our ribs, which we know come very close to our hearts, and thus to explain the mutual sympathy of man and woman, and thereby to account for that compassion and tenderness man feels for her, and also for the manner in which she flies to man's side as her true resting-place in peril and doubt. But we have a cosmogony of our own, elucidated from internal convictions, assisted by all the modern appliances of table-rapping and clairvoyancy. According to our cosmogony, woman is compounded of three articles, sugar, tincture of arnica, and soft soap. Sugar, because of the sweetness which is apparent in most women—alas! that in some it should have acidulated into strong domestic vinegar; arnica, because in woman is to be found that quality of healing and soothing after the bruises and wounds which afflict us men in the great battle of life; and soft soap, for reasons too obvious to need specification.

[1] Jones, Trad. N. American Indians (1830), vol. iii. 175.

"FLAGELLUM SALUTIS"

There is a strange old book with the above title to be found in the libraries of the curious, so quaint in character as to deserve to be better known. It was composed by Christian Franz Paullini, a German physician, and was published at Frankfort-on-Maine in 1608. It is a treatise on the advantage of the whip for curative purposes in various disorders.

Dr. Paullini, in the first section of his work, directs attention to the consecration of corporal punishment by Scripture and the Church. Did not St. Paul assert, "Castigo corpus meum et in servitutem redigo"? Does not the bishop in confirmation box the ear of the candidate, in token that he is to be ready to endure suffering and shame as a good Christian soldier? And look at the saints of the calendar, were they not mighty in flagellation, fervent in rib-whacking?

> Shall precious saints and secret ones,
> Break one another's outward bones?
> When savage bears agree with bears,
> Shall secret ones lug saints by the ears?

asks the Puritan in his metrical version of Psalm lxxxiii, and Dr. Paullini promptly answers: "Certainly, it is good for health of soul and body that they should so act towards one another."

> Scorpius atque fabæ nostra fuere salus.

Had our learned author been acquainted with the Rabbinical gloss on the account of the Fall of Man, he would, maybe, have hesitated to attribute universal benefit to the application of the rod. For, say the Rabbis, when Adam pleaded that the woman gave him of the tree, and he did eat, he means emphatically that she gave it him palpably. Adam was recalcitrant, Eve dedit de ligno; the branch was stout, the arm of the "mother of all living" was muscular, and the first man succumbed, and "did eat" under compulsion.

There is nothing like the rod, says the doctor; it is a universal specific, it stirs up the stagnating juices, it dissolves the precipitating salts, it purifies the coagulating humours of the body, it clears the brain, purges the belly, circulates the blood, braces the nerves; in short, there is nothing which the rod will not do, when judiciously applied.

> Antidotum mortis si verbera dixero, credas!
> Attonitum morbum nam cohibere valent.

65

Having laid down his principle, the doctor proceeds to apply it to various complaints, giving instances, the result of experience.

And first as to melancholy.

One predisposing cause of melancholy, observes Paullini, is love, and that eventuates in idiotcy or insanity.

To parents and guardians our author gives the advice, when the first symptoms of this complaint appear in young people under their charge, let them grasp the rod firmly, and lay it on with vigour and promptitude. The remedy is infallible. Valescus de Taranta says, in the case of a young man—and his words are words of gold— "Whip him well, and should he not mend immediately, keep him locked up in the cellar on bread and water till he promises amendment."

I saw, continues our author, an instance of the good effect of this treatment at Amsterdam. A stripling of twenty, comely enough in his appearance, the son of an artisan in the town, fell in love with the mayor's daughter. He could neither eat, drink, sleep, nor do anything in the remotest degree rational. The father, unaware of the cause, put him into the hands of a medical practitioner, who did his utmost to cure him, but signally failed. At last the father's eyes were opened by means of an intercepted letter. Like a sensible man he packed his son off to the public whipping-place, there to learn better moralia. And this had the desired effect; for the youth returned perfectly cured and in his right senses.

But for this treatment he might have sunk into his grave, like him mentioned by P. Boaysten, who died of a broken heart through unrequited love; and, at the post-mortem examination, his bowels were discovered to be uncoiled, his heart shrivelled, his liver shrunk to nothing, his lungs corroded, and his skull entirely emptied of every trace of brains.

For short sight there is nothing like a good thrashing, or at least a violent blow, says our doctor.

An old German, aged eighty, who had all his lifetime suffered from short sight, was one day jogging to market on his respectable mare, Dobbin. Dobbin tripped on a stone and flung her rider. The old man fell upon a stone, which pierced his skull. The dense vapours which had obscured his vision for so long were enabled to escape through the aperture, and on his recovery the venerable gentleman had the sight of an eagle.

A cavalier was troubled with the same infirmity. He saw a large salmon hanging up outside a fishmonger's shop, and, mistaking it for a young lady of his acquaintance, removed his cap and addressed it with courtesy. Another youth having made great fun of the mistake, the short-sighted cavalier felt himself constrained in honour to call him out. In the duel he received a sword wound over his left eye, and this completely cured his vision.

For deafness Dr. Paullini recommends a box on the ear. Especially successful is this treatment in the case of children who do not attend to the commands and advice of their parents on the plea of "not having heard." In such cases the employment of corporal punishment cannot be too highly estimated. The doctor tells the story of a boy destined for the ministry who ran away from school and apprenticed himself to a tailor, and who was cured of deafness and tailoring propensities by the application of a large pair of drumsticks to a sensitive part of his person, and who eventually became a Lutheran pastor, and was, to the end of his days, able to mend his own clothes.

This story furnishes the author of Flagellum Salutis with matter for a digression on clerical education. He quotes with approval the sentiments of his old patron, Dr. Schupp, expressed thus: "Nowadays that every bumpkin makes his son study for the ministry, we have them scrambling about the country begging for promotion, and grumbling because it does not come as fast as they expect. The learned son is a poor curate, with no benefice. Such a to-do about this—complaints, murmurs, and what not! Why did he not learn a trade in addition to his theology? Luke the Evangelist was a theologus and medicus as well, and a painter to boot. Paul in his youth studied divinity at the feet of Gamaliel, but he was a carpet manufacturer besides. Was the Kaiser Rudolph a worse Emperor for being as well a clever craftsman? 'If I could recall my past years and begin life again,' said Dr. Schupp, 'I would not become a student only, but learn a trade besides. Then, if the thankless world kicked me, I would measure its foot for a boot; if it made faces at me, I would paint its portrait for it; if my divinity did not agree with its stomach, I would dose it with purgatives like Luke. I would make the world respect me for my diligence in trade, if it turned up its nose at my theology. Anyhow, I would not go about snivelling and crying poverty and want of promotion.'"

To this speech of Dr. Schupp, Paullini adds a few pertinent remarks. "The lad I was telling you about," he says, "had a hankering after tailoring. Well, tailoring is an honourable and useful profession. Was not Moses bidden, 'Thou shalt make holy garments for Aaron thy brother, for glory and for beauty. And thou shalt speak unto all that are wise-hearted, whom I have filled with the spirit of wisdom, that they may make Aaron garments.' Tailors filled with the spirit of wisdom! Why despise the craft which God has honoured?"

It must be allowed that there is sense in this little digression.

Doubtless it would be well if not only those destined for the ministry, but all the sons of the higher classes of society, were taught some manual employment in addition to the cultivation of their intellectual faculties. That our grammar schools should take the hint is not to be anticipated; masters and governors have the same implicit confidence in classic studies as the universal panacea that Dr. Paullini professes for the rod and Dr. Sangrado for cold water and blood-letting. I do not dispute the fact that the most useful knowledge for a lad to acquire who is destined for colonial farming, or for a mercantile life at home, is Greek prosody; but I suggest that an acquaintance with carpentering, land-surveying, or book-keeping might be found advantageous in a secondary degree.

Lockjaw is to be treated in the same manner, asserts our author, and he tells an amusing anecdote on the subject from Volquard Iversen.

Nicolas Vorburg was an Oriental traveller. In the course of his wanderings he reached Agra, the capital of the Great Cham. The European was introduced to His Majesty at the dinner-hour, and found the monarch just returned from the expedition, and as hungry as a hunter. A bowl of rice was brought in. The Great Cham dipped his hands into it, and ladled so much rice as they would hold into his capacious mouth, distended to the utmost conceivable extent. But the Great Cham had overestimated the capabilities of the distension of his jaws, and they became dislocated. At the sight, the servants were distracted with fear. The nobles stroked their chins in uncertainty how to act, the priests had recourse to their devotions, but no one assisted the monarch out of his dilemma. He sat upon his imperial throne purple in the face, his eyes distended with horror, his mouth gaping, and full of rice. Suffocation was imminent. Nicolas Vorburg, without even prostrating himself before the emperor, ran up the steps of his throne, and hit him a violent crack with the palm of his hand upon the cheek. The rice fell out of his mouth upon the imperial lap, some, it is surmised, descended the imperial red-lane. Another slap accomplished the relief of the monarch, and set the jaw once more in working order. At the same moment the servants screamed at the outrage committed upon the sacred majesty of the emperor, the nobles drew their swords to avenge it, and the priests converted their prayers for the recovery of their king into curses on the head of him who had sacrilegiously raised his hand to violate his divinity. Poor Vorburg would have been made into mincemeat, had not the emperor providentially recovered his breath in time to administer a reproof to his over-zealous subjects. He acknowledged the relief afforded him by the stranger by a present of a thousand rupees.

A tailor had a son who was half-witted. The father was out one day, and the child, who was left in the house, after the manner of children, looked about him in quest of some mischief which he might perpetrate. A pair of elegant breeches, just completed by his father, and designed for the legs of a nobleman, hung suspended from the wall. The child made a figured pattern upon the amber silk with his finger, dipped at intervals in the ink-pot. The mother was the first to discover the transformation of the breeches, and, not regarding the alteration in the same light as did her child, caught up the yard-measure and administered a castigation to the culprit, sufficient to "stir up the stagnating juices, dissolve the precipitating salts, and purify the coagulating humours," in at least one portion of the lad's body. The youth, under the impression that high art is never appreciated at first sight, made himself scarce for some hours. The father, on his return, used every effort to obliterate the flowering of ink which his son had drawn over the amber breeches, but with only a limited degree of success—so limited, in fact, that the nobleman for whom they were destined utterly refused to invest his person in them, and they were returned on the tailor's hands. The boy, towards evening, impelled by hunger, had returned home, and was soothing his injured feelings with bread and butter, when the father re-entered the house. In a moment the parental left hand had grasped the scruff of his neck, whilst the right hand dexterously completed the stirring up the stagnant juices, dissolving of precipitating salts, and purifying of coagulating humours with such success, that Dr. Paullini assures us the child grew up a miracle of discretion, and never after decorated articles of clothing other than his own pinafore.

Under the heading of "Swollen Breasts," the learned doctor gives us his ideas on the subject of schoolmasters and their titles. These remarks are sensible enough in their way, but hardly come under the heading he has selected for the chapter. Connected still more vaguely with swollen breasts is the commentary on some verses in the twenty-first chapter of St. John's Gospel, which closes the section.

To those who suffer from toothaches he recommends the practice of a learned professor under whom he studied. This man suffered excruciating torture from his teeth at night. The professor, the moment that his sufferings began, was wont to leave his bed and spend his night in jumping on to his table, and then jumping down again, till the pain ceased. Paullini does not state the feelings of those who slept in the room immediately underneath that occupied by Dr. Erasmus Vinding; neither does it seem clear at first sight how the jumping diversion is connected with the subject of the rod, concerning the merits of which the book treats; but on further consideration the connection becomes apparent. Dr. Paullini being silent on this point, we have but the light of nature to guide us to the conclusion that the saltatory performances of Dr. Erasmus would arouse and exasperate the other lodgers into an application of the universal panacea to his scantily protected person.

For constitutional indolence the rod is inestimable; the monotony of its use as a specific may, however, be pleasingly varied by an application of corporal punishment in the following disguised form, which, if severe, is nevertheless infallible as a cure. Hermann Habermann, a native of Mikla, deserves the credit of being the first to communicate it to the medical profession. Habermann had spent many years in Iceland, and it was there that he saw the treatment in use. An artisan suffering from indolence was recommended by a native doctor to let himself be sewn up in a sack stuffed with wool, and then be dragged about, rolled down hill, thumped, kicked, and jumped upon by his friends and acquaintances. When he emerged from the sack he was to take a draught to open his pores, and to go to bed. The remedy was tried, and succeeded.

A somewhat similar cure came under Paullini's personal observation. A nobleman had a jester who was dotingly fond of fowls. He stole all his master's poultry, so that his master was obliged to do without eggs for his breakfast. The fool, moreover, was deficient in fun, and was by no means worth his keep. At last his master determined on correcting him severely. He had him sewn up in a hop-bag and well thrashed, and then rolled down hill and thrashed again. The fool never stole eggs from that day forward, and from being but a poor fool he became one famous for his brilliant parts and sparkling humour.

For tertian fever, the rod is an admirable specific. A lawyer once suffered from this complaint, which left him at times able to continue his avocation. He had brought upon himself the ill-feeling of a certain gentleman whom he had, in one of his pleadings, turned into ridicule. This person determined to punish the advocate as soon as a convenient opportunity presented itself. The opportunity came. The lawyer was riding home one day, past the house of the nobleman, when the latter descried him, and immediately sent him a message requesting a moment's private conversation. The unfortunate advocate fell into the trap. Expecting to get employment in a fresh suit, he hurried eagerly to the castle, only to find the gates closed upon him and all egress prevented. In another moment the insulted gentleman stood before him.

"Vile bloodhound of the law!" he exclaimed, "you have long escaped the punishment due to you for your insolence and temerity.

You disgraced me publicly, and I shall revenge myself upon you by degrading you in a manner certain to humble your pride. Yet I am merciful. I give you your choice of two modes of suffering. You shall either sit on an ant-hill, in the clothing provided you by nature, till you have learned by heart the seven penitential psalms; or you shall run the gauntlet in the same dégagé costume round my courtyard, where will be ranged all my servants armed with rods wherewith to belabour you."

The hapless lawyer cast himself on his knees before the nobleman, and implored mercy. He pleaded that he had his wife and children to provide for; but the other replied that this was not to the point, as he had no intention of injuring the lady or the infants. Then the lawyer alleged his illness, saying that the access of fever would be on him next day, and that the punishment wherewith he was threatened—either of them in fact—might terminate fatally.

"That," replied the injured gentleman, "can only be ascertained by experiment. My own impression is that the ants or the whips will produce a counter irritation, which may prove beneficial. Still," he continued, stroking his chin, "we mortals are all liable to err, and my impression may be unfounded. I will frankly acknowledge my mistake if convinced by the result taking the direction you anticipate."

Reluctantly the poor advocate made his election of the treatment he was to undergo. From the ants and the penitential psalms he recoiled with horror, and he chose shudderingly to run the gauntlet. So he ran it.

Black and blue, bruised and bleeding, the wretched man was dismissed at last, to return to the bosom of his family. The nobleman was right, the lawyer was forever cured of his tertian fever.

In another work of the same author (Zeitkürzende, erbauliche Lust, 8vo, Frankfort, 1693) the doctor argues the case, whether an honourable man may thrash his wife; and concludes that such a course of action entirely depends on the behaviour and temperament of the wife.

Woman was created to be good, quiet, and orderly; when she is otherwise she is going contrary to her vocation, and art must be employed to correct nature. Eve was given to Adam, reasons Paullini, to be a helpmeet to him, and not to be the plague and worry of his life. Woman's vocation is to be a modest and gentle angel, and not to be a brazen, furious demon. Every woman is either one or the other. If she is as heaven made her, she takes to the bit and rein readily, is easily managed without the whip, and is perfectly docile. If, however, she is what the evil one would have

71

her, she takes the bit in her teeth, sets back her ears, plunges, and kicks; and woe to the man who comes within reach of her tongue, her claws, or her toes. Then there is need for the rod. To a good wife, "there is a golden ornament upon her, and her bands are purple lace: thou shalt put her on as a robe of honour, and shalt put her about thee as a crown of joy." But as for the bad wife, deal with her after the advice of the poet Joachim Rachel:—

> Thou wilt be constrained her head to punch,
> And let not thine eye then spare her:
> Grasp the first weapon that comes to hand—
> Horsewhip, or cudgel, or walking-stick,
> Or batter her well with the warming-pan;
> Dread not to fling her down on the earth,
> Nerve well thine arm, let thy heart be stout
> As iron, as brass, or stone, or steel.

For no wrath is equal to a woman's wrath; and better is it to live in the cage of an African lion, or of a dragon torn from its whelps, than to live in the house with such a woman. Of all wickedness the worst is woman's wickedness. Why, asks the doctor, what sort of a life did Jupiter lead in heaven with his precious Juno? Poor god! he let her get the upper hand of him. Had he but taken his stick to her instead of scolding, he might have had Olympus quiet, and have saved himself from being badgered through eternity.

They managed things better in Rome. A man had a wife full of bad tempers. He went to the oracle and asked what should be done with a garment which had moths in it. "Dust it," was the oracular response. "And," added the man, "I have a wife who is full of her nasty little tempers; should not she be treated in a similar manner?" "To be sure," answered the oracle, "dust her daily." And never was a truer or better bit of advice given by an oracle.

The work of Dr. Paullini called forth others in response, and doubtless enthusiastic devotees of the rod abounded. His views were, however, combated by others. From a tract against the use of the rod I cull one curious and droll story, wherewith to conclude this article:—

A husband accompanied his wife to confession. The lady having opened her griefs, the father who was shriving her insisted on administering a severe penitential scourging. The husband, hearing the first stroke inflicted on his better half, interfered, and urged that his wife was delicate, and that as he and she were one flesh, it would be better for him, as the stronger vessel, to receive the scourging intended for his helpmate. The confessor having consented to this substitution, the man knelt in his wife's place, while she retired from the confessional. Whack! whack! went the cat, followed by a moan from the good man's lips.

"Harder!—harder!" ejaculated the wife; "I am a grievous sinner!"

Whack! whack! whack!

"Lay it on!" cried she; "I am the worst of sinners."

Whack! whack! and a howl from the sufferer.

"Never mind his cries, father!" exclaimed she; "remember only my sins. Make him smart here, that I may escape in purgatory."

"HERMIPPUS REDIVIVUS"

"Man," said the learned Prioli, "is composed of soul, body, and goods. In his pilgrimage through life these component parts are constantly exposed to three mortal enemies: the devils, who are ever seeking the destruction of his soul; the doctors, who are intent on ruining his constitution; and the lawyers, who seek to rob him of his goods."

We will put the devils aside for a moment, the lawyers, too, with the tongs, and devote our attention to the doctors. We have already examined the medical treatise entitled Flagellum Salutis, wherein was exposed the excellence of the whip for the cure of every disorder to which mortality is heir. We propose considering another equally startling tractate in this paper, one more modern by a few years than that of Dr. Paullini, but its superior in absurdity. The title of the work is "Hermippus Redivivus, or a curious physico-medical examination of the extraordinary manner in which he extended his life to 115 years by inhaling the breath of little girls; taken from a Roman memorial, but now supported on medical grounds, as also illustrated and elucidated by a wondrous discovery of philosophical chemistry, by Johan Heinrich Cohausen, M.D." 8vo, 1743.[2] This extraordinary book is adorned with an illustration, representing a

---

[2] Original edition in Latin. A translation by John Campbell, LL.D., under the title of Hermippus Redivivus, London, 1743. A second edition much enlarged, under the title Hermippus Redivivus, or the Sage's Triumph over Old Age and the Grave, London, 1749, 8vo. We have seen also an Italian translation. That from which we quote is the German edition.

pedagogue with a big nose, of Brobdingnagian proportions, keeping a mixed school of solemn little girls in jackets and aprons, and little prigs of boys in stocks, knee-breeches, coats, and wigs. One little boy, whose body is the size of the master's hand, sits reading a book on his right knee. On the ground at his left is a little maiden, just reaching to the top of the master's gaiters. A tiny dog is sitting up begging in the midst of a class in the middle distance; and in the background, behind a row of urchins who are not looking at their books, is a cat as big as any one of them, attacking a cage containing a singing bird. The whole of this strange work is built on a Roman inscription, said to have been found in the seventeenth century, and figured by Thomas Reinsius in his Syntagma Inscriptionum Antiquarum, and afterwards by Johann Keyser in his Parnassus Clivensis. This inscription, which is almost certainly not genuine, runs as follows:—

AESCULAPIO . ET . SANITATI .
L . CLODIUS . HERMIPPUS.
QUI . VIXIT . ANNOS . CXV . DIES . V .
PUELLARUM . ANHELITU .
QUOD . ETIAM . POST MORTEM
EIUS.
NON . PARUM . MIRANTUR . PHYSICI .
IAM . POSTERI . SIC . VITAM . DUCITE .

That is to say: "To Æsculapius and to health, L. Clodius Hermippus dedicates this, who lived 115 years, 5 days, on the breath of little girls, which, even after his death, not a little astonishes physicians. Ye who follow, protract your life in like manner."

Other old writers, as Cujacius and Dalechampius, quote similar inscriptions, as "L. Clodius Hirpanus vixit Annos CXV. Dies V. alitus Puerorum anhelitu," and "L. Clodius Hirpanus vixit Annos CLV. Dies, V. Puerorum halitu refocillatus et educatus."

These inscriptions are sufficiently like and unlike to make it more than probable that they are all forgeries. It is hardly to be conceived that there should have been two individuals with names so very similar, living similar lengths of time,[3] the one on little girls' breath, the other on that of little boys. If, however, we are to suppose them genuine, we have:—"Lucius Clodius Hermippus dying aged 115 years, 5 days"; "Lucius Clodius Hirpanus dying aged 155 years, 5 days."

---

[3] It is possible that, by the engraver's fault, the L in the last inscription may have been substituted for an X.

74

However, the authenticity of these monuments is of little importance. Let us to our book.

Dr. Cohausen enters on a minute verbal commentary on the words of the inscription, after having relieved his enthusiasm in a lengthy preface, and a still longer epistle dedicatory to a doctor of his acquaintance.

The commentary is as careful as though life hung upon each letter of the text. Having completed this portion of his work, the author gives rein to his fancy, and elaborates from his internal consciousness a life of L. Clodius Hermippus. This is too curious to be passed over. Dr. Cohausen asks how the subject of the inscription managed to live upon the breath of little girls. He inquires whether Hermippus was a very wealthy man, and enters into reasons which appear to him conclusive to the contrary. He makes elaborate calculations as to the number of children who would have been necessary to supply breath to Hermippus, supposing them to have been changed every five years, and he to have adopted his system of prolonging life at the age of sixty. After having discussed the question whether Lucius Clodius were a schoolmaster, or the director of an hospital for children, he concludes that he was the head of an orphanage supported by Government; and when he has quite satisfied his mind upon this point, Dr. Cohausen proceeds to sketch the daily routine of the life of Hermippus, as follows:—

"The orphanage, which was like a palace, had many handsome dwelling and dining-rooms, adapted for the daily uses of himself and the children, so that the breath and exhalations from such a number of little girls might fill the enclosed air, and might mingle to compose a salubrious vapour; which, absorbed into the lungs of Hermippus, might the better exercise the desired properties. In these rooms he spent with them the greater part of the day, occupying the time in friendly and agreeable conversation, unfolding to them good rules of life, relating innocent stories, and wisely pronouncing exhortations on the practice of virtue. Early in the morning, when the noise of the awaking children aroused him, at his command they kindled in the room a fire, in order that the air, which had become thickened during the night, might be rarified. In damp weather they perfumed it with the best perfumes several times in the day, because they had been instructed by their master how necessary this was to the preservation of health. When the aged man left his room the little damsels waited on him in the breakfast-chamber, and wished him a happy morning. Often he explained to them the dreams which they related to him, making them conduce to their moral edification. Some of those sufficiently old to have an inkling of the art of flattery, combed out his snow-white hair; others smoothed out his long white beard; others, again, rubbed his back with a coarse towel, which is considered good for the health of old people. And if, at that period, tea or coffee had been drunk, unquestionably they would have supplied him with it. At all events, we may conclude, as these beverages were not then in vogue, that it is quite possible to reach a great age without imbibing them. When school-time was over they passed the rest of the day in childish sports, with the permission of Hermippus. They jumped about, they played with their dolls, sometimes they also sang, for old people consider nothing so good for health, and so invigorating, as vocal music. And in this manner everything conduced to assist the expirations of the little girls in supporting our old man. If ever he was compelled to leave the room, one might see the children dragging at his coat-tails to detain him, and fervently desiring his return. Adjoining the orphanage was a pleasant garden, in which were plants and flowers calculated by their odour to quicken the vital spirit, and assist in the prolongation of life. With these the maidens daily adorned the rooms. Into this garden Hermippus betook himself with all the little girls, each provided with a doll; and he walked about with them in it, chaffed them, romped, danced and sang, acting as though his limbs were those of youth. A thousand little rogueries, a thousand little jokes on the part of the tiny lasses assisted in enlivening him, for they possessed the art of making themselves cheerful. They wreathed flowers, and placed a crown of spring-blossoms on the white head of Hermippus, and thus he spited the fates and reached an advanced age."

Will it be believed that all this detail is pure invention on the part of Dr. Cohausen?

The learned author next proceeds to reason upon the cause producing these results; he solves the question why the breath of little girls should tend to prolong life.

"The breath," says Dr. Cohausen, "consists of an inhalation and an exhalation: and if I speak scientifically, I say that when man breathes he lets forth the thick and thin airs through his mouth and nostrils, which he had before received into his lungs, where they had become impregnated with the evaporations from his body, the subtilised watery particles and vitalising blood, the balsamic and sulphuric atoms. Wherefore the human breath when outside the spiracles has a material character, namely, an exhalation from the vapours and gases which are intermixed with the blood and sap of the human body; and it is so especially in the breath of little girls. So observes Ficinus. This air is warm or tepid, and it moves and is endowed unmistakably with life, and like an animal is composed of joints and limbs, so that it can turn itself about, and not only so, but it has a soul also; so that we may certainly predicate that it is an animal composed of vapour, and endowed with reason. Consequently, any one who draws into his lungs this breath or conglomerated vapour, must necessarily absorb into his system the properties of that body from which it emanated, and from which it derived its being. For we know by experience that the air which enters the lungs dry, goes forth carrying with it moisture, as may be seen by breathing on a glass, or in cold weather. Also, when we inhale the breath of any one who is ill, we are conscious of receiving infection. On the other hand, it is manifest that the breath of a young and vigorous person, charged with powerful volatile salts, will have a balsamic and vitalising capacity, or at the least a mechanical elasticity, which must communicate vigour." The doctor quotes with approval the opinion of Van Helmont, that the air absorbed into the lungs penetrates the whole system, and circulates through every part, to the very hair, catching up volatile salts on its passage. Thence he concludes that the exhalations of little girls, who are brimming over with vitality, and heaven knows what life-giving salts, must be charged with some of their redundant vitality; and if this breath be inhaled by an old man, he assumes into himself, and absorbs into his constitution, that life which had been cast off as superfluous by the children.

> Quæ spiramina dat puella? Nectar.
> Dat rores animæ suave olentes,
> Dat nardumque thymumque cinnamumque,
> Et mel, quale jugis tegunt Hymetti
> Aut in Cecropiis apes rosetis,
> Quæ si multa mihi voranda dentur,
> Immortalis in iis repente fiam.

The third line, with its repetition of "umque," is peculiar rather than elegant. The doctor rates the schoolmasters of his day for smoking during class hours: he tells them that they are losing an opportunity of inhaling the most invigorating salts at no expense.

> Quando doces pueros, tibi fistula semper in ore est,
> Atque scholæ fumos angulus omnis habet.

"Oh, my Orbilius!" he exclaims, "wherefore dost thou do so? Dost thou complain of the stuffiness of the schoolroom. Thou art mistaken, Orbilius, these vapours are full of volatile salts, by which, if thou wert wise, thou wouldst attain a long life. Away with thy nasty pipe, and suck in rather these redolent exhalations whereby thou mayest become healthy and aged."

It must not be supposed that the scientific—or physico-

77

medical, as the doctor calls it—portion of the subject is dismissed in
such few words. The author dilates on the theory, turns it over,
tosses it about, takes a bite, squeezes it, holds it up for admiration,
and then reluctantly puts it aside. In the course of his physico-
medical argument, he introduces a few illustrative anecdotes. One
of these, taken from P. Borellus, is to this effect: A servant much
devoted to his master, on his return from a journey, found his lord
dead and prepared for burial. Full of grief, he cast himself on the
deceased, and kissing his pallid lips poured forth a whirlwind of
sighs. The breath thus emitted penetrated to the lungs of the corpse,
inflated them, and the dead opened his eyes, winked, and sat up.
The sighs of the faithful domestic had fanned into flame the
expiring, and as all had deemed expired, vital spark. From
Orubelius our author quotes another story in confirmation of his
hypothesis:—

A woman had died in her first confinement, or, at all events,
had fallen into a state which was believed by the attendants and by
Orubelius, who was the physician present, to be death. She lay thus
for a quarter of an hour devoid of sense and feeling, with pale face,
stationary pulse, and with lungs which had ceased to play. A maid-
servant who thus beheld her, opened her mouth, and breathed into
it; whereupon the patient revived. The physician then asked the girl
where she had learned the use of this simple yet efficient
restorative, and the servant replied that she had seen it practised
upon new-born children with the happiest results. The author also
assures us of the beneficial effect produced by wringing the necks of
poultry before a person in articulo mortis, and making the cocks
and hens breathe out their souls into the mouth of the dying,
whereby he is not unfrequently restored, and becomes quite well
and chirrupy.

But, continues Dr. Cohausen, it is not only the exhalations
from the lungs which are life-generative, but also those from the
pores. The pores are little mouths situated all over the body,
constantly engaged in the aëration of the blood; they inhale the
surrounding atmosphere and then exhale it again, charged with
balsamic and sulphurous particles taken up from the system. Men's
bodies are pneumatic-hydraulic machines, composed of fluid and
solid materials, and health depends on the fluids being prevented
from coagulating, by being stirred up by the constant operations of
the currents of air which penetrate the frame through the pores and
mouth. The solid portion of the body is disposed to harden and dry
up and become stiff, and this produces age and decay; but if the
circulation of the fluids be kept up by the healthful infusion of fresh

vital force and living energies, then decrepitude and death may be almost indefinitely postponed.

Now the lips of the little mouths or pores all over the person can be kept flexible by oil, and therefore enabled to perform their functions with facility. Thus Pollio, an ancient soldier of the Emperor Augustus, when asked how he had succeeded in prolonging his energies over a hundred years, replied that he had daily moistened his outer man with oil, and his inner man with honey. Dr. Cohausen proceeds to lay down that it is better to absorb the exhalations of little girls than those of little boys, because females are more oily than males—a view we in no way feel inclined to dispute, without having recourse to the receipt of Mocrodius for wholesale incremations, which the doctor quotes to establish the fact:—"Lay one female body to six male bodies, in a great pyre, for thereby the male corpses are the more speedily consumed." No doubt about it: there is enough combustible material in one woman to set any number of men in a blaze.

Johannes Fabricius, in his Palladium Chymicum, relates that he knew of a lady whose hair when combed emitted sparks.

Bartholinus mentions in his Tractatus de Luce Hominum the case of a female who flashed fire whenever her limbs or back were rubbed with a towel. These examples lead our author to conclude that in women there is not merely a considerable amount of oil, but that there is also no small item of latent fire; we are inclined to add, explosive material as well.

The advantage of old men marrying young wives is next discussed by Dr. Cohausen; and he strongly urges all who have entered on the sere and yellow leaf, to take to themselves wives of very early age; that, if Providence has not made them superintendents of orphanages, or schoolmasters, they may be enabled at small expense to inhale youthful breath. Men already possessed of wives are to spend their days in the nursery. As an instance of the advantage of patriarchs taking girl-wives, he relates the story of a certain ancient man with snow-white hair and beard, who married at the advanced age of eighty. After a while the old man fell ill; all his hair and skin came off. On his recovery, he had a fresh transparent complexion, and a magnificent bushy head and chin of vivid red hair.

"Whatever you do!" earnestly entreats the doctor, "never marry an old woman; she will absorb all the vital principle from your lungs. Alas for him who, in hopes of gaining money, marries a rich old spinster! She becomes youthful, and he prematurely aged. For old women," he continues, "are like cats, whose breath is poisonous to life. From the eyes and mouth a cat discharges so much that is hurtful, that it has been the cause of innumerable complaints. Indeed, Matthiolus relates that a whole monastery of Religious died because they kept a number of cats."

"My dear reader," says Cohausen, "if you are young and wish to marry, follow the advice of Baron von Hevel, late member of the Imperial Council, which he gives in his 'Psalmodia Sacra':—

> "Si cupis uxorem quæ præstet ubique decorem,
> Formidetque marem, dilige sorte parem,
> Prolificam, bellam, prudentem quære puellam,
> Non genium vanum, nec viduam nec anum.

That is:—If you want a wife who may be a credit to you, and respect her husband, choose a girl your equal, prolific, comely, prudent; not a giddy head, nor an old widow." If this is a specimen of the Baron's Sacred Psalmody, we must allow the book to be very light reading for a Sunday.

In reading this extraordinary work, one is astonished at the manner in which the author seems to regard the fair sex as merely pharmaceutic agents, putting them much on a level with pills and powders, created for the purpose of keeping men in good health, and prolonging their lives. The idea scarce suggests itself to him, that they may object to be so regarded and administered. Dr. Cohausen would, as soon as look at you, write a prescription containing, among other items, so many respirations of the breath of little girls to be taken in scented smoke.

		lb.	oz.	drm.
℞ Gum	Olibani	1	8	
"	Styrac		2	
"	Myrrhi		2	
"	Benz.		4	
Corb. casc. pulv.				4
Anhel. puellarum.		quant. suff.		

When the question does arise, how the damsels will like this treatment, the doctor brushes it aside with imperturbable coolness. It will be a great honour to them, to be thus rendered conducive to the prolongation of male life. Indeed, it will cause them not to be held as cheap as they are now. At present they are good-for-noughts; but employed to infuse the breath of life into men's lungs, they will be respected and valued.

And now, with a flourish of horns, he introduces the "Wondrous discovery of philosophical chymistry," of which he boasted on his title-page. "Now then, O ye cooks of Gebri, or, that I may give you your better title, ye sons of Hermes, who has taught you to extract the marvellous stone of the philosophers from the fire, that thereby ye may be skilled to sustain a protracted life! Now will I disclose to you a new philosophy! The once famous hermetic philosopher in France, Johann Petsus Faber of Montpelier, boasted of a certain arcanum animale which would cause any one who used it to be free from injury caused by the inclemency of the weather, from the gray hairs of age, from exhaustion through bodily fatigue, or through mental tension, whom no sickness would enfeeble, but who would reach the term fixed by Providence for his days, free from injury from every foe. I shall prove that Hermippus protracted his life by the use of such an arcanum. For although, hitherto, it has been an unknown arcanum to use the crude breath of little maidens for the prolongation of the mortal existence, still it will be regarded a far higher arcanum if this can be concentrated and cooked into an essence by chymical process, so that it should have in itself the invisible spirit of nature, and the subtilised fundamental principle of life. Let no one consider what I am now about to relate as a fable, but let him hold it as genuine fact. In my youth I had the good fortune to have the entrée of the house of an illustrious personage, whose lady was immeasurably learned in the hermetic science, and laboured at it along with her husband; with her I had the opportunity of discussing the primordial matter of universal substance, which the philosophers have veiled under enigma and fable. She boasted that she had learned the secret of this from an Italian Adeptus at Rome, and thereby she aroused my curiosity to hear what it was: although, at the time, I was by no means slightly acquainted with hermetic philosophy.

"Once, as I urgently besought her to do me the favour of disclosing to me this mystery, she began, after the manner of philosophers, to speak in similitude: she said the ens spirituale was that without which no man could exist. It was common to all, to rich and poor alike. Adam brought it with him out of Paradise, and in it lay a nourishing principle of life attenuated in water and exhaled in air. I will not refer to other enigmas, which she knew how to propound from the writings of philosophers.

"In order to make the matter more conclusive, she ordered to be brought from her cabinet a vessel containing cold water, which she held under my nose, telling me that it was the true subjectum of science, distilled, as one might conclude, from female exhalations, which Flamellus terms corporeal vapour. With this she roused to the highest pitch my anxiety to thoroughly sound the mystery, as I had already seen hints of these properties in the writings of

81

Sandivogius and other philosophers. I did not fail to use my utmost persuasion on every available opportunity to penetrate the secret of this Lixivium microcosmi. At last the favour was accorded me, and I ascertained that this holy arcanum consisted in human breath, which was collected from this lady's servant girls, and liquefied in glass instruments curved like trumpets. The water thus gathered was concentrated in retorts and other chymical apparatus, and was the very essence fixed of impalpable matter.

"By means of this discovery, life may be easily prolonged over a hundred years, for this vapour of breath collected from maidens in trumpets, when distilled, becomes an elixir of life, and by the copious use of this concentrated vitality steamed down to an essence, man becomes interpenetrated with living energy capable of resisting disease and repelling the inroads of age."

If we consider that the substances we absorb into our bodies become part of ourselves, and that our systems are undergoing a perpetual assimilation of the particles taken into us and renovation thereby, so that every seven years we have totally changed our substance, it is evident that, in the words of a learned friend of Doctor Cohausen, "This entire Hermippus, since he lived over one hundred years, must have been completely composed of the transmutated breath and porous exhalations of little girls; so that his career must have closed by evaporation."

It is certain that men can live a long time on what they inspire, without eating; for the famous laughing philosopher Democritus, who lived to a hundred and nine, when near his death observed that his sister was depressed, and on inquiring the cause, ascertained that she had anticipated great pleasure by attending an approaching festival of Ceres, but that she feared his death would render it an infringement of etiquette for her to be present at the public festivities. Democritus consoled her by promising to live over the day. And, in order to extend his life the required time, he ordered her to keep warm bread poultices under his nose, that by constantly inhaling the nourishing vapours he might be preserved. When the festival was over he ordered the bread pap to be removed, whereupon he gently expired.

Now, argues our doctor,—and this is a signal illustration of his method of drawing conclusions from insufficient premises,—if the vapour of bread could sustain the fleeting spirit of Democritus,—then the still more invigorating outbreathings of little maidens will prolong life indefinitely;—for only consider how much better are little girls than soft pap!

At the startling results of this discovery:—

therefore ye—

Posteri, sic vitam ducite!

THE BARONESS DE BEAUSOLEIL

"Madame de Beausoleil, astronomer and alchemist in the seventeenth century, who came from Germany to France in the exercise of her profession, was incarcerated at Vincennes in 1641, by order of Cardinal Richelieu; the date of her death is unknown." Such is all that the great French biographical dictionaries have to say concerning a woman of surprising talent, indomitable perseverance, and a martyr of science. She was the first to draw attention to the mineral resources of France, and to indicate the profit which might accrue to the treasury by the working of the mines. And how did France repay her services? By despoiling her of her private wealth, by casting her into prison, and leaving her to perish forgotten in its dungeons. And even now her very name and services are passed over and ignored. A sad chapter is that in the history of science which relates the names of its martyrs, and records their services and the ingratitude and ignominy with which they have been repaid. Among these martyrs the good Baroness of Beausoleil deserves commemoration, and merits now the attention that the age in which she lived refused to yield to her.

The date and place of her birth cannot be fixed with accuracy; but, as a memoir published in 1640 says that for thirty years she had been engaged in mineralogical studies, it seems probable that she was born about 1590. She belonged to the noble family of Bertereau, in the Touraine; her Christian name was Martine. In 1610 she married Jean du Châtelet, Baron de Beausoleil and d'Auffenbach, a Brabantine nobleman of great learning and abilities. The Baron had borne arms in his youth, but his natural tastes lay in the direction of natural philosophy, and his attention was chiefly directed to mineralogy, then a science in its earliest infancy. Following the bent of his inclinations, and impelled by the desire of obtaining a practical acquaintance with the working of mines, and the character and conditions of the different metal ores in situ, he visited in order the mines of Germany, Hungary, Bohemia, Tyrol, Silesia, Moravia, Poland, Sweden, Italy, Spain, Scotland, and England. By this means he obtained a practical knowledge of his subject possessed by no other in his day, and an intimate acquaintance with ores and their indications, which made him the first of mineralogists. The German Emperors, Rudolph and Matthias, recognised his abilities, and constituted him Commissary-General of the Hungarian mines. The Archduke Leopold created him Director-in-Chief of the Trentin and Tyrolean mines, and the Dukes of Bavaria, Nieubourg, and Cleves conferred upon him similar offices in their territories; lastly, a brevet of like nature was given him by the Pope for the States of the Church. In 1600, at the recommendation of Pierre de Beringhen, Controller-General of the French mines, the Baron came to France.

Ten years after he married Martine de Bertereau, who thenceforth became his companion in all his travels, his fellow-labourer in the same field of science, and who even surpassed him in ability and skill in detecting the indications of ore. The couple examined together the German, Italian, and Swedish mines. She then crossed the Atlantic to investigate those of the New World. She next applied herself to the study of chemistry, geometry, hydraulics, and mechanics, and became accomplished in each of these sciences. She was able to speak fluently Italian, German, English, Spanish, French, and was a Latin and Hebrew scholar. In 1626, Cinq-Mars, then superintendent of the mines, gave the Baron a commission to traverse several of the provinces, and open mines wherever he found indications of ore. Whilst thus engaged, the Baron published a volume on The True Philosophy concerning the First Matter of Minerals, a work of no great value, as it is overloaded with the absurd theories of the metamorphosis of metals then in vogue.

The course of his investigations led him and his wife to Morlaix, in Brittany, and there, in 1627, an event took place which gave them considerable annoyance, as well as proving a severe pecuniary loss. The Baron was engaged in examining a mine in the forest of Buisson-Rochemarée, and his wife was at Rennes seeing to the registration of their commission. Taking advantage of the absence of both at the same time, a provincial provost, Touche-Grippé by name, of the race of Dogberry, made an entry into their house, under the plea of search after magical apparatus, for, as the provost said, "How can mortal man discover what is underground without diabolical aid?" On this pretext, then, the house was ransacked, and Dogberry laid violent hands on every article which aroused his curiosity or attracted his cupidity. The boxes were broken open, the cupboards burst into, the drawers searched, and gold, silver, jewels, mineralogical specimens, scientific instruments,

84

legal documents, notes of observations made in the course of travel, every fragment of manuscript, private letters, and maps, were carried off by Touche-Grippé and appropriated to his own use.

On the return of the Baron and Baroness to Morlaix they found that, in addition to this robbery in the name of justice, a charge was laid against them of magic. They were constrained to appear before Touche-Grippé and a fellow-magistrate of like nature, and free themselves of the charge. They were allowed to depart exculpated, but without their property, which the magistrate refused to surrender. The Baron appealed to the Parliament of Brittany, but without obtaining any redress; he then applied to that of Paris, but Touche-Grippé had friends at court, and the appeal of the Baron was rejected. Twelve years after, in 1640, we find the Baroness still asking for redress, and still in vain.

The failure of the couple in obtaining any attention so irritated them that they left France and returned to Germany, which had always recognised their services, and treated them with the respect due to their abilities and attainments. Ferdinand II. at once placed the Baron de Beausoleil in charge of the Hungarian mines.

But, unfortunately, the nobleman and his wife were not content to remain in Germany, and after a few years resolved on trying their fortune once more in France. This time they determined on carrying on their operations upon a more extensive scale, and in 1632 they entered the kingdom of Louis XIII., accompanied by fifty German and ten Hungarian miners, together with private servants. The king at once renewed the commission given by Cinq-Mars in 1626, and the Baron commenced a series of explorations in Brittany and in the south of France. The Parliaments of Dijon and Pau having objected to the commission, the king issued an order to them to recognise the Baron and his wife, and to aid them in their search after minerals by affording them every facility which lay in their power. Notwithstanding this apparent royal support, the two mineralogists obtained no pecuniary assistance from Government, but were expected to carry on all their operations at their private expense. The maintenance of sixty miners, the prosecution of extensive works, and the travelling from province to province, could not fail to reduce the means of the couple very considerably. A little glory might accrue to them, but they were sure of becoming the objects of jealousy; they obtained praise from the king, but no money; and after having expended 30,000 livres—in fact, their whole fortune—they were as far from obtaining any pecuniary acknowledgment of their services as they were when first entering France. In 1632 the Baroness addressed a memoir to the king on the mineral treasures of the country; it was entitled, "Veritable

Declarations made to the King and his Council of the rich and inestimable Treasures lately discovered in the Kingdom"; but as this met with no response, she reprinted it under the title "Veritable Declarations of the Discovery of Mines and Minerals in France, by means of which his Majesty and his subjects will be enabled to do without Foreign Mineral Trade; also concerning the Properties of Certain Sources and Mineral Waters lately discovered at Château-Thierry by Madame Martine de Bertereau, Baroness de Beausoleil." In this interesting memoir one hundred and fifty mines are indicated as having been discovered by the Baron and his wife. The Government, satisfied of the value of the services of the two foreigners, but unwilling, for all that, to pay them, now, as acknowledgment, conferred on them a new brevet, giving them extended powers, and elevating the Baron to the grade of Inspector-General of all the mines in France. If glory alone could suffice as a reward to merit, the Baron du Châtelet and Madame de Bertereau must have felt content with the dignity now conferred upon them. But a glory which cost them their whole fortune, and which in no way repaid their labours, must have seemed to them a bitter deception.

Little by little the worthy couple had to reduce their retinue and to curtail their expenses, and after ten years of unrequited exertion in behalf of the crown, their train was scanty enough. However, their hopes were not yet exhausted, promises had been made to them of the most brilliant description, and they relied upon the honour of the French crown to redeem them.

In 1640 the Baroness appealed to Cardinal Richelieu in a pamphlet entitled "La Restitution de Pluton à l'Eminentissime Cardinal Duc de Richelieu," a second title-page adds, "with a refutation of those who believe that mines and subterranean matters are only discovered by magic and by the aid of the devil."

Whether the Cardinal read the memoir or not, we cannot say, but undoubtedly he perused the dedicatory epistle, or, at all events, the sonnet it contains, which sums up its flatteries and hyperbolic compliments.

Esprit prodigieux, chef-d'œuvre de nature,
Elixir épuré de tous les grands esprits,
Puisque vous conduisez notre bonne aventure
Arrêtez un peu l'œil sur ces divins écrits.

Ces écrits sont dressés pour une architecture,
Dont la sainte beauté vous rendra tout épris;
Le soleil et les cieux conduisent la structure,

86

Et vous, vous conduisez cet ouvrage entrepris.

La France et les Français vous demandent les mines;
L'or, l'argent, et l'azur, l'aimant, les calamines,
Sont des trésors cachés par l'esprit de Dieu.

Si vous autorisez ce que l'on vous propose,
Vous verrez, Monseigneur, que, sans métamorphose,
La France deviendra bientôt un Riche-Lieu.

The Restitution of Pluto is a book most interesting, not only
on account of the erudition and rare acquaintance with natural
philosophy which it displays, but also from the stately and vigorous
writing of the authoress. It contains passages glowing with energy,
and is composed in a style of dignified and manly eloquence. Maybe
the publication of this work opened the eyes of the Cardinal to the
fact that the State certainly was indebted to this illustrious couple
for services gratuitously rendered during upwards of ten years. The
most convenient method of paying them was that of silencing the
voices which cried for acknowledgment, and thus stifling the claims
on the royal exchequer. Slanderous reports were circulated relative
to the Beausoleils, and they were accused of various crimes. The
suspicion of magic, which had attached to them from the time of the
inquisition of the provost of Morlaix, was revived, and the
prejudices of the age tended to give it force to overthrow the noble
pair. Old superstitions concerning gnomes of the mines and
subterranean demons were not yet extinct. The Baroness herself
believed in them, and in one of her works speaks of her having
encountered some of them. In the mines of Neusol and Chemnitz in
Hungary, she says, "I saw little dwarfs about three or four palms
high, old, and dressed like miners, that is, clothed in an old suit, and
with a leather apron, a white tunic and cap, a lamp and staff in
hand—terrible spectres to those who are unaccustomed to mines."
Several times already, as appears from her writings, she and her
husband had been exposed to the violence of the rude and ignorant
rustics, who thought their scientific instruments means for
conjuring up the devil, and the authorities were, as we have seen at
Morlaix, quite prepared to second the popular superstition when
profit could be obtained thereby. The divining rod, then much in
vogue in Germany, was used by the Baron and his wife, who had
strong belief in its magnetic properties, and the employment of it
may have given some colour to the charges now raised against them
on all sides of being necromancers in league with evil spirits.

In 1642, by order of Cardinal Richelieu, the Baron de

Beausoleil was cast into the Bastille, and the Baroness was shut up in the state prison of Vincennes, without trial and sentence. Thus, after forty years of labour together in the same pursuits, in the same manner of life, in the decline of their days this worthy couple were separated, to spend the rest of their life in prison. Such was the reward accorded to them for their devotion to the cause of science, and the recompense for the benefits they had afforded to France.

The Baroness died in the prison of Vincennes. The date of her death is unknown, but probably it was not long deferred. Her ardent soul would not long endure the torture of imprisonment, and the sorrows of finding all her labours repaid with ingratitude. Her husband died in the Bastille after lingering for three years behind bars.

One last glimpse of the noble woman we obtain from the Mémoires de Lancelot touchant la vie de M. de Saint-Cyran. The Abbé de Saint-Cyran was shut up in Vincennes in 1638 as a Jansenist. On the 14th of May in that year he was arrested by Richelieu, who then made use of the remarkable words, "Had Luther and Calvin been imprisoned the moment they began to dogmatise, Government would have been spared much trouble." Saint-Cyran remained in Vincennes till 1642. He died the next year. During his imprisonment he observed in church the Baroness de Beausoleil and her daughter, prisoners like himself. Touched with the scantiness of their clothing, he endeavoured to procure for them the dresses which they needed, and those necessaries which the sickness of the noble lady demanded. The following are the words of the memoir:—"Whilst M. de Saint-Cyran was in Vincennes he met a lady named the Baroness de Beausoleil, who was there with her daughter, whilst her husband was prisoner in the Bastille. Seeing her in church, poorly clad, he made inquiries about her, and sent to Madame le Maître, telling her whom he had seen, and begging her to purchase some chemises for this person, expressly desiring that they might be long, for nothing escaped his charity, and also that the material should be good. When they had been sent, it was ascertained that what had been made for the mother would only fit the daughter, and he gave them to the latter, and ordered fresh ones for the mother. Afterwards he requested to have fustian under-garments, shoes and stockings, sent to them according to measures which he procured, and also after the fashion of the day.

"At the approach of winter he wrote to say that he found that the lady was menaced with dropsy, and that she was extremely sensitive to cold. He therefore begged the person I have mentioned to make for her a dress of thick ratteen, of the best description, and trimmed with black lace, because he heard that such was the fashion, and he added that his maxim was, that people should be served according to their rank. He also had a gown made for the daughter.... He also sent to the Bastille to have the husband well dressed; and I know that the person who brought the tailor to him asked him to choose his material and the trimmings, for he had orders to have him dressed as suited his taste."

In Saint-Cyran's own letters we find additional details, very sad they are, but full of interest to those who have followed this worthy couple through their labours into disgrace.

"This letter," writes the Abbé to his friend M. de Rebours, "is to entreat you, at your convenience, to execute with the utmost secrecy, without allowing it to transpire who sends you and who you are who make the inquiries, a work of great charity upon which I am engaged. There is a person imprisoned here who is the authoress of the book I send you; will you kindly go to M. Maréchal, glassmaker, and consequently a gentleman, and inquire what has become of the children of the Baroness de Beausoleil, a German lady; and lest he should mistrust you, say you do it in charity; and should he still have suspicions, promise him any token of sincerity which he may require. He lives near the House of Charity in the Faubourg St. Germain. Perhaps you had better inquire at the House of Charity for M. Maréchal, and of the girl named Madlle. Barbe, with whom the Baron de Beausoleil, now in the Bastille, and his wife, now here in prison, had left one of their daughters, named Anne du Châtelet, aged twelve, whom her mother had instructed in Latin, so as to make her useful in the search after mines, a science hereditary in the family. By this means you may be able to learn what has become of the other children.

"If you know yourself, or by any of your friends, M. Maturel, advocate, or his brother, who favoured these good people, and who know all their affairs, and are aware of all the circumstances of the robbery committed upon them in Brittany, and estimated at a hundred thousand crowns, you will obtain their entire confidence, and be able to learn what has become of the children. This must be done with the utmost circumspection. You must say that your friends, who lived formerly in Paris, want to know particulars of the family. The eldest son, having gone to the Bastille without proper precautions, to make inquiries concerning his father, was arrested. But we desire to learn something about the other children, some five or six, and who has got charge of them.... What a strange thing it is, that there is no surer means of falling into trouble than to love the faith and Catholic verity."

Such is the last glimpse we obtain of this unfortunate family. Two noble and devoted servants of science cast into dungeons, and their children scattered or imprisoned—because they served the State too well.

On the 4th of December 1642 Richelieu was called to his account before the throne of a just Judge, to answer for that as well as his other crimes; and in another century the accursed Bastille was torn down stone from stone by an exasperated people and laid low in the dust, never to rise again.

SOME CRAZY SAINTS

Among the ignorant there is always admiration for the not-understood, and in former times nothing was less understood than hysteria. The original source of a thousand superstitions, and of most idolatries, lies in the sense of surprise, wonder, into which the mind is thrown by seeing that which it cannot explain. A remarkable rock, a queer shell, peculiar eyes in a man or woman, a curious fruit, like the coco-de-mer, awaken admiration, perplex the untaught mind, and superinduce religious reverence. What strikes the imagination thenceforth provokes the instinctive awe felt for the supernatural. Now nothing is more calculated to astonish those who know naught of nervous disorder than the phenomena attending hysteria and its allied maladies. Consequently, not only have hysteric patients been for a long period regarded as specially allied with the spiritual powers, but so also have the insane, because insanity is particularly amazing to the man with his wits about him. To the present day in the East epilepsy is regarded as something sacred, and idiocy and madness as divine possession. It is not marvellous that some men and women in rude times, who were subject to fits, were scrofulous, hysterical, and lived out of the ordinary mode of life, should have been given a character for sanctity that scarcely perhaps was their due. Hysterical persons have a strange craving after sympathy, a hunger after notoriety, and will endure much self-imposed torture to obtain that which to their vanity is dearer than bodily ease.

Motives in this world are much mixed, and nowhere more mixed than in hysterical saints, where the glory of God and the glorification of self are inextricably involved.

It is not in the least surprising that some of the crazy saints we shall now consider should have been canonised by the popular voice; what is extraordinary is that they should have been accepted and inserted in the lists of those who are recognised by the Church as models of holiness, and that in a later and more critical age they have not been kicked out of the association to which they were ill qualified to belong. We will begin with the story of St. Symeon the Fool.

I
ST. SYMEON SALOS

The life of this saintly personage comes to us on excellent authority. The patron of Symeon in Edessa, and the witness of his acts, was a certain simple-minded John the Deacon. Leontius, Bishop of Neapolis in Cyprus, whose Apology for Sacred Images was accepted and approved by the Second Council of Nicæa, was acquainted with this John the Deacon, and from his account of the doings of Symeon wrote the life, in Greek, which has come down to us entire. It is one of the most curious and instructive of early Christian biographies.

Evagrius, the historian, also a contemporary of Symeon, makes mention of him in his Church History (lib. iv. c. 34).

The story of Symeon is as follows:—

In the reign of the Emperor Justinian, two young Syrians came to Jerusalem to assist at the Feast of the Exaltation of the Holy Cross. The name of one was John, and the name of the other was Symeon. John, a young man of two-and-twenty, was accompanied by his bride, a beautiful and wealthy girl, to whom he had been very lately married, and by his old father. With Symeon was his widowed mother, aged eighty.

The festival having terminated, the pilgrims started on their return to Edessa, and had reached Jericho, when John, reining in his horse, bade the caravan proceed, whilst he and his comrade Symeon tarried behind. The two young men flung themselves from their horses on the coarse grass. In the distance, near Jordan, glimmered the white walls of a monastery, and a track led towards it from the main road followed by the caravan.

"What place is that?" asked Symeon.

"It is the home of angels."

"Are the angels visible?" Symeon inquired.

"Only to those who elect to follow their manner of life," answered John, and descanted to his companion on the charms of a monastic life. "Let us cast lots," he said, "whether we shall follow the road to the convent, or that which the caravan has pursued." They cast lots, and the decision was for the life of angels.

So they turned into the road that led to Jordan and the monastery, and as they went they encouraged each other. For, we are told, John feared lest the love Symeon bore to his old widowed mother would draw him back, and Symeon dreaded the effects of the remembrance of the fair young bride on John.

On reaching the monastery, which was that of St. Gerasimus, the abbot, named Nicon, received them cordially, and gave them a long address on the duties and excellences of the monastic life. Then both fell at his feet and besought him at once to shear off their hair. The abbot hesitated, and spoke to each in private, urging a delay of a year, but Symeon boldly said, "My companion may wait, but I cannot. If you will not shear my head at once, I will go to some other monastery where they are less scrupulous." Then he added, "Father, I pray thee, ask the Lord to be gracious to and strengthen my comrade John, that the remembrance of his young wife, to whom he has been only lately married, draw him not back."

And when the abbot spoke to John, "My father," said he, "pray for my comrade Symeon, who has a widowed mother of eighty years, and they have been inseparable night and day; he dearly loves her, and has been wont never to leave the old woman alone for two hours in the day. I fear me lest his love for his mother make him take his hand from the plough and look back."

So the abbot cut off their hair, and promised on the morrow to clothe them with the religious habit. Then some of the members crowding round them congratulated the neophytes that on the morrow "they would be regenerated and cleansed from all sin." The young men, unaccustomed to monastic language, were alarmed, thinking that they were about to be rebaptized, and went to the abbot to remonstrate. He allayed their apprehensions by explaining to them that the monks alluded to their putting on the "angelic habit."

John and Symeon did not long remain in the abbey before a wish came upon them to leave it. Accordingly, in the night, they made their escape, and rambled in the desert to the east of the Dead Sea, till they lighted on a cave which had once been tenanted by a hermit, but was now without inhabitant. The date-palms and vegetables in the garden grew untouched, and the friends settled in the cave to follow the lives of the desert solitaries.

Their peace of mind was troubled for long by thoughts of the parent and wife left behind. "O Lord, comfort my old mother," was the incessant prayer of Symeon; "O Lord, dry the tears of my young wife," was the supplication of John. At length Symeon had a dream in which he saw the death of his mother, and shortly after John was comforted by a vision which assured him that his wife was no more.

After a while Symeon informed his comrade that he could not rest in the cave, but that he was resolved to serve God in the city. He felt there were souls to be saved in the world, and that he had a call to labour for their conversion.

This announcement filled John with dismay. He wept, and entreated Symeon not to desert him. "What shall I do, alone, in this wild ocean of sand? O my brother, I thought that death alone would have separated us, and now thou tearest thyself away of thine own will. Thou knowest I have forsaken all my kindred, and I have thee only, my brother, and will my brother desert me?"

"Do thou, John, remember me in thy prayers here in the desert, whilst I struggle in the world; and I will also pray for thee. But go I must."

"Then," said John solemnly, "be on thy guard, brother Symeon, lest what thou hast acquired in the desert be lost in the world; lest what silence has wrought, bustle destroy. Above all, beware lest that modesty, which seclusion from women has fostered, fail thee in their society; and lest the body, wasted with fasting here, surfeit there. Beware, also, lest laughter take the place of gravity, and worldly solicitude break up the serenity of the soul."

He had good cause to give this advice, as the sequel proves; but Symeon gave no heed to the exhortation, answering, "Fear not for me, brother; I am not acting on my own impulse, but on a divine call."

Then they wept on one another's shoulders, and Symeon promised to revisit his friend before he died.

John accompanied Symeon a little way, and then again they wept and embraced, and after that John sorrowfully returned to his cell, and Symeon set his face towards the world, and came to Jerusalem.

He spent three days in the Holy City, visiting the sacred sites, and then went to Emesa.

Hitherto his life had been, if not altogether commendable, yet at least respectable. But from this point his character changes. He simulated madness, his biographer says, with the motive of drawing down on himself the ridicule of the world.

This ill-conditioned fellow is venerated by Greeks and Russians as a saint, and Cardinal Baronius with culpable negligence introduced his name into the modern Roman Martyrology.

Alban Butler, the Père Giry, and the Abbé Guérin, and indeed all Roman Catholic hagiographers, give the former part of this history with some detail, and draw a curtain of pious platitudes over the second act of the drama. They state that the saint made himself a fool for Christ, but are very careful not to give the particulars of his folly.

It is hardly necessary to point out how untrue to history, how morally dishonest, such a course is.

The Jesuit Fathers, who continued the work of Bollandus, give the original Greek Life in their volume for July, but with searchings of heart. "If," say they, "our lucubrations could be confined to such small space as would suffice to give only the lives of those men whose memory is edifying and deserves imitation, never for a moment would it have entered into our heads to give and illustrate the life of St. Symeon Salos. For towards the close of that life many things occur, silly, stupid, absurd, scandalous to the ignorant, and to the learned and better educated worthy of laughter rather than of faith."

But the unfortunate Bollandists were not at liberty to avoid the unpleasant task, as Symeon figured among the Saints of the Roman Calendar in these words: "At Emesa (on 1st July) St. Symeon, Confessor, surnamed Salos, who became a fool for Christ. But God manifested his lofty wisdom by great miracles." 1st July is a mistake for 21st July, the day on which St. Symeon is venerated in the East. Baronius was misled by a faulty manuscript of the Life, which gave α for κα, as the day on which the saint died. It is a pity that, when he was transferring the day, he did not place St. Symeon Salos on the more appropriate 1st of April.

The only way in which I can account for this insertion in the Calendar is that Baronius read the first part of the Life, and was pleased with it, and did not trouble himself to conclude the somewhat lengthy manuscript. He therefore placed Symeon in his new Roman Martyrology, which received the approbation and imprimatur of Pope Sixtus V. and afterwards of Benedict XIV.

But to return to St. Symeon.

On reaching the outskirts of Emesa, Symeon found on a dung-heap a dead, half-putrefied dog. He unwound his girdle and attached the dog with it to his foot, and so entered the gate of the city and passed before a boys' school. The attention of the children was at once diverted from their books, and, in spite of the expostulation of their preceptor, they rushed out of school after Salos, like a swarm of wasps, shouting, "Heigh! here comes a crack-brained abbot!" and kicked the dog and slapped the monk.

Next day was Sunday. Symeon entered the church with a bag of nuts before him, and during the celebration of the divine mysteries threw nuts at the candles and extinguished several of them. Then, running up into the ambone, or pulpit, he threw nuts at the women in the congregation, and hit them in their faces. Laughter and outcries interrupted the sacred service, and Symeon was expelled the church, not, however, without offering a sturdy resistance.

Outside, the market-place must have resembled one on a Sunday abroad at the present day, for it was full of stalls for the sale of cakes. In rushing from the church officials, he knocked over the stalls,[4] and the sellers beat him so unmercifully for his pains that he groaned in himself: "Humble Symeon, verily, verily, they will maul the life out of you in an hour!"

A seller of sour wine[5] saw him racing round the market-place, and, being in want of a servant, hailed him, and said, "Here, fellow; if you want a job, sell pulse for me."

"I am ready," answered Symeon. So he gave him pulse and beans and peas to sell, but the hermit, who had eaten nothing for a week, devoured the whole amount.

"This will never do," said the mistress of the house; "the abbot eats more than he sells. Here, fellow, what money have you taken?"

Symeon had neither money nor vegetables to show, so the woman turned him out of the house. The monk placidly seated himself on the doorstep, and proceeded to offer up his evening devotions. But these were not complete without the ritual adjunct of smoking incense. Symeon looked about for a broken pot in which to put some cinders; but finding none, he took some lighted charcoal in the palm of his hand, and strewed a few grains of incense upon it. The mistress of the house, smelling the fumes, looked out of the window, and exclaimed, "Gracious heaven! Abbot Symeon, are you making a thurible of your hand?"[6] At that moment the charcoal began to burn his palm, and he threw the ashes into the lap of his coarse goat's-hair mantle.

The taverner and his wife were so moved by the piety of Symeon that they received him into the house, and employed him in selling vegetables, which duty he executed satisfactorily when his appetite was not exacting. They speedily found that Silly Symeon drew customers to their house, for Symeon laid himself out to divert them, and it became the rage for a time in Emesa for folk to visit the tavern, saying, "We must have our dinner and wine where that comical fool lives."

One day Symeon Salos saw a serpent put its head into one of

---

4 Ἔστρεψεν τὰ ταβλία τῶν πλακουνταρίων.
5 Εἶς φουσκάριος.
6 Εἶς Θεὸς, ἀββᾶ Συμεὼν, εἰς τὸν χεῖρα σου θυμιᾷς.

the wine pitchers in the tavern, and drink. He took a stick and broke
the pitcher, thinking that the serpent had spit poison into the wine.
The publican was angry with Symeon for breaking the amphora,
and, catching the stick out of his hand, cudgelled the poor monk
with it, without listening to his explanation. On the morrow the
serpent again entered the tavern, and went to the wine jars. The
host saw it this time, and rushed after it with a stick, upsetting and
breaking several amphoræ. "Ha, ha!" exclaimed Symeon, peeping
out from behind the door, where he had concealed himself, "who is
the biggest fool to-day?"[7]

The taverner did not show much kindness to Symeon; but this
is hardly to be wondered at, when we hear that, summoned to his
wife's bedroom by her cries one night, he found it invaded by the
saint, who was deliberately undressing in it for bed. This he did,
says Leontius, Bishop of Neapolis, in order to lower the high
opinion entertained of him by his master.[8] After this, as may well be
believed, the taverner told the tale over his cups with much laughter
to his guests, and with confusion to his man. In Lent the saint
devoured flesh, but would not touch bread. "He is possessed," said
the inn-keeper; "he insulted my wife, and he eats meat in Lent like
an infidel."

In Emesa he picked up a certain John the Deacon, who
admired his proceedings. To this John, the saint related the events
of his former life; and from John Leontius heard the story.

One day John the Deacon was on his way to the public baths,
when he met Symeon. "You will be all the better for a wash, my
friend," said the Deacon; "come with me to the baths."

"With all my heart," answered the monk, and he forthwith
peeled off his clothes, wrapped them in a bundle, and set them on
his head.

"My brother!" exclaimed the Deacon, "put on your clothes
again. I cannot walk with you in the public street in this condition."

"Very well, friend, then I will walk first, and you can follow."
And stark naked, bearing his bundle "like a faggot" on his head, he
stalked down the crowded thoroughfare.

The baths were divided into two parts, one for women, the
other for men. Symeon ran towards the women's entrance.

"Not that way!" shouted the Deacon in alarm; "the other side
is for men."

---

[7] Τί ἐστιν ἔξηχε, ἴδε, οὐκ εἰμὶ ἐγὼ μόνος ἀπέργης.

[8] Θέλων οὖν ὁ Ὅσιος ἀναλῦσαι τὴν οἰκοδομὴν αὐτοῦ, ἵνα μὴ θριαμβεύσῃ αὐτὸν, ἐν
μιᾷ κοιμωμένης τῆς γυναικὸς αὐτοῦ μόνης, κἀκείνου προβάλλοντος οἶνον, ἐπέβη
πρὸς αὐτὴν ὁ ἀββᾶς Συμεὼν, καὶ ἐχηματίσατο ἀποδύεσθαι τὸ ἱμάτιον αὐτοῦ, κ.τ.λ.

"Hot water here, hot water there," answered Symeon; "one is as good as the other"; and throwing down his bundle, he bounded into the ladies' compartment, and splashed in amongst the female bathers.

The women screamed, flew on him, beat, scratched, pushed him, and drove him ignominiously forth.

The biographer gravely informs us that on another occasion an unbelieving Jew saw Symeon privately bathing with two "angels," and would have told what he had seen had not Salos silenced him. It was only after the death of the saint that the Jew related the circumstance. The Christians concluded that the two lovely forms with whom Symeon was enjoying a dip were angels. "To such a pass of purity and impassibility had the saint attained," continues the Bishop of Neapolis, "that he often led the dance in public with an actress on each arm; he romped with actresses, and by no means infrequently allowed them to tickle his ribs and slap him."[9]

Indeed, his biographer tells some stories of his association with very fallen angels, which are anything but edifying.

His antics in the streets and market-place became daily more outrageous. "Sometimes he pretended to hobble as if he were lame, sometimes he capered, sometimes he dragged himself along to the seats, then he tripped up the passers-by, and sent them sprawling; sometimes at the rising of the moon he would roll on the ground kicking. Sometimes he pretended to speak incoherently, for he said that this above all things suited those who were made fools for Christ. By this means he often refuted vice, or spat forth his bile against certain persons, with a view to their correction."

A Count, living near Emesa, heard of him, and said, "I will find out whether the fellow is a hypocrite or not."

As it happened, when the Count entered the city, he found that Symeon's housekeeper[10] had hoisted her master upon her back, whilst another young woman administered to him a severe castigation with a leather strap. The Count, we are told, went away much scandalised. Salos wriggled off his housekeeper's back, ran after the Count, struck him on the cheek, then stripped off his own clothes, and danced in complete nudity before him up the street and down again.

Passing some girls dancing one day, and noticing that some of them had a cast in their eyes, he said, "My dears, let me kiss your pretty eyes and cure you of your squint."

---

[9] Ὥστε ἔστιν ὅτε ἔβαλλον τὰς χεῖρας αὐτῶν τὰ ἄσεμνα γύναια εἰς τὸν κόλπον αὐτοῦ,καὶ ἐσίαινον, καὶ ἐκόπταζον, καὶ ἐγαργάλιζον αὐτόν.
[10] Ἐβάσταζεν αὐτὸν μία προϊσταμενὴ, καὶ ἄλλη ἑλώριζεν αὐτόν.

One or two of the young women permitted him to kiss them, and, we are assured, were cured; after which, all the girls who thought they had something the matter with their eyes ran after Symeon to have theirs kissed. The Deacon John invited him to dinner one day. Symeon went, and devoured raw bacon which was hanging up in the chimney, instead of what was provided for the guests. Symeon was fond of frequenting the houses of the wealthy, where, says his biographer, he sported with and kissed the maids.[11]

Two Fathers were troubled that Origen should be regarded as a heretic, and they asked the hermit John the reason. John bade them inquire of Symeon in Emesa. On reaching Emesa they found the monk in the tavern, with a bowl of boiled pulse before him, eating as voraciously "as a bear." "What is the use of consulting this Gnostic?" said one of the Fathers; "he knows nothing but how to crunch pulse."

"What is the matter with the pulse?" asked Symeon, starting up and boxing the hermit on the ears, so that his face bore the mark for three days. "The pulse has been soaking for forty days, and is soft enough, I warrant ye! As for your Origen, he can't eat pulse, for he is at the bottom of the sea. And now take this for your pains!" and he flung the scalding pulse in their faces. His reason, Leontius tells us, was to prevent them from telling all men how he had read their purpose before they had spoken about Origen.

One Lord's Day, Symeon was given a chain of sausages.[12] He hung it over his shoulders like a stole, and filled his left hand with mustard. He ate all day at the sausages, flavouring them with the mustard, and smearing his face with it. This highly amused a rustic, who mocked him. Symeon rushed at him, and threw the mustard in his eyes. The man cried with pain, and Symeon bade him wash the mustard out of his eyes with vinegar. Now it happened that this man was suffering from ophthalmia, and the mustard and vinegar applied to his eyes loosened the white film that was forming over them, and it peeled off, and thus the man was cured.

Symeon had long ago left the service of the publican, and had taken a small cottage, which was only furnished with a bundle of faggots and a housekeeper. John the Deacon supplied him with food, but somehow Symeon managed to secure a store of excellent provisions, and the beggars and tramps of the town were

---

[11] Πολλάκις δὲ προσποιεῖσθαι καταφιλεῖν τὰς δούλας. No wonder if one of them said, "Ὁ Σαλὸς Συμεὼν ἐβιάσατό με." The maid's mistress indignantly scolded Symeon, who replied with a smile, "Ἄφες, ἄφες, ταπεινή, ἄρτι γεννᾷ σοι, καὶ ἔχεις μικρὸν Συμεών."

[12] Σειρὰν σαλσικίων.

accustomed to assemble in his hut occasionally for a grand feast. John the Deacon unexpectedly dropped in on one of these revels, and wondered where the "white wheaten bread, cheesecakes, buns, fish, and wine of all sorts, dry and sweet, and, in short, whatsoever is to be found most dainty,"[13] had come from, which Symeon and his housekeeper were serving out to the beggars and their wives. But when Symeon assured him that these good things had come down straight from heaven in answer to prayer, the Deacon went away wondering and edified. In the same way Symeon always had his pockets full of money. We find him bribing a woman of bad character with a hundred gold pieces to be his companion.[14] Many of these ladies sought his society with eagerness, "for," says his pious biographer, "he was always showing them large sums of money, for he had as much as he wanted, God always invisibly supplying him with funds for his purpose." Whence came this money? For what purpose was it used? Why was the saint so continually found in the society of these women, or among the female servants of the wealthy citizens?

Early in the morning Symeon was wont to leave his hut, twine a garland of herbs, break a bough from a tree, and thus crowned and sceptred enter the city. John the Deacon asked the monk how it was that he never saw him having his hair cut, nor with his hair long. Symeon assured him that this was in answer to prayer. He had supplicated Heaven that he might be saved the trouble of having recourse to a barber, and Heaven had heard him; all which John the Deacon fully believed.

When death approached, Symeon revisited his friend John in the wilderness, who probably did not find his old comrade much improved in morals and manners by his residence in town.

He then returned to Emesa, and was found dead one morning under his bundle of faggots.

The remarks of Alban Butler are not a little amusing. "Although we are not obliged in every instance to imitate St. Symeon, and though it would be rash even to attempt it without a special call; yet his example ought to make us blush"—we should think so, indeed—"when we consider"—ah!—"with what an ill-will we suffer the least things that hurt our pride." Symeon slipped into the Roman Martyrology by an inadvertency. Let us trust that at the next revision, he may be turned out.

---

[13] Σιλίγνια, καὶ πλακοῦντας, καὶ σφαίρια, καὶ ὀψάρια, καὶ οἰνάρια διάφορα, ψαθύρια, καὶ γλυκὺ, καὶ ἁπλῶς ὅσα πάντα ἔχει ὁ βίος λιμβά.
[14] Ἔστι γὰρ ὅτε καὶ τοῦτο ἔλεγε πρὸς μίαν τῶν ἑταιρίδων· θέλεις ἔχο σε φίλην καὶ δίδω σοι ἑκατὸν ὁλοκοτίνα.

II

ST. NICOLAS OF TRANI

The life of this extraordinary man is given to us with much detail by two eye-witnesses of his doings. Bartholomew, a monk, who associated himself with Nicolas, travelled with him, admired, and after his death worshipped him, wrote one of these lives. He had heard from the lips of Nicolas the account of his childhood and youth, and he faithfully recorded what he heard. Therefore Nicolas himself is our authority for all the earlier part of his history, whilst he was in Greece. For the latter part we have the testimony of Bartholomew, his companion night and day.

Secondly, we have an account of the close of his strange career by a certain Adalfert of Trani, also an eye-witness of what he describes; thus there is every reason for believing that we have an authentic history of this man.[15]

Nicolas was the child of Greek parents, near the monastery of Sterium, founded by St. Luke the Stylite. His parents were poor labouring people, and the child was sent, at the age of eight, to guard sheep. About this time he took it into his head to cry incessantly, night and day, "Kyrie eleison!" The mother scolded and beat him, thinking that she might have too much even of a good thing. But as he did not mend or vary his monotonous supplication when he had reached the age of twelve, she angrily bade him pack out of the house, and not come near her again till he had learned to keep his noisy cries to himself.

The boy then ran away to the mountains, where he turned a she-bear out of her cave, and settled himself into it, living on roots and berries; and climbing to dizzy heights, spent his days in yelling from the crags where scarce a goat could find a footing, "Kyrie eleison!"

His clothes were torn to tatters, so that scarce a shred covered his nakedness, his feet were bare, and his hair grew long and ragged.

The poor mother, becoming alarmed at his disappearance, offered a small sum of money to any one who would find the boy and bring him home. The peasants of the village scattered themselves among the mountains, caught the runaway, and at the mother's request took him to the monks of St. Luke's monastery to have the devil exorcised out of him, for she believed he must be mad. But Nicolas in his cave had one night seen come to him an old

---

[15] Both are published in the Acta Sanctorum for June, T.I., pp. 237-260, with notes by Papebroeck, the Bollandist.

man of venerable aspect, with long beard and white hair, stark naked,[16] who bade him be of good cheer, and pursue his admirable course of conduct. The monks of Sterium brought him into the church and endeavoured to exorcise the demon, first with prayers, and afterwards with kicks and blows. Nicolas rushed from the gates of the church shrieking, "Kyrie eleison!" He was brought back and shut up in a tower, with a slab of stone against the door, to keep him in. During the night the sleep of the monks was broken by the muffled cries of "Kyrie eleison!" issuing from the old tower. A thunderstorm burst over the monastery at midnight, and Nicolas dashed the door open, threw down the stone, and leaped forth, shouting between the thunder crashes, "Kyrie eleison!" The monks caught him, put shackles on his wrists, and thrust him into a cell. As they sat next day at their meal in the refectory, the door flew open, and in stalked Nicolas with the chains broken in his hands; he clashed them down on the table before their eyes, and shouted "Kyrie eleison!" till the rafters and walls shook again. The monks rose from table, and thrust him forth, whilst they proceeded with their meal.

Nicolas ran to the church, scrambled up the walls—how no one knew; his biographer Bartholomew thinks he must have swarmed up a sunbeam—reached the dome, and mounting to the apex, began to shout his supplication, "Kyrie eleison!"

In the meantime the monks had retired for their nap after dinner, when the reiterated cries from the top of the church cupola roused them and made sleep impossible. They came forth in great excitement. One, by order of the hegumen, or abbot, took a stout stick, and ascending to the roof by a spiral staircase, crawled after the boy, reached him, dislodged him, and with furious blows drove him off the roof.[17]

The monks now thought the best thing they could do would be to get summarily rid of the maniac by drowning. Papebroeck, the Bollandist, at this point appends the curious note: "If amongst ourselves, better instructed, it is customary to suffocate those who have been bitten by a mad dog—an atrocious custom—lest they should bite and hurt others, and this is regarded as a rough sort of mercy, is it any wonder that these rude monks should have supposed it proper to make away with a madman upon whom exorcism had failed to produce any effect?"

---

[16] "Monachus aspectu venerabilis, barba prolixa, corpore nudus, capillis canus." This old monk was St. Luke the Stylite, appearing in vision.
[17] "Unus—cum gravi baculo ascendens ad eum, ipsum graviter ac dure cædens, de ecclesiæ trullo descendere fecit, cum multa festinantia et furore."—Fr. Barth.

The monks accordingly tied the hands and feet of Nicolas, drew him down to the shore, threw him into a boat, rowed some way out to sea, and flung him overboard.

But Nicolas broke his bonds,[18] as he had shivered the shackles, and swimming ashore, reached land before the monks, and mounting a rock, roared to them as his greeting, "Kyrie eleison!"

The monks despaired of doing anything to him, and abandoned him to follow his own devices. He ran wild among the mountains, and constructed a little hut of logs and wattled branches for his residence. One day he descended to his mother's house and carried off a hatchet, a knife, and a saw, and amused himself fashioning crosses out of the wood of the cedars he cut down, and erecting them on the summit of rocks inaccessible to every one else.

On another occasion he carried off his brother; but the boy was so frightened at the wild gestures and cries of Nicolas, that he refused to remain more than a night in his cell and ran away home, to the inexpressible relief of his mother.

Nicolas rambled over the country, dirty, dishevelled, and naked, asking and enforcing alms. He was well known to the monks of the monasteries throughout the neighbourhood as an importunate beggar at their doors. The lonely traveller hastily flung him an offering, glad to escape so easily. On one occasion Nicolas waylaid the steward of the monastery of Sterium, and arresting the horse he rode, reproached him with stinginess. The monk, who was armed with a cudgel, bounded from his saddle, fell on Nicolas, and beat him unmercifully, then mounted and joyfully pursued his road.

Nicolas picked himself up, and followed him at a distance with aching bones to the village where the steward slept that night. Then, stealing to his bedside in the dark, he roared into his ear, "Kyrie eleison!" and woke him with a start of terror.

The monk jumped out of bed, called up the house; the watch-dogs were let loose, and Nicolas fled from their fangs up a tree, where he crouched till daylight.

On the Feast of SS. Cosmas and Damian, Nicolas went to the monastery of Sterisca to receive the Holy Communion, but was repulsed as being in an unsound state of mind, and driven out of the church, where his religious emotions found noisy vent, to the confusion of the singers and the distraction of the congregation. Nicolas was much distressed at the treatment he had received; he cried bitterly, and then resolved, as he was despised in the Greek Church, to secede to the Roman obedience; and according to his

---

[18] The biographer thinks a dolphin must have bitten his cords, and thus freed him.

own account this excommunication was the reason of his flying from his native land to visit Italy.

But he makes an admission which gives this pilgrimage West quite another complexion. He started on his journey with a very pretty girl as his companion, whom he seduced from her home, whose hair he cut short with his own hands, and whom he disguised in male costume. But the parents of the damsel, anxious at her loss, made search for her, and found her, to their dismay and disgust, in company with Nicolas, dressed as a boy, sharing his bed and board, yelling "Kyrie eleison!" with him through the Greek villages, and making the best of their way to the sea to escape to Italy.

It is not difficult to see through this incident as it comes to us with Nicolas's own explanation. The motive which Nicolas gave afterwards to Bartholomew to account for his running away from his native land was an afterthought. He had formed this discreditable connection, and the couple were escaping when caught by the parents and brought before the magistrates. Nicolas was tried for the seduction of the young girl. According to the young man's own account, the girl took all the blame on herself, and Nicolas was allowed to depart unpunished. How far this is true we cannot say.

Greece was now too hot for Nicolas, and he hurried to Lepanto, to take ship for Italy. There he met Brother Bartholomew, who was so edified by his frantic piety and the odour of sanctity which pervaded the vagrant, that he attached himself to the young pilgrim as an ardent disciple.

Nicolas and Bartholomew took ship and crossed over to Otranto. Before entering the port, however, Nicolas cried, "Kyrie eleison!" and jumped overboard. Every one on board ship supposed he would be drowned, and Brother Bartholomew tore his beard with dismay.

But Nicolas was not born to be drowned. He came ashore safely, and declared that he had seen a beautiful lady draw him out of the water by the hair of his head.

One day at Otranto a procession was going through the town, bearing an image of the Virgin, when Nicolas, who had walked for some time gravely in the train, suddenly started out of it to make humble obeisance to an old man who attracted his respect.

"See! he is worshipping a Jew!" exclaimed the people; "this strange fellow is no good Christian. Bring hither the image."

Then the Madonna was brought before Nicolas, and he was told to bow before it. He refused. Then the people fell on him with their fists and sticks, and beat and kicked him into a ditch.

Papebroeck suggests that his reason for refusing to worship the image was humility, hoping to draw on himself the indignation of the multitude, and thereby acquire the merit of enduring insult and suffering wrongfully. Perhaps, as a Greek, Nicolas was unaccustomed to images other than pictures; perhaps he did not understand the language of his assailants; but probably he was actuated by no reason but a mad freak. In the Italian versions of the Life of St. Nicolas sold at Trani, this incident is omitted for obvious reasons.

Leaving Otranto, Nicolas came to Lecce, which he entered bearing a cross on his shoulders, and uttering his usual cry. He spent the alms given to him in the purchase of apples, which he carried in a pouch at his waist, and these he threw among the boys who followed him in crowds and shouted after him, "Kyrie eleison!"

The noise he made in the streets, the uproar caused by the children, were so intolerable that two brothers named John and Rumtipert seized Nicolas, and binding him hand and foot, locked him into a room of their house. But he suddenly disengaged himself from his bonds, and was again in the street, calling, "Kyrie eleison!"

Early in the morning he went under the windows of the bishop, and broke his slumbers by his shouts. The bishop ordered him to be severely beaten and driven out of the city. Nicolas went forth triumphantly bearing his cross, shouting, "Kyrie eleison!" followed by a train of capering boys roaring, "Kyrie eleison!" and then bursting into peals of laughter. Nicolas gravely turned, cast a handful of apples among them, and passed out of the gates.

He took up his abode outside the town, and continued to astonish and edify the peasants who came into Lecce to market.

One day an officer of the prince was issuing from the gate, followed by a troop of servants. Nicolas rushed before his horse brandishing his cross and howling, "Kyrie eleison!" The horse plunged and threw his rider, and Nicolas was well beaten for his pains.

At St. Dimitri he was locked up in the church, heavily ironed; but at midnight he broke off his chains, and entering the tower pealed the bells.

Thence he went to Tarentum, where he stationed himself outside the bishop's palace, under his bedroom window, and through the night yelled, "Kyrie eleison!" It was the duty of the bishop to watch and pray, and not to sleep, thought Nicolas. But the prelate differed from him in opinion, and sent his servants to dislodge Nicolas. He returned to his post, and continued his monotonous howls. The bishop could endure it no longer, and revenged his sleepless night on the back and ribs of Nicolas, already blue with the bruises received at Lecce and St. Dimitri; and he was ignominiously expelled the city.

He proceeded thence to Trani, which he entered on 26th May 1094, carrying his cross and distributing apples among the boys who crowded about him and made a chorus to his cry.

The archbishop, hearing the disturbance, had him apprehended and brought before him. He asked Nicolas what he meant by his eccentric conduct. The crazy fellow replied, "Our Lord Jesus Christ bade us take up our cross and follow after Him, and become as little children. That is precisely what I am doing."

The archbishop began a long discourse, but Nicolas impatiently shook himself free from his guards, and without waiting for the end of it, bounded out of the hall to the head of the steps leading into the street, crying, "Kyrie eleison!" which was responded to by a shout from the boys eagerly awaiting him without.

At the head of a swarm of children he rushed madly through and round the city, making the streets resound with his monotonous appeal, and bringing the wondering citizens to their doors and windows.

But the blows he had received at Tarentum had done him some serious internal injury, and he now fell sick at Trani. There was hardly an inhabitant of the city who did not visit his sickbed, that he might hear the poor madman howl, "Kyrie eleison!" with his fevered lips, and depart marvelling at his sanctity.

The boys who had run after him and partaken of his apples came to see him, and the dying man gave them his cross, and bade them march about the dormitory of the hospital where he lay, bearing the cross, and vociferating, "Kyrie eleison!" Night and day the dormitory was crowded, and the excitement of the fevered man kept constantly stimulated. He died on 2nd June 1094, and till his burial his body attracted ever-increasing crowds.

He was buried at Trani with considerable ceremony, for already the notion had spread that the crazy Greek was a great saint, and the infatuated Brother Bartholomew did his utmost to fan the growing popular enthusiasm into a flame. Almost immediately after the burial highly imaginative individuals began to believe they had been miraculously healed of diseases at his tomb. He appeared in visions, cured cripples, uttered forebodings. The Archbishop of Trani made formal investigation into the miracles, after the manner of ecclesiastical investigations, and pronounced them genuine. Trani was without a patron; no blood of martyrs had reddened its soil, no saint had occupied its episcopal throne. It was discreditable to be without a patron, and the good people of Trani were not nice as to whom they had as patron so long as they had one whom they could claim as peculiarly their own.

A statement of the virtues, acts, and miracles of Nicolas was forwarded with gravity by the Archbishop of Trani to the Pope and Council at Rome in 1099. Urban II. with equal gravity, by special bull, canonised this pitiable fool, and hoaxed Christendom into worshipping a man in whose career no single spark of godliness appears; a man driven, to all appearance, from his own country for having led astray an innocent girl, whom he persuaded to elope with him from her home, and join him in his vagabond life.

III
ST. CHRISTINA THE WONDERFUL

The life of this extraordinary saint, so extraordinary that even those who canonised her—the vulgar and ignorant—called her "The Wonderful," comes to us on the best possible authority. Her life was written by Thomas de Chantpré, or Catimpré, born at Leuve in the Low Countries in 1201; he was canon in the abbey of Catimpré, and then entered the Dominican Order in a convent at Louvain, in 1232, and there taught theology. He was a contemporary and fellow-countryman of Christina; he had all the particulars necessary from those who had seen and conversed with Christina, whom he survived by many years. Indeed, she died when he was aged twenty-three. Christina the Wonderful was born at the village of Brustheim, near St. Trond in Hesbain, in the year 1150. When aged fifteen she was left an orphan, the youngest of three sisters, and spent her childhood in the fields tending sheep and cows. As now, so then, there were no hedges, and cattle sent into pasture had to be subjected to supervision lest they transgressed into the land of neighbours. Christina was employed as thousands of little girls have been employed since in Germany and Belgium. It was a solitary occupation for a child, and she was thrown much in on herself, on her own thoughts, her own imaginations.

Nothing remarkable about her was observed till she began to pass from childhood into womanhood, a critical period, and then it was that her malady first manifested itself. She fell down one day in a cataleptic fit, and was taken up as dead. Her sisters, with whom she lived, had her washed, laid out, placed on a bier, and conveyed to church, where the funeral mass was ordered to be said.

Christina had been in a cataleptic fit, or had been shamming death. All at once she scattered the funeral party and the worshippers by a leap off her bier, in winding-sheet, with a shrill cry, and then by a scramble up one of the pillars of the sacred edifice, which she managed to surmount. She then got upon one of the tie-beams of the roof, and there seated herself, as her biographer tells us, "like a bird." The congregation, frightened out of their wits, ran helter-skelter in all directions. One of her sisters alone had courage to remain, or possibly knew enough of Christina's eccentricities not to be alarmed. The priest at the altar faltered, stopped, turned and looked about him, and went forward headlong with the service to the end. When he had retired to the sacristy, probably, Christina's sister came to him and explained matters. Anyhow we learn that he reappeared in the church showing no signs of fear, and very peremptorily ordered the young woman down from her perch, and demanded the reason of this extraordinary freak. Christina meekly descended, and on being again asked the reason of her proceedings, condescended to inform the priest that she had scrambled aloft to escape the strong odour emitted by the peasants, which to her refined perceptions was especially repugnant. It must be admitted that it continues the same to the present day, and that to the noses of those who are not saints.

Christina was now conducted home by her sisters, and was given something to eat. When she had fed, she told them a long and marvellous story of her having visited the regions of the dead; she said that she had been in Hell, where she recognised the familiar features of a good many acquaintances, no doubt of all such as had slighted and offended her in the past and were dead. Then she had visited Purgatory, where also she found herself among acquaintances. After that she ascended to Heaven, where she was offered her choice, whether she would remain there eternally, or return to earth and there perform the meritorious work of liberating, by her prayers and self-tortures, the souls of those still undergoing purification in Purgatory. With the utmost heroism and self-denial she chose the latter alternative, probably not to the satisfaction of her sisters, who seem to have regarded her as a self-willed, troublesome piece of goods, and would have preferred to have her at a distance, as an intercessor in heaven, than on earth an object of much solicitude and annoyance.

She speedily gave them cause enough to regret the choice she had made, for she took it into her head to race about the country, leaping hedges, climbing walls, as she pretended, to get away from the scent of men, which specially distressed her. She did not specify whether this odour was spiritual or carnal, but left it to be inferred that moral turpitude was the most odoriferous. She was repeatedly found on the tops of trees, or on the summit of church towers, balancing herself beside the weathercocks, gasping for wholesome air.

Naturally enough her relatives held her to be deranged; and they proceeded to have her bound, as mad folk were chained and held in bondage till comparatively recently. But one night she broke away from her prison, tore off her fetters, declaring that the "odour of men" was suffocating her, and ran away into the nearest forest, where she swarmed to the tops of the highest trees and there gasped for untainted air. There for a while her relatives left her, she must starve or return to them. As Thomas of Chantpré says, she lived for a while like a bird among the boughs of the trees, and though sorely in want of food, would not return to association with odoriferous human beings.

Her biographer gives us an outrageous story which accounts for the way in which she lived; but in all likelihood she fed on eggs.

After five weeks thus spent, she was recaptured and again put in chains, stronger than before.

Again she broke loose, ran to Liège, where she rushed headlong into the Church of St. Christopher, and insisted on the priest whom she found there giving her the Holy Communion. He naturally enough demurred to do so. Her wild appearance, with hair flying, her galled wrists, her flashing, frantic eyes, the condition of dirt and raggedness in which she was, made him conclude she was an escaped maniac. He made an excuse, and she was unable to force him to act against his conscience by any representation she made. Then, as suddenly as she appeared, so suddenly did she rush away again into another church, where she frightened the priest into compliance. But what was his disgust and dismay to see the communicant jump up, leave the church in flying leaps, and run as fast as she could tear down the steep hill that falls towards the Meuse. He hastily laid aside his surplice and stole, and ran after her. Then he came on the priest of St. Christopher, who was also in pursuit, and the two ran after her to the quay, where she made a plunge, went head foremost into the water, and swam to the farther shore. The Meuse, as any one who is acquainted with Liège knows, is no inconsiderable stream there, and the two priests watched, breathless and alarmed, till the girl had reached the farther shore. Then only did they breathe freely.

Christina's conduct became daily more outrageous. She crept into bakers' ovens, and there howled with pain at the heat, but would not come forth, till dragged out by the heels. Sometimes she would run into a fire and kick the brands about with her bare feet. When she saw water hot in large vessels for a washing, in she leaped, souse, and then shrieked with the pain. In winter she would run into the river and remain there squealing with cold, till the parish priest came and ordered her out. One of her favourite pursuits was to dive under the sluice of a miller's water-conduit, and go with the water, head over heels, over the wheel. These exploits attracted a crowd, and excited her to renewed attempts, not always most decorous, but greeted with roars of approval and encouragement to re-attempt the feat.

Another of her freaks was to frequent the places of execution, and climb the poles with wheels at top on which robbers and murderers had been broken, and to writhe her own legs and arms in and out of the spokes, with more dexterity than delicacy, to amuse the vulgar rabble that followed and applauded her proceedings. Or she would provide herself with a rope and hang herself between two criminals on the public gallows, with happy indifference to the savour the corpses emitted. All these proceedings were, she affirmed, eminently grateful to the souls in Purgatory, and afforded them consolation and relief.

At night it was her delight to run through the streets of St. Trond, with all the dogs of the town barking and snapping after her; she led them a chase over the country, running like the wind, they tearing her tattered garments, and also biting and wounding her limbs. She, however, seemed insensible to pain, in her enjoyment of the race. Finally, when exhausted, she went up a tree like a chased cat.

One great source of entertainment she provided during divine service was to coil herself up into a ball, so that neither head, hands, nor feet appeared, and so roll about the church. Then all at once, when no one was expecting it—snap! out flew head, feet, and hands, and she lay flat on the floor, rigid as a log of wood, all her limbs extended and motionless. Another of her devotional vagaries was to pirouette on one toe on the top of a paling, whilst vociferously praying. All which not only edified the living, but afforded vast gratification to the souls in Purgatory.

At length her sisters could stand her vagaries no longer,—her biographer candidly admits that Christina put them to the blush,— and they engaged a strong man to catch her and chain her up again. He went after her, and she ran. Unable to catch her, he flung a club at her that brought her down and, as was thought, broke her thigh. As she could not walk, a cart was brought to the spot, and she was placed in it and conveyed to a surgeon, who had a bed of straw strewn for her in his cellar. He put her leg in splints, but to ensure her remaining quiet and not tearing at the bandages, bound her hands and fastened them to a ring in the cellar wall. In the night she succeeded in disengaging her hands. Then she ripped off the bandages, threw away the splints, and stood up. Her thigh was not broken. She got a stone, and with it broke a way through the wall of the cellar, and escaped into the open country once more.

After this her relatives gave up all further attempts to control her.

Finding herself unmolested, she ventured back to the haunts of men, and begged for food or whatever she required. If refused what she wanted, she became angry and took it. Few dared resist her importunities or violence. When she had a sleeve of her gown torn off she went to the first woman she encountered and asked for hers. If not at once given, she rushed at the person, and with teeth and claws tore the sleeve off the gown, and then, with crazy laughter, she slipped her own bare arm into it. Her dress was a mass of tatters and incongruous patches, sewn on with willow-bark thread, or pinned together with thorns. Her hair, dark, utterly uncombed, hung wildly about her head, and fell over her tanned, dirty face. Her limbs were covered with scars. One day she visited the parish church of Wellen, near St. Trond, and finding the cover off the font, and the sacred vessel pretty full, since the recent benediction of the sacred water, with one jump reached the brim, and then flopped herself down in the hallowed water. This, says her biographer solemnly, had the effect of subduing in her the more extraordinary manifestations of ecstatic devotion; and after this souse in the baptismal water, she professed herself less distressed by the odour of human beings.

She was not gracious to those who gave her food. As she ate what she had begged, she growled, "Why am I eating this nastiness? Why am I thus plagued?" and told them that what they gave her tasted like the insides of newts and toads.

Her biographer assures us that "she avoided, with the utmost solicitude, all human honour and praise," but it would be hard to find that either was shown or offered her whilst alive; for then she certainly was esteemed crazy. Only after her death did it occur to people that she was a saint.

In her old age she was often given shelter by the kind sisters of St. Catherine at St. Trond, and she returned their hospitality by her amusing antics. One day, as she was talking with them, she suddenly curled herself up into a ball, and began to roll round the room, "like a boy's ball, without any token of her limbs appearing." Then, all at once, she expanded flat on the floor, and ventriloquised. "No voice or breath issued from her mouth and nose, but only her breast and throat resounded with an angelic harmony." She concluded this exhibition by singing the "Te Deum" from the pit of her stomach, and then jumped up and ran away.

We can understand that at a time when hysterical disorders

110

were completely misunderstood, such marvellous contortions and tricks were reputed to be due to spiritual agency, either divine or diabolic. Towards the close of her days she spent most of her time in the Convent of St. Catherine, and she was there when attacked by her mortal sickness.

When she was apparently insensible the Superior, Sister Beatrice, said to her, "Christina! you have always been obedient to me; return now to life, I have something I desire to ask of you."

Then Christina opened her eyes and said, "Why have you disturbed me? Be quick, I cannot tarry; tell me what you want, that I may be gone."

Then the Superior put the question, received her reply, and the next moment the poor clouded spirit fled. She died on 24th July 1224, at the age of eighty-four.

Twenty-five years after her death an old woman told the Superior, "I have come to you with a divine revelation, to say that the body of that most holy woman, Christina, is not receiving proper respect from you. If you neglect to give it sufficient honour it will fare ill with you."

On the strength of this vague message the body of the poor old creature was dug up, and enshrined. Miracles attended the elevation of the bones, and thenceforth St. Christina the Wonderful came to be regarded as a saint in the Low Countries. Her body is still preserved as that of one of the elect of God in the Church of St. Catherine at Milin, near St. Trond; and her name has been inserted in a good number of martyrologies—amongst others, that of France. It is not in the Roman Martyrology, where, however, she has a better right to figure than have St. Symeon Salos and St. Nicolas of Trani, who were loose fishes as well as fools.

THE JACKASS OF VANVRES

A CAUSE CÉLÈBRE

On the 1st July 1750 Madame Ferron, washerwoman of Vanvres, entered Paris riding on a jackass in the flower of its age. The good lady had come a-marketing; and on reaching the house of M. Nepveux, grocer, near the Porte S. Jacques, she descended from Neddy's back, and entered the shop, leaving the animal attached to

111

the railings by his halter. After having made some purchases of soap and potash she asked the shopman to keep his eye on her ass whilst she went a few doors off to purchase some salt. This he neglected to do—Hinc illæ lacrymæ. A few moments after Madame Ferron had disappeared there passed Madame Leclerc, wife of a florist in Paris, mounted on a she-ass of graceful proportions and engaging appearance.

It has been questioned by some whether love at first sight is not altogether a fiction of poets and romancers. We are happy to be able to record an instance of this on unimpeachable historical evidence. A mutual passion kindled in the veins of these two asses simultaneously, during the brief space of time occupied by Madame Leclerc in passing before the grocer's shop. Their eyes met.

The she-ass, unable to express the ardour of her affection by any other means, brayed thrice in the most tender and impassioned manner. The jackass replied with corresponding sentiment. He panted to approach her, but was restrained by his halter. To love, however, nothing is impossible; or, as the Latin syntax has it, "Amor omnia vincit." He tossed his head, broke the cord, and trotted after the mistress of his affections.

Madame Leclerc adjured Neddy. Ladies do not like their servants to encourage followers. She shook her head at the lover and bade him return. But passion sometimes renders its victims insensible to the dictates of duty; Neddy still pursued.

On arriving at her door, near the Porte du Demandeur, the florist's wife caught up a stick, and charged from her doorstep upon the young and ardent lover. The lady was exasperated at the silent contempt he had exhibited for her entreaties and objurgations. She hit him on the nose, she whacked his ribs, she beat his back, and the poor ass brayed with pain and rising indignation. The she-ass brayed sympathetically.

Madame Leclerc's blows fell faster and more furiously, and then the lion under the ass's skin became apparent. Neddy reared, and falling on the old lady, bit her in the arm.

The brayings of the animals and the cries of the lady attracted a crowd, and the combatants were parted. The washerwoman's ass was consigned, with back-turned ears and palpitating sides, to confinement in a stable. Madame Leclerc retired to her apartment exhausted from her battle, and fainted, with feminine dexterity, into the extended arms of monsieur the florist, her husband, and monsieur the deputy florist, his assistant. By slow degrees the lady was brought round, by means of feathers burned under her nose, and a drop of cordial distilled down her throat. And where was the she-ass, the cause of all this mischief? She had been turned out into a clover-field. Such is the way of the world.

Next day the gardener's wife sent notice to the shop of M. Nepveux that "If any one had lost an ass he would find it at the house of a floral gardener, Faubourg S. Marceau, near the Gobelins."

Jacques Ferron, husband of the lady who had gone a-marketing on Neddy, had spent the night, as we learn from his express declaration in Court, on the borders of insanity. Not a wink of sleep visited his eyes during the hours of darkness, and the dawn broke upon him tossing feverishly on his pillow, with all the bedclothes in a heap upon the floor.

The news of his Neddy's whereabouts being discovered, restored his spirits to equanimity. He wept for joy, and despatched his wife to claim the truant, whilst he himself remained in his doorway, with palpitating bosom and extended arms, ready to embrace the returning prodigal.

But, alas! Madame Ferron, on reaching the gardener's house, learned to her dismay that she was involved in further misfortune. Madame Leclerc demanded damages for the bite she had received, to the amount of 1500 livres, and the ass would not be given up till the sum demanded was paid. Tears and entreaties were in vain; and the washerwoman returned to her husband with drooping head and a soul ravaged by despair.

On the following day, 4th July, a claim against Jacques Ferron for the sum of 1500 livres damages, and 20 sous a day for the keep of the ass, was lodged with the Commissaire Laumonier.

On the 21st August the Court ordered Leclerc to bring forward evidence to establish his claim, and the defendant was bidden challenge it. The case was heard on the 29th of the same month.

The plaintiff urged that his wife had been brutally assaulted by an enraged jackass belonging to the defendant, had been seriously alarmed by its ferocity, and had been severely bitten in the arm.

The damages claimed were reduced to 1200 livres, and payment was demanded, as before, for the keep of the delinquent.

The defence of Ferron was to this effect:—

"The ass of the washerwoman was tied to a railing. It was not likely to break away unless induced to do so by some one else. The she-ass of the plaintiff was the cause of the jackass breaking its halter and pursuing Madame Leclerc. Consequently the defendant was not responsible for what ensued.

"The distance between the Porte S. Jacques and the Gobelins is considerable, and the streets full of traffic. Had the florist's wife wished to get rid of the jackass, there were numerous persons present who would have assisted her; but from her not asking assistance, it was rendered highly probable that she had deliberately formed the design of profiting by the circumstance, and of appropriating to herself the pursuing ass.

"The plaintiff pretends that 1200 livres are due to her because she was bitten by the ass of the defendant. No medical certificate of the date is produced, but only one a month after the transaction. No evidence is offered that this bite was given by Ferron's ass, and the wound attested by the medical certificate may have been given by the ass of the plaintiff. But supposing the bite were that of Ferron's ass, was not the poor beast driven to defend itself from the blows of the defendant? Is an ass bound to suffer itself to be maltreated with impunity?

"Asses are by nature gentle and pacific animals, and are not included amongst the carnivorous and dangerous beasts. Yet the sense of self-preservation is one of the rudimentary laws of nature, and the most gentle and docile brutes will defend themselves when attacked. Is it to be wondered at that the tender-spirited and love-lorn Neddy, when fallen upon by a ferocious woman armed with a thick club, her eyes scintillating with passion, her face flaming, her teeth gnashing, and foam issuing from her purple lips, whilst from her labouring bosom escape oaths and curses, at once profane and insensate—such as sacré bleu, and ventre gris, suggesting the probability that the utterer of the said expressions was a raving maniac; is it to be wondered at that Neddy when thus assaulted, and by such a person, should fall back on the first law of nature and defend himself?

"The opinion of Donat. (Loix Civiles, tom. i. lib. 2, tit. 8) is conclusive, for it enunciates the law (xi. tit. 2, lib. 9) Si quadrupes paup. fec., ff.

"'If a dog or any other animal bites, or does any other injury because it has been struck or wilfully exasperated, he who gave occasion to the injury shall be held responsible for it, and if he be the individual who has suffered he must impute it to himself.'

"Now the woman Leclerc was not content with merely exasperating the jackass of Ferron, she almost stunned it with blows. She has therefore little reason for bringing so unfounded a claim for damages before the Court. Si instigatu alterius fera damnum dederit, cessabit hæc actio (Liv. i. § 6, lib. I).

"The more one reflects," continued the counsel for the defendant, "upon the conduct of Madame Leclerc on this occasion, the less blameless appear her motives. If, as seems probable, she designed to gain possession of the donkey, she richly deserved the bite which she complains of having received. Pierre Leclerc cannot plead that his wife did not irritate the ass, for this is proved by the very witnesses whom he summoned to sustain his case. They stated in precise terms that 'they saw Madame Leclerc pass, mounted on a she-ass, followed by a jackass, to which the said woman Leclerc dealt sundry blows, with the intention of driving it off; that, on reaching her door, and the animal approaching nearer, she beat him violently, and that then the said jackass bit her in the arm.'

"But further, who induced the ass to break his halter and follow the woman Leclerc as far as the Gobelins? Madame Leclerc's ass, and none other but she. Having thus drawn another person's animal away from its owner, and having placed it in her own stable, she claims 20 sous a day for the keep of an ass which Pierre Leclerc has retained on his own authority, against the will of the legitimate owner, from 1st July to 1st September, using it daily for going to market; thus, in all, he demands 60 livres for the keep of the beast. Although the price is twice the value of the ass itself, Ferron does not dispute the amount; he contents himself with observing that the woman Leclerc having brought upon herself the wound from the bite of the ass, which is the subject of litigation, she was not thereby morally or legally justified in detaining the animal that bit her till her demand for compensation was satisfied. If she fed and tended it, she was amply repaid by the use she and her husband made of it for carrying heavy burdens daily to market.

"On the other hand, Ferron has suffered from the loss of his ass, through its unjustifiable detention. He has been compelled to hire a horse during two months to carry on his business, and this has involved him in expenses beyond his means. For this loss Ferron will claim indemnification at the hands of Leclerc."

Such was the case of the defendant. Along with it were handed in the two following certificates, the latter of which, as giving a character for morality and respectability to a donkey, is certainly a curiosity.

Certificate of the Sieur Nepveux, grocer, at whose shop-door the ass was tied.

I, the undersigned, certify that on the 2nd July 1750 the day after the ass of the defendant Jacques Ferron, which had been attached to my door, had followed the female ass of the person Leclerc, there came, at seven o'clock in the morning, a woman to ask whether an ass had not been lost here; whereupon I replied in the affirmative. She told me that the individual who had lost it might come

115

and fetch it, and that it would be returned to her; and that it was at a floral gardener's in the Faubourg St. Marcel, near the Gobelins: in testimony to the truth of which I set-to my hand.

(Signed) Nepveux, grocer.
Porte Saint Jacques, Paris,
20th August 1720.

Certificate of the Curé, and the principal inhabitants of the parish of Vanvres to the moral character of the Jackass of Jacques Ferron.

We, the undersigned, the Prieur-Curé, and the inhabitants of the parish of Vanvres, having knowledge that Marie Françoise Sommier, wife of Jacques Ferron, has possessed a jackass during the space of four years for the carrying on of their trade, do testify, that during all the while that they have been acquainted with the said ass, no one has seen any evil in him, and he has never injured any one; also, that during the six years that it belonged to another inhabitant, no complaints were ever made touching the said ass, nor was there a breath of a report of the said ass having ever done any wrong in the neighbourhood; in token whereof, we, the undersigned, have given him the present character.

(Signed) Pinterel, *Prieur et curé de Vanvres*.
Jerome Patin,
C. Jannet,
Louis Retore,   }*Inhabitants of Vanvres*.
Louis Senlis,
Claude Corbonnet,

The case was dismissed by the Commissaire. Leclerc had to surrender the ass, and to rest content with the use that had been made of it as payment for its keep, whilst the claim for damages on account of the bite fell to the ground.

But if dismissed by the Commissaire, it was only that it might be taken up by the wits of the day and made the subject of satire and epigram. Some of the pieces in verse originated by this singular action are republished in the series Variétés Historiques et Literaires; allusions to it are not infrequent in the writers of the day.

About the same time an action was brought by a magistrate of position and fortune against the curé of St. Etienne-du-Mont, a M. Coffin, for refusing him the sacrament on account of a gross scandal

116

he had caused. A wag contrasted the conduct of the two priests in the following lines:—

De deux curés portant blanches soutanes,
Le procédé ne se ressemble en rien;
L'un met du nombre des profanes
Le magistrat le plus homme de bien;
L'autre, dans son hameau, trouve jusqu'aux ânes
Tous ses paroissiens gens de bien.

A MYSTERIOUS VALE

In the Gretla, an Icelandic Saga of the thirteenth century, is an account of the discovery of a remarkable valley buried among glacier-laden mountains, by the hero, a certain Grettir, son of Asmund, who lived in the beginning of the eleventh century. Grettir was outlawed for having set fire, accidentally, to a house in Norway, in which were at the time the sons of an Icelandic chief, too drunk to escape from the flames. He spent nineteen years in outlawry, hunted from place to place, with a price on his head. The Saga relating his life is one of the most interesting and touching of all the ancient Icelandic histories.

In the year 1025 Grettir was in such danger that he was obliged to seek out some unknown place in which to hide. In the words of the Saga:—About autumn Grettir went up into Geitland, and waited there till the weather was clear; then he ascended the Geitland glacier and struck south-east over the ice, carrying with him a kettle and some firewood. It is supposed that Hallmund (another outlaw) had given him directions, for Hallmund knew much about this part of the country. Grettir walked on till he found a dale lying among the snow-ranges, very long, and rather narrow, and shut in by glacier mountains on all sides, so that they towered over the dale.

He descended at a place where there were pleasant grassy slopes and shrubs. There were warm springs there, and he supposed that the volcanic heat prevented the valley from being closed in with glaciers.

A little river flowed through the dale, and on both banks there

117

was smooth grassy meadow-land. The sunshine did not last long in the valley. It was full of sheep without number, and they looked in better condition and fatter than any he had seen before. Grettir now set to work, and built himself a hut with such wood as he could procure. He ate of the sheep, and found that one of these was better than two of such as were to be found elsewhere.

An ewe of mottled fleece was there with her lamb, the size of which surprised him. He fattened the lamb and slaughtered it, and it yielded forty pounds of meat, the best he had tasted. And when the ewe missed her lamb, she went up every night to Grettir's hut and bleated, so that he could get no sleep. And it distressed Grettir that he had killed her lamb, because she troubled him so much. Every evening, towards dusk, he heard a lure up in the dale, and at the sound all the sheep hurried away towards the same spot. Grettir used to declare that a Blending,[19] a Thurse named Thorir, possessed the dale, and that it was with his consent that Grettir lived there. Grettir called the dale after him, Thorir's dale. Thorir had two daughters, according to his report, and Grettir entertained himself with their society: they were all glad of his company, as visitors were scarce there. When Lent came on, Grettir determined to eat mutton-fat and liver during the long fast. There happened nothing deserving of record during the winter. But the place was so dull that Grettir could endure it no longer; so he went south over the glacier range, and came north over against the midst of Skjaldbreid. There he set up a flat stone, and knocked a hole through it, and was wont to say, that "if any one looked through the hole in the slab, he would be able to distinguish the place where the gill ran out of Thorir's dale."

It is surprising that this account should not have stirred up the interest and curiosity of the natives to rediscover the rich valley, but we know of only two such attempts having been made: one by Messrs. Olafsen and Povelsen, at the close of last century, which was unsuccessful, and another, made in 1654, by Björn and Helgi, two Icelandic clergymen, an account of which is found among the Icelandic MSS. in the British Museum, and which has been kindly communicated to the writer of this paper by a native of the island, now in London. This account is of exceeding interest; it corroborates the description in the Gretla in several points, and opens a field for exploration and adventure to members of the Alpine Club more novel than the glacier world of Switzerland, and not less interesting to science.

The writer, who visited Iceland in 1862, purposed exploring this mysterious valley from the south, but was unable to find grass

---

[19] A blending is a changeling, or one who is half troll, half human.

for his horses within a day's ride of the glaciers, and was obliged to relinquish his attempt; had he then seen the account of the visit of Björn and Helgi to the valley, he would have attempted to reach it from the north.

In order that the position of this valley, and the course pursued by its explorers, may be understood, it will be necessary briefly to describe the glacier system in the midst of which it is situated.

Lang Jökull is an immense waste of snow-covered mountain, extending about forty-three miles from north-east to south-west, of breadth varying between eight and twelve miles. The mass rises into points of greater elevation along the edge than, apparently, towards the centre; and these mountains go by the names of Ball Jökull, Geitlands Jökull, Skjaldbreid Jökull, Blàfell Jökull, and Hrutafell. Skjaldbreid Jökull is opposite the volcanic dome of Skjaldbreid, an extinct volcano, with its base steeped in a sea of lava. Due east of Geitlands Jökull is another glacier-crowned dome, called Ok, from which it is cut off by a trench of desolate ruined rock filled with the rubbish brought down by the avalanches on either side—a rift between black walls of trap, crowned with green precipices of ice, which are constantly sliding over the rocky edges and falling with a crash into the valley: this valley is called Kaldidalr, or the cold dale—a title it well deserves. Those who traverse it from the south encamp at a little patch of turf around some springs, at the foot of Skjaldbreid, Brunnir by name, and thence have twelve hours' hard riding before they see grass again on the Hvitá, north of Ok. Half-way through this Allée Blanche is a mountain of trachyte, which has been protruded through the trap, from which it is clearly distinguishable by its silvery gray and ruddy streaked precipices, so different in colour from the purple-black of the trap.

This mountain is called Thorir's Head, and is popularly supposed to mask the dale discovered by Grettir.

The elaborate map of Iceland published by Gunnlaugson indicates the valley as winding from opposite Skjaldbreid to this point, but this is conjectural; and it will be seen by the sequel that it is inaccurate.

North of Geitlands Jökull is an extraordinary dish-cover-shaped cake of ice raised on precipitous sides, called Eîrek's Jökull, a magnificent, but peculiar pile of basalt, ice, and snow.

Before proceeding with the narrative of Messrs. Olafsen and Povelsen, and of the two clergymen, we may observe that several circumstances tend to give a colour of probability to the account in the Gretla.

In the first place, the phenomenon of the edges of the great

119

glacier region of Lang Jökull rising above the centre, makes it possible that towards that centre there may be a considerable depression. Next, the stone asserted to have been set up by Grettir on Skjaldbreid still stands, but has fallen out of the perpendicular, so that the hole in it does not point to any opening in the glaciers; but a little to the right appears a small ravine between piles of ice, through which runs a small river, which shortly after enters a lake, and, after having fed two other lakes, finally enters the Tungafljot, and flows past the geysers. And once more, throughout Iceland, the junction of the trap and trachyte is marked by boiling jetters; so that the mention of the hot-springs in the Gretla is quite in accordance with what the geological structure of Thorir's Head would lead us to expect.

The suspicious portion of the account is the mention of Thorir and his daughters; but in all probability this Troll was nothing more than an outlaw, like Grettir himself, and, indeed, Hallmund, who is alluded to as having given Grettir his direction to the valley, and who was a personal friend of Grettir's, and an outlaw, is called a Troll in the Barda Saga, which speaks of him and the Thorir of the mysterious vale.

It is a curious fact that, in the south-east of the island, in the Vatna Jökull, a tract very similar in character to Lang Jökull, but on a far larger scale, is a valley full of grass and flowers and glistening birch, completely enclosed by glaciers, which sweep down on this little fairy dell from all sides, leaving only one narrow rift for the escape of the water, and as a portal to the glen.

The expedition of Messrs. Olafsen and Povelsen is given in their own words. "On the 9th of August we started from Reykholtsdal on our way to the glacier of Geitland; our object was not so much to discover a region and inhabitants different from those we had quitted, as to observe the glacier with the most scrupulous accuracy, and thus to procure new intelligence relative to the construction of this wonderful natural edifice. The weather was fine and the sky clear, so that we had reason to expect that we should accomplish our object according to our wish, but it is necessary to state that in a short time the Jökulls attract the fogs and clouds that are near. On the 10th of August in the morning the air was calm, but the atmosphere was so loaded with mist that at times the glacier was not visible. About eleven o'clock, however, it cleared up, and we continued our journey from Kalmanstúnga.

"The high mountains of Iceland rise in gradations, so that on approaching them you discover only the nearest elevation, or that whose summit forms the first projection. On reaching this you perceive a similar height, and so pass over successive terraces till you reach the summit. In the glaciers these projections generally commence in the highest parts, and may be discovered at a distance, because they overtop the mountains that are not themselves glacier-clad. We found that it was much farther to the Jökull than we had imagined, and at length we reached a pile of rocks which, without forming steps and gradation at the point where we ascended, were of considerable height and very steep: these rocks extend to a great distance, and appear to surround the glacier, for we perceived their continuance as far as the eye could reach.[20] Between this pile of rocks and the glacier there is a small plain, about a quarter of a mile in width, the soil of which is clay without pebbles and flakes of ice, because the waters which continually flow from the glacier carry them off. On ascending farther, we discovered, to the right, a lake situated at one of the angles of the glacier, the banks of which were formed of ice, and the bed received a portion of the waters that flowed from the mountains. The water was perfectly green, a colour it acquired by the rays of light that broke against the ice.[21]

"After many turnings and windings we found a path by which we could descend with our horses into the valley. On arriving there we met with another embarrassment, as well in crossing a rivulet discharged from the lake, as in passing the muddy soil, in which our horses often sank up to the chest. In some parts this soil is very dangerous to travellers, many of whom have been engulphed and have perished in it.

"Our object was so far attained, that we were now on Geitland, but we found it a very disagreeable place. We observed a mountain peak rising above the ice, and which, as well as the other peaks, had been formed by subterranean fires. We led our horses over the masses of ice, after which we left them, and travelled the remainder of the way on foot. We had taken the precaution of providing ourselves with sticks armed with strong points, and with a strong rope in case of either of the party falling into a crevasse, or sinking in the snow. Thus prepared we began to escalade the glacier at two o'clock in the afternoon; the air was charged with dense fog covering all the mountain, but, hoping it would disperse, we continued our difficult and dangerous route, though at every instant we had to pass deep crevasses, one of which was an ell and a half in width, and the greatest precaution was required in crossing it.

"As we mounted higher the wind blew much stronger, and drove larger flakes of snow before it: fortunately we had the wind in

---

[20] They form a huge ancient moraine.
[21] It much resembles the beautiful Marjelen Sea, familiar to the visitor to Aegischhorn.

121

our backs, which facilitated our ascent; but we met at the same time with so much loose snow that our progress was but slow. Hoping, however, that the weather would change, we agreed not to return till we had gained the summit, from which arose a black rock.

"At length, after two hours' longer tramp, we found that we could discover nothing in the distance. A rampart of burnt rock of no considerable height rose above the ice, and at this we paused to rest. The snowflakes now obscured the air so much that we hardly knew how we should get back: we examined the compass, but without observing any change; and we were prevented by our guides from going towards the north-west, where the mountain is highest and least accessible. The weather continued the same, so that we found it impossible to resist the cold much longer, and deemed it prudent to return.

"Although the sky was very heavy and dark, we discovered, on our return, the entrance to a valley; if the weather had been more favourable we should doubtless have had the pleasure of investigating it; but we doubt whether we should have found Thorir's dale. As we descended we found the wind in our face, which threw the snow so much against us that we could not discover the traces of our ascent."

This expedition was frustrated by the inclemency of the weather. Messrs. Olafsen and Povelsen made the mistake of starting in the morning. In Iceland vapours form over the mountain tops directly that the evening sun loses its power, and although there is no night, the air is sensibly colder after 6 P.M. They had the fine part of the day for the ascent from Kalmanstúnga to the snow, and their journey over the glacier was at a time when they might almost have calculated on cloud and snow.

Probably they had not seen the description of the discovery made by Björn and Helgi in 1654. They allude to the expedition of these clergymen, but give one of them a wrong name, and speak of their journal as vague and confused, which it is not.

The account of the expedition of the two clergymen, Björn and Helgi, written in the same year that it was undertaken, is now, in Icelandic, in the British Museum. It is full of interest, and sufficiently curious to deserve attention. Björn and Helgi were brothers-in-law. In the summer of 1654, they met at Nes, where they had some conversation about Thorir's dale, and Helgi told his brother-in-law that he was convinced that either the valley itself, or some traces of it, could be seen by any one who would ascend the highest ridge of Geitlands Jökull. In consequence of this conversation, Björn, attended by two men, rode to Húsafell, where lived his sister and brother-in-law, and persuaded Helgi to accompany him on the glacier. Húsafell lies just under Ok. They started at an extremely early hour on St. Olaf's Day (28th July), without mentioning their intention to any one. This was on Thursday. They soon turned from the highway, following the west side of a cleft that enters a trunk-ravine near Húsafell,[22] and then, reaching the north side of Ok glacier, they halted. There was a young man, Björn Jónsson by name, with the two clergymen, a well-educated man; to him they now, for the first time, told their purpose, and they positively declared that they were determined to go at once across Kaldidalr, and thence ascend Geitlands Jökull, striking due east. His curiosity was aroused, and he agreed to go with them. They took with them, also, a little boy, intending, if they reached a precipice commanding the valley which they could not descend themselves, to let the boy down by a rope, that he might examine the place. They had with them a tent, and provisions for several days.

"They now struck due east, and kept their eyes fixed on a point where they thought they could discern a black ridge of mountains on the north side of the Jökull, and a hollow on the south. Till they reached the glacier, they met with no obstacle except a stony ridge of hills, which stretches all the way from the glaciers in the east, and crosses Kaldidalr in a northern direction. On the north side of this ridge was a heap of snow, and a small lake, formed by the water from the glaciers. Apparently, the horses could not descend; but Björn pushed his horse down a narrow pass, into a small river, flowing below the rocks. The river is very deep, but is full of soft mud, and sluggish. From the eastern bank of it, towards the glacier, is a sandy, muddy plain; here they saw a raven flying from the north side of the glacier towards Ok. It did not make any noise, but seemed to be rather startled by the sight of human beings in that solitude. After a while they lost sight of it and saw it no more. They crossed the sandy plain towards the glacier, and scrambled up a spur of loose shingle, till they reached a river that burst out from beneath the ice. There the glacier became very steep, and they did not see how to take their horses farther, as on all sides were seracs of ice, and fissures and crevasses of immense depth. Then Björn made a vow that he would take his horse, named Skoli, over the glacier, and not leave the ice-mountain except on the eastern side, provided this was not contrary to the will of God. Then Helgi made a vow that if he met with any human beings, male or female, in Thorir's dale, he would endeavour to Christianise them; and Björn

---

[22] The writer has been over this portion of the ground, and knows the course pursued.

promised to assist him in this to the best of his power. And they agreed to baptize immediately all the people in the valley who might be willing to embrace Christianity. They thought it prudent to leave behind them one of their horses, their baggage and the tent, at a rock near the river. On this rock they piled up three cairns as evidence that they had been there; and there, also, they left the boy in charge of the horse, with strict orders not to stir till their return, which would be in the night or on the following day. They took with them a bottle of corn-brandy, remarking that the men of Aradalr would probably be quite ignorant of its properties. They took no weapons, except small knives, and each had a spiked staff, to assist him in climbing the ice. Both the clergymen and Björn Jónsson rode all the way over the glacier, and on its northern side ascended a strip of rubble as far as they could. Then they pushed the horses down on a snowdrift, above the course of the river and the ravine through which it flowed. This snow-bed extended over the glacier an almost interminable way due south, or perhaps a little south-west. The crust was sufficiently hard to bear up the horses. Where the glacier began to rise again, it was entirely free from snow and ice, full of drifts and chasms in a direction from north to south, and as they were bearing to the east they had to cross every one of them. Most were filled with water which overflowed the glacier, and disappeared in the snowdrift, and in some places they rode through the water on the ice. None of these rifts were too broad to be crossed in one place or another, either higher up the glacier towards the south, or at its lower and north end. If they had met with a rift which they could not pass, they intended to have made a snow-bridge over it, rather than return. In this way they crossed the ice of the glacier. Next came another bed of snow, over which they rode for some while; but it was very heavy, as the day was exceedingly warm and mild.

"When they were within a short distance of what seemed to them to be the highest point of the glacier on the east, a mist set in on both sides from the north and south, leaving a clear space towards the east, so that they could see the bright sky exactly opposite their faces; and the reason of this was that the mountains rose on either side, leaving a sort of depression between them, along which they were going as they held on due east. This was not discouraging, as it showed that the mountain peaks caught the mist, and left the lower ground clear. At the same time, they heard the rush of water beneath their feet without being able to see the stream. The noise indicated a volume much larger than that which they had seen pouring through the ravine, and they conjectured that

124

the sub-glacial river divided into several streams before discharging itself.

"They now passed from the snow to a gravelly soil, devoid of grass. It was a smooth ridge of sandstone, like the bank of a mountain torrent. The glaciers now sloped towards the north-east, whilst some tended towards the east; but right across the glaciers there lay a hollow trough, and in many places along the edge black rocks shot out of the snow. On the north side were lofty and craggy fells, connected by snowdrifts and strips of shale; and the glacier range rose considerably on the north side.

"The party followed the sandstone ridge till it terminated abruptly in a precipice with ledges. Then they climbed a height, and looked about them. On the east of the glaciers they saw distinctly a desert track, not covered with snow, which they conjectured lay in a straight line north of Biskupstungur sands. East of the glacier were two brown fells; that which was most to the south was not large, and it had a castellated appearance, whilst the other was oblong, stretching from north to south, and full of snowdrifts. From the same height they saw a great valley, long and narrow, running in a semicircle. At the end were heaps of shingle, precipices, and ravines. The valley began about the middle of the glacier, and ran north-east; then bent towards the east, and finally turned south. Towards the east the glacier became lower, and in the same proportion as the mountain ranges fell, did the valley become shallower; but it seemed nowhere to dive to the very bottom of the mountains. Towards the higher end of the valley, the glacier hemmed it in with steep sides. Where the valley was deepest, the mountain slopes were bare and weather-beaten, consisting of swarthy or brown terraces and hollows, having a colour like that of the fell close to the southern extremity of Geitland.[23]

"In some places there were dry watercourses. It was so far to the bottom of the valley that the explorers could not discover exactly whether there was not grass on one of the slopes; but possibly the hue was the peculiar colour of the sandstone. Anyhow, they could not discover green pasturage. At the bottom of the valley were sandy flats, and in some places avalanches had fallen from the glaciers, and strewn the ground with blocks of ice and other débris. The slopes were very uneven. No water or waterfalls were to be seen, except two pools glittering towards the south, where the valley became shallow, and where it spread into gravelly plains, with the glacier sliding almost to the bottom of the vale on both sides. At the

---

[23] It is not easy to make out what fell is meant. Possibly it may be the ridge called Thorir's Head.

north-east bend of the valley were two small bare hills, beneath which the explorers thought they perceived two grassy plains on both sides of a watercourse. Neither hot spring, wood, heather, nor grass, beside these patches, were visible anywhere." In one point the account of these men differs from that in the Gretla, for there it is stated that the valley was narrow, and covered with grass; but possibly the ice has encroached on the turf and destroyed it.

"The clergymen having erected a pile of stones in memorial of their visit, they went towards an immense rifted rock at the higher extremity of the valley, and there discovered a cave, with an opening towards the north, and looking down the valley. There was another opening, like a window, into the cavern, commanding the east. The door was exactly square, and just opposite it was a big square stone. This, as well as the cave, was of sandstone. This was the only block of stone thereabouts. The clergymen found that they were half the height of the cave; so that it must have been from ten to twelve feet high. The window on the east was oblong, and they conjectured that it had been made by the wind and rain, though it had possibly been the work of former inhabitants of the cave. The explorers supposed that the slab opposite the door had been thrown down from above, and that there had originally existed no door, except the rift they first discovered. The rift faces the west, and to enter the cave one must climb several ledges in the rock. This cavern is sufficiently extensive to hold a couple of hundred persons. Its floor is of sand, and it is well lighted through the window. They did not find any antiquities; but they supposed this to have been the cave occupied by Thorir and his daughters.

"The men cut their initials on the rocks; Björn cut B. S. on that opposite the door, and Helgi cut a single H. on the eastern wall of the cave, just below the window. Björn Jónsson cut his opposite, but Helgi's was the deepest engraved, and will stand longest. When they had finished this, they sat down and took some refreshments, and remarked, as they drank their brandy, that this was in all probability the first time that the smell of brandy had been snuffed in that place.

"It was now getting late; however, they ascended a mountain peak, on the west side of the cave, and separate from it by a sweep of snow, and this peak they believed to be visible from Kaldidalr; it was very steep and difficult to climb, so they rested twice on their way. They went up on different sides as the clink-stone rolled away beneath their feet on those behind. Björn, the priest, was the first to attack the peak, but Helgi reached the summit first, and found it so sharp at the top as to afford hardly enough standing-ground for the three. They heaped a cairn on the top and put in it a flat stone, which they placed in a vertical position, and made fast with other stones. In it is a small rift; and they arranged it so that, by placing the eye at this rift, it looks eastward, through the door of the cave.

"The party then returned the same way that they had come, and parted in the morning in the middle of Kaldidalr, Björn going southward, and Helgi towards the north."

We think that the clergymen were mistaken in supposing that this clink-stone cone is visible from Kaldidalr, for we saw no appearance of it. From Skjaldbreid a peak is distinguishable, however, but more to the south-west than that described by the priests.

Apparently, three ways of entering the mysterious vale present themselves, that which we ourselves intended being impracticable. One is to follow the route of the bold explorers, Björn and Helgi; a second is to camp the horses at Hlitharvellir, grassy plains between Skjaldbreid and Hlothufell, and to follow the stream that issues from the glacier ravine into the recesses of the Jökull. A third course, and that which we expect would prove the easiest, though the least interesting, would be to encamp on the grass-land round the lake Hvitarvatn, to the east of the Jökull, where the mountains are lower, and the existence of a large sheet of water, from which issues a considerable river—the Hvitá—points to this being a place to which the drainage of a very considerable portion of the glacier converges.

It is not a little remarkable that the huge extent of Lang Jökull feeds scarcely any other rivers. It is true that the Nordlinga fljot, another Hvitá and Asbrandsá, have their sources under the Lang Jökull, but they are only small streams, whereas the Hvitá bursts out of its lake a wide and deep river; and we think that this is accounted for by the presence of a depression towards the interior of the range which gathers the drainage from the surrounding glaciers, and then pours the flood in a sub-glacial torrent into the lake. The opening to this valley we suppose to be blocked above the lake by the glaciers from Hrutafell and Blàfell's Jökull, which meet and overlap.

KING ROBERT OF SICILY

Next to the Saga of King Olaf, without doubt the most beautiful and successful of the Tales of a Wayside Inn, is that of King Robert of Sicily. The legend is of a remote antiquity, has passed through various modifications and recastings, and, after having lain by in forgotten tomes, has been vivified once more by the poetic breath of Longfellow, and popularised again. It is singular to trace the history of certain favourite tales; they seem to be endowed with an inherent vitality, which cannot be stamped out. Born far back in the early history of man, they have asserted at once a sway over the imagination and feelings; have been translated from their original birth-soil to foreign climes, and have undergone changes and adaptations to suit the habits and requirements of the new people amongst whom they have taken root. Political disturbances cannot obliterate them; war sweeps over the land they have adopted, famine devastates it, pestilence decimates its inhabitants, and for a while the ancient tales hide their heads, only to crop up again green and fresh when the springtide of prosperity returns.

Sometimes a venerable myth disappears for an exceptionally long period, and its vitality is, we suppose, extinguished. But though ages roll by, if it have in it the real essential power of development and assimilation, it is only waiting for its time to start a fresh career, full of concentrated vigour. Like the ear of wheat in the hand of the mummy, it has lain by, wrapped in cere-cloths, without giving token of germ, till the moment of its liberation has arrived, when, falling on good ground, it brings forth a hundredfold.

Such was the history of Fouque's exquisite romance, Undine. It was a very ancient tale, but it had been forgotten. The German poet found it in the dead hand of the whimsical pedant, Theophrastus Paracelsus, swathed in barbarous Latin. He writes:— "I ceased not to study an old edition of my speechmonger, which fell to me at an auction, and that carefully. Even his receipts I read through in order, just as they had been showered into the text, still continuing in the firm expectation that from every line something wonderfully magical might float up to me, and strike the understanding. Single sparks, here and there darting up, confirmed my hopes, and drew me deeper into the mines beneath ... then, at last, as a pearl of soft radiance, there sparkled towards me, from out its rough-edged shell—Undine." And he tells us how that his story has been translated into French, Italian, English, Russian, and Polish. The mummy wheat was soon multiplied.

The legend of King Robert of Sicily, which the American poet has rescued from oblivion, is one of those few which can be traced with rare precision through its various changes, and tracked to the country where it originated. It is instructive to note how in one form, it did service in the cause of one religion, and how, in another form, it pointed a striking moral in behalf of an entirely different creed.

Two methods of procedure lie open to us in the examination of this story, analysis and synthesis. We might trace the legend back from the form in which it is known to the modern public, by sure stages, to the ultimate atoms out of which it is developed, or we might take the original germ, and follow it in its expanding and varying forms, till it has assumed its present shape in the pages of the Tales of a Wayside Inn.

We shall adopt the latter method, as the most suitable in this peculiar instance.

In the Pantschatantra, a Sanscrit collection of popular tales, the date of the compilation of which is uncertain, but that of the tales is unquestionably earlier than the Christian era, is the following story:

"In the town of Liavati, lived a king, called Mukunda. One day he saw a hunchback performing such comical actions that he invited him to become an inmate of his palace, and, as his court fool, to divert him in his hours of idleness and depression. The king was so taken up with this droll rascal, that his prime minister was seriously displeased, and he said, in reproof, to his master—

'Far flies rumour with three pairs of ears.'

To which the king laughingly replied—

'The man is an idiot, so have no fears.'

"Grumbling still, the old and prudent minister said—

'The beggar may rise to royal degree,
The monarch descend to beggary.'

"One day a Brahmin came to the palace, and offered to teach the king various magical arts. The monarch agreed with delight, and for a small sum of money acquired power to send his soul from his own body into any disengaged carcass that he wished to vivify. The hunchback was in the room when the king learned his lesson.

"A few days after, Mukunda and his fool were riding in the forest, when they lit on the corpse of a Brahmin who had died of thirst. Here was an opportunity for the king to practise what he had learned. But first he asked the hunchback if he had given attention

129

to the instruction of the Brahmin. The fool replied that he never bothered his head with the pedantry of professors. The king, satisfied with the answer, pronounced the magical words. Down fell his body, senseless, and his soul animating the corpse, the dead Brahmin sat up and opened his eyes. Instantly the crafty hunchback repeated the incantation, and took possession of the carcass of his majesty, mounted the king's horse, and rode off to Liavati, where he was received by the courtiers, the servants, the ministers, and the queen as if he were the true Mukunda, whilst the real monarch, in the shape of a begging Brahmin, roved the forests and the villages, cursing his folly, half starved on the scanty charity of the faithful.

"Suspicions that all was not right forced their way into the queen's mind, and she mentioned her doubts to the minister.

'Far flies rumour with three pairs of ears,'

said he, addressing the false king, who shrugged his shoulders, and laughed. Again the minister tried him with—

'The beggar may rise to royal degree,'

and received a peremptory order to be silent as he valued his head.

"'He is not the king,' said the minister to the queen. 'We must find the true Mukunda, wherever he may be.'

"In order to effect this, to every one whom the vizier addressed he uttered the two half-verses—

'Far flies rumour with three pairs of ears,'

and

'The beggar may rise to royal degree,'

but with no results. One evening, however, as he was walking home, deep in thought, a poor Brahmin clamoured for alms. The minister made no answer; but when the pauper continued his importunities, he said, sharply,—

'Far flies rumour with three pairs of ears';

to which the Brahmin promptly answered—

'The man is an idiot, so have no fears.'

"Hearing this, the old man was arrested by his interest. He hastily continued—

'The beggar may rise to royal degree';

and the Brahmin responded without hesitation—

'The monarch descend to beggary.'

130

"The minister caught him at once by the hand, and insisted on hearing his story. No sooner was he made aware of what had been done by the hunchback, than he hastened to the palace, where he found the queen bathed in tears over a favourite parrot, which lay dead on her lap. The old man concerted with her a plan for the destruction of the hunchback and the restoration of the true king; then he secretly introduced the transformed Mukunda into the chamber, and summoned the false king.

"'O sire,' said the queen, 'if you love me restore my pretty parrot to life.'

"'That is easily effected,' answered the fool.

"In an instant his body fell rigid, and his soul entered the bird, which sat up, plumed its feathers, and began to chatter. At the same moment the true Mukunda pronounced the magic words, dropped his adopted body, and darted into that which had originally been his. At the sight of the reviving monarch, the queen wrung the parrot's neck, and thus destroyed the impostor."

This story is based on the great Buddhist doctrine of the transmigration of souls, and was evidently a very popular illustration of that fundamental dogma, for variations of it are common in most ancient Sanscrit collections. Thus in the Katha Sarit Sagara, a work of Soma Deva, written between A.D. 1113-1125, the story reappears considerably altered, but still told with the design of insisting on the doctrine of transmigration of souls. Soma Deva's tale is this in brief:—

Vararutschi, Vyâdi, and Indradatta desired to learn the new lessons of Varscha, but could not pay the stipulated fee—a million pieces of gold. They determined to ask King Nanda—a contemporary of Alexander the Great, by the way—to pay it for them, and they visited his capital. They are too late: Nanda is just dead. However, determined to obtain the requisite sum, Indradatta leaves his body in a wood, guarded by his companions, and sends his soul into the dead king. Then Vararutschi goes to him, asks, and receives the gold, whilst Vyâdi sits beside the deserted body.

But the prime minister suspected that the revived master was not quite identical with the deceased master. Indeed, King Nanda now exhibited an intelligence and vigour which had been sadly deficient before. The minister knew that the heir to the throne was but a child, and that he had powerful enemies. He therefore formed the resolution of keeping the false king on the throne till the heir was of age to govern. To effect his purpose, he issued orders that every corpse in the kingdom should be burnt. Amongst the rest was consumed that of Indradatta, and the Brahmin found himself, with horror, obliged to remain in the body of a Sudra, though that Sudra was a king.

There is another story, similar to that in the Pantschatantra, told of Tschandragupta, the founder of the Maurya dynasty, and one of the most renowned of the ancient Indian kings. But, indeed, the variations occurring in the ancient Sanscrit Buddhist tales are very numerous.

From India the story travelled into Persia—when, is not known; but it was probably there long before A.D. 540 when the Persian translation of the Pantschatantra was made. In Persian it occurs in the Bahar Danush, and in the version of the Çukasaptati. It is in the Turkish Tûtînâmeh. It is in the famous Arabian Nights, as the story of the Prince Fadl-Allah. It is also in the Mongolian Vikramacarita. But, though it was translated with small variations from the Sanscrit in these works, popularly the story had gone through great adaptations and alterations to suit creeds which did not believe in the transmigration of souls.

When it was made known to the Jews is not certain; probably at the captivity. Yet there are passages in the Psalms, and especially in the song of Hannah, which bear a striking resemblance to the verses of the prime minister, and seem almost like an allusion to the fable. Thus, "The Lord maketh poor, and maketh rich: he bringeth low, and lifteth up. He raiseth up the poor out of the dust, and lifteth up the beggar from the dunghill, to set them among princes, and to make them inherit the throne of glory." This may be a reference or it may not. The sentiment is not unlikely to have been uttered without knowledge of the Indian fable; but if Hannah had been acquainted with it, no doubt to it allusion was made.

It is certain, however, that the story did popularise itself among the Jews, and when it did so, it was in a form adapted to their belief, which had nothing in common with metempsychosis. And it is exceedingly probable that they derived it from Persia, for one of the actors in the tale, Asmodeus, is the Zoroastrian Aêshma. The story is found in the Talmud and is as follows:—

"King Solomon, having completed the temple and his house, was lifted up with pride of heart, and regarded himself as the greatest of kings. Every day he was wont to bathe, and before entering the water, he entrusted his ring, wherein lay his power, to one of his wives. One day the evil spirit, Asmodeus, stole the ring, and, assuming Solomon's form, drove the naked king from the bath into the streets of Jerusalem. The wretched man wandered about his city scorned by all; then he fled into distant lands, none recognising in him the great and wise monarch. In the meanwhile the evil spirit reigned in his stead, but unable to bear on his finger the ring graven with the Incommunicable Name, he cast it into the sea. Solomon, returning from his wanderings, became scullion in the palace. One day a fisher brought him a fish for the king. On opening it, he found in its belly the ring he had lost. At once regaining his power, he drove Asmodeus into banishment, and, a humbled and better man, reigned gloriously on the throne of his father David" (Talmud, Gittim, fol. 68).

The Arabs have a similar legend, taken from the Jews:—

"One day Solomon asked an indiscreet question of an evil Jinn subject to him. The spirit replied that he could not obtain the information required without the aid of Solomon's seal. The king thoughtlessly lent it, and immediately found himself supplanted by the Jinn. Reduced to beggary, he wandered through the world repeating, 'I, the preacher, was king over Israel in Jerusalem.' The constant repetition of this sentence attracted attention; the disguised demon took alarm and fled, and Solomon regained his throne."

Finally the Jews or Arabs introduced the story to Western Europe, where it soon became popular. In the Gesta Romanorum, a collection of moral tales made by the monks in the fourteenth century, the Emperor Jovinian takes the place of Solomon, and the story is thus told:—

"When Jovinian was emperor, he possessed very great powers; and as he lay in bed reflecting upon the extent of his dominions, his heart was elated to an extraordinary degree. 'Is there,' he impiously asked, 'any other god than me?' Amid such thoughts he fell asleep.

"In the morning he reviewed his troops, and said, 'My friends, after breakfast we will hunt.' Preparations being made accordingly, he set out with a large retinue. During the chase the emperor felt such extreme oppression from the heat, that he believed his very existence depended upon a cold bath. As he anxiously looked round, he discovered a sheet of water at no great distance. 'Remain here,' said he to his guard, 'until I have refreshed myself in yonder stream.' Then, spurring his steed, he rode hastily to the edge of the water. Alighting, he divested himself of his apparel, and experienced the greatest pleasure from its invigorating freshness and coolness. But whilst he was thus employed a person similar to him in every respect arrayed himself unperceived in the emperor's dress, and then mounting his horse, rode to the attendants. The resemblance to the sovereign was such, that no doubt was entertained of the reality; and straightway command was issued for their return to the palace.

"Jovinian, however, having quitted the water sought in every possible direction for his clothes, but could find neither them nor the horse. Vexed beyond measure at the circumstance, for he was completely naked, he began to reflect upon what course he should pursue. 'There is, I remember, a knight residing close by; I will go to him and command his attendance and service. I will then ride to the palace, and strictly investigate the cause of this extraordinary conduct. Some shall smart for it.'

"Jovinian proceeded naked and ashamed to the castle of the aforesaid knight, and beat loudly at the gate. 'Open the gate,' shouted the enraged emperor, as the porter inquired leisurely the cause of the knocking, 'you will soon see who I am.' The gate was opened, and the porter, struck with the strange appearance of the man before him, exclaimed, 'In the name of all that is marvellous, what are you?' 'I am,' replied he, 'Jovinian, your emperor. Go to your lord and command him to supply the wants of his sovereign. I have lost both horse and clothes.'

"'Infamous ribald!' shouted the porter, 'just before thy approach, the emperor, accompanied by his suite, entered the palace. My lord both went and returned with him. But he shall hear of thy presumption.' And he hurried off to communicate with his master. The knight came and inspected the naked man. 'What is your name?' he asked roughly.

"'I am Jovinian, who promoted thee to a military command.'

"'Audacious scoundrel!' said the knight, 'dost thou dare to call thyself the emperor? I have but just returned from the palace, whither I have accompanied him. Flog the rascal,' he ordered, turning to his servants: 'flog him soundly, and drive him away.'

"The sentence was immediately executed, and Jovinian, bruised and furious, rushed away to the castle of a duke whom he had loaded with favours. 'He will remember me,' was his hope. Arrived at the castle, he made the same assertion.

"'Poor mad wretch!' said the duke, 'a short time since, I returned from the palace, where I left the very emperor thou assumest to be. But, ignorant whether thou art more fool or knave, we will administer such a remedy as will suit both. Carry him to prison, and feed him with bread and water.' The command was no sooner delivered than obeyed; and the following day Jovinian's naked body was submitted to the lash, and again cast into the dungeon. In the agony of his heart, the poor king said, 'What shall I do? I am exposed to the coarsest contumely, and the mockery of the people. I will hasten to the palace and discover myself to my wife,— she will surely know me.'

"Escaping therefore from his confinement, he approached the imperial residence. 'Who art thou?' asked the porter.

"'It is strange,' replied the aggrieved emperor, 'that thou shouldest forget one thou hast served so long.'

"'Served thee!' returned the porter indignantly; 'I have served none but the emperor.'

"'Why!' said the other, 'though thou recognisest me not, yet I am he. Go to the empress; communicate what I shall tell thee, and by these signs, bid her send the imperial robes, of which some rogue has deprived me.' After some demur, the porter obeyed; and orders were issued for the admission of the mad fellow without.

"The false emperor and the empress were seated in the midst of their nobles. As the true Jovinian entered, a large dog, which crouched on the hearth, and had been much cherished by him, flew at his throat, and but for timely intervention would have killed him. A falcon also, seated on her perch, no sooner saw him than she broke her jesses, and flew out of the hall. Then the pretended emperor, addressing those who stood about him, said: 'My friends, hear what I will ask of yon ribald. Who are you? And what do you want?'

"'These questions,' said the suffering man, 'are very strange. You know I am the emperor, and master of this place.'

"The other, turning to the nobles who stood by, continued, 'Tell me, on your allegiance, which of us two is your lord?'

"They drew their swords in reply, and asked leave to punish the impostor with death.

"Then, turning to the empress, he asked, 'Tell me, my lady, on the faith you have sworn, do you know this man who calls himself thy lord and emperor?'

"She answered, 'How can you ask such a question? Have I not known thee more than thirty years, and borne thee many children?'

"Hearing this the unfortunate monarch rushed, full of despair, from the court. 'Why was I born?' he exclaimed. 'My friends shun me; my wife and children will not acknowledge me. I will seek my confessor. He may remember me.' To him he went accordingly, and knocked at the window of his cell.

"'Who is there?' asked the priest.

"'The Emperor Jovinian,' was the reply; 'open the window that I may speak with thee.' The window was opened; but no sooner had the confessor looked out than he closed it again in great haste.

"'Depart,' said he, 'accursed creature! Thou art not the emperor, but the devil incarnate.'

"This completed the miseries of the persecuted man. 'Woe is me,' he cried, 'for what strange doom am I reserved?'

"At this crisis, the impious words which in the arrogance of

135

his heart he had uttered, crossed his recollection. Immediately he beat again at the window of the confessor.

"'Who is there?' asked the priest.

"'A penitent,' answered the emperor.

"The window was opened. 'What is your majesty pleased to require?' asked the confessor, recognising him at once. Then he made his confession, and received of the old father a few clothes to cover his nakedness, and by the priest's advice returned to the palace. The soldiers presented arms to him, the porter opened immediately, the dog fawned on him, the falcon flew to him, and his wife rushed to embrace him. Then the feigned emperor spoke:—'My friends, hearken! That man is your king. He exalted himself, to the disparagement of his Maker, and God has punished him. But repentance has removed the rod.' So saying, he disappeared. The emperor gave thanks to God, and lived happily, and finished his days in peace."

The same story, with some alterations, is told of Robert of Sicily. An old poem or metrical romance on the subject is given by Warton; and on it Longfellow has founded his poem.

> Robert of Sicily, brother of Pope Urbane
> And Valmond, Emperor of Allemaine,
> Apparelled in magnificent attire,
> With retinue of many a knight and squire,
> On St. John's eve, at vespers, proudly sat
> And heard the priests chant the Magnificat.
> And, as he listened, o'er and o'er again
> Repeated, like a burden or refrain,
> He caught the words: 'Deposuit potentes
> De sede, et exaltavit humiles.'

He inquired of a clerk the meaning of these words; and, having heard the explanation, was mightily offended:—

> "Tis well that such seditious words are sung
> Only by priests, and in the Latin tongue;
> For, unto priests and people be it known,
> There is no power can push me from my throne.'
> And, leaning back, he yawned, and fell asleep,
> Lulled by the chant monotonous and deep.

When he awoke he was alone in the church. An angel had assumed his likeness, and had swept out of the minster with the court. The story then runs in the same line as that of Jovinian.

136

Robert is unrecognised, and is at last received into the palace as court fool. At the end of three years there arrived an embassy from Valmond, the emperor, requesting Robert to join him on Maundy Thursday, at Rome, whither he proposed to go on a visit to his brother Urban. The angel welcomed the ambassadors, and departed in their company to the Holy City. We place side by side the Old English metrical description of Robert's appearance, as he accompanied the false emperor, with the modern poet's rendering:

OLD ENGLISH

The fool Robert also went,
Clothed in loathly garnement,
With fox-tails riven all about:
Men might him knowen in the rout.
An ape rode of his clothing;
So foul rode never king.

LONGFELLOW

And lo! among the menials, in mock state,
Upon a piebald steed, with shambling gait;
His cloak of fox-tails flapping in the wind,
The solemn ape demurely perched behind,
King Robert rode, making huge merriment
In all the country towns through which they went.

Robert witnessed in sullen silence the demonstrations of affectionate regard with which the pope and emperor welcomed their supposed brother; but, at length, rushing forward, he bitterly reproached them for thus joining in an unnatural conspiracy with an usurper. This violent sally, however, was received by his brothers, and by the whole papal court, as an undoubted proof of his madness; and he now learnt for the first time the real extent of his misfortune. His stubbornness and pride gave way, and were succeeded by remorse and penitence.

After five weeks in Rome, the emperor, and the supposed king of Sicily, returned to their respective dominions, Robert being still accoutred in his fox-tails, and accompanied by his ape, whom he now ceased to consider as his inferior. When the angel was again at the capital of Sicily, he felt that his mission was accomplished.

And when once more within Palermo's wall,
And, seated on the throne in his great hall,
He heard the Angelus from the convent towers,
As if a better world conversed with ours,
He beckoned to King Robert to draw nigher,
And, with a gesture, bade the rest retire;
And when they were alone, the Angel said,
'Art thou the king?' Then, bowing down his head,
King Robert crossed both hands upon his breast,
And meekly answered him: 'Thou knowest best!
My sins as scarlet are; let me go hence,
And in some cloister's school of penitence,
Across those stones that pave the way to heaven
Walk barefoot, till my guilty soul is shriven!'
The Angel smiled, and from his radiant face
A holy light illumined all the place,
And through the open window, loud and clear,
They heard the monks chant in the chapel near,
Above the stir and tumult of the street:
'He has put down the mighty from their seat,
And has exalted them of low degree!'
And through the chant a second melody
Rose like the throbbing of a single string,
'I am an angel, and thou art the king!'
King Robert, who was standing near the throne,
Lifted his eyes, and lo! he was alone!
But all apparelled as in days of old,
With ermined mantle, and with cloth of gold;
And when his courtiers came they found him there,
Kneeling upon the floor, absorbed in silent prayer.

We think it would be scarcely possible to find a more pointed illustration of the purifying, humanising, and refining nature of Christianity, than to observe the course pursued by this story. Among Buddhists the false king is vivified by a crafty rogue's infused soul; among Jews he is a transformed devil; but among Christians he is an angel of light.

SORTES SACRÆ

It is not an uncommon case, nowadays, for pious persons at times of great perplexity to seek a solution to their difficulties in their Bibles, opening the book at random and taking the first passage which occurs as a direct message to them from the Almighty.

The manner in which this questioning of the sacred oracles is performed is serious. A considerable time is previously devoted to prayer, after which the inquirer rises from his knees and consults the family Bible in the way described. Whether such a manner of dealing with the Word of God be under any circumstances justifiable, I do not pretend to judge. St. Augustine in his 119th letter to Januarius seems not to disapprove of this custom, so long as it be not applied to things of this world.

Gregory of Tours tells us what was his practice. He spent several days in fasting and prayer, and in strict retirement, after which he resorted to the tomb of St. Martin, and taking any book of Scripture which he chose, he opened it, and took as answer from God the first passage that met his eye. Should this passage prove inappropriate, he opened another book of Scripture.

The eleventh chapter of Proverbs, which contains thirty-one verses, is often taken to give omen of the character of a life. The manner of consulting it is simple; it is but to look for the verse answering to the day of the month on which the questioner was born. The answer will be found in most cases to be exceedingly ambiguous.

The practice of consulting certain books for purposes of augury is of high antiquity. Herodotus speaks of the custom, and of the fraud of Oxomacritus, a celebrated diviner, who made use of Musœus for reference, and who was driven out of Athens by Hipparchus, son of Pisistratus, because he had been detected inserting in the verses of Musœus an oracle predicting the disappearance in the waves of the islands near Lemnos. Homer, and afterwards Virgil, were the poets most frequently consulted, but Euripides was also regarded as divinely inspired to foretell the future.

Two hundred years after the death of Virgil, his poems were laid up in the temple at Prœneste, for consultations. Alexander Severus sought the oracle in the reign of Heliogabalus, who feared and hated him; and the line of Virgil he read told him that "if he could surmount opposing fates, he would be Marcellus." The

Emperor Heraclius, when deliberating where to fix his winter quarters, was determined by an oracle of this sort. He purified his army during three days, and then opened the Gospels. The passage he found was understood by him to indicate that he should winter in Albania.

Nicephorus Gregoras relates how Andronicus the Elder was reconciled to his nephew Andronicus in consequence of lighting on the verse of the Psalm (lxviii. 14), "When the Almighty scattered kings for their sake, then were they as white as snow in Salmon." Whereby he concluded that all the troubles that had been undergone by him had been decreed by God for his purification.

With the same intent during the consecration of a bishop, at the moment when the book of the Gospels was placed on his head, it was customary to open the volume and gather from the verse at the head of the page an augury of the prelate's reign. This is illustrated in a curious ancient painting of the consecration of St. Thomas à Becket by Van Eyck, shown in the Leeds Fine Art Exhibition of 1868.

Chroniclers and biographers have not failed to mention several prognostications given in this manner which were verified in the event.

At the consecration of Athanasius, nominated to the patriarchate of Constantinople by Constantine Porphyrogenitus, a patriarchate which he stained with his crimes, "Caracalla, bishop of Nicomedia, having brought the Gospel," says the historian Pachymerus, "the congregation prepared to take note of the oracle which would be manifest on the opening of the book, though this oracle is not infallibly true. The bishop of Nicæa, noticing that he had lighted on the words, 'Prepared for the devil and his angels,' groaned in the depth of his heart, and putting up his hand to hide the words, turned over the leaves of the book, and disclosed the other words, 'The birds of the air come, and lodge in the branches': words which seemed far removed from the ceremony which was being celebrated. All that could be done to hide these oracles was done, but it was found impossible to conceal the truth. It was said that they did not forbid the consecration, but that, nevertheless, they were not the effect of chance, for there is no such a thing as chance in the celebration of the Sacred Mysteries."

"Landri, elected bishop of Laon," says Guibert de Nogent, "received episcopal unction in the Church of St. Ruffinus; but it was of sad portent to him, that the text of the Gospel for the day was, 'A sword shall pierce through thine own soul also.'" After many crimes he was assassinated. He was succeeded by the Dean of Orleans, whose name is not known. "The new prelate having presented himself for consecration, people looked to see what the Gospel would prognosticate; but it was opened at a blank page, as though God had said, 'I have nothing to foretell of this man, because he will be, and will do, nothing.' And in fact he died at the end of a very few months."

Guibert tells a story of himself, which shows that the same practice was in vogue at the installation of an abbot. "On the day of my entry into the monastery," he writes, "a monk who had studied the sacred books desired, I presume, to read my future; at the moment when he was preparing to leave with the procession to meet me, he placed designedly on the altar the book of the Gospels, intending to draw an omen from the direction taken by my eyes towards this or that chapter. Now the book was written, not in pages, but in columns. The monk's eyes rested on the middle of the second column, where he read the following passage, 'The light of the body is the eye.' Then he bade the deacon, who was to present the Gospel to me, to take care, after I had kissed the cross on the cover, to hold his hand on the passage he indicated to him, and then attentively to observe, as soon as he had opened the book before me, on what part of the pages my eyes rested. The deacon accordingly opened the book, after I had, as custom required, pressed my lips upon the cover. Whilst he observed, with curious eyes, the direction taken by my glance, my eye and spirit together turned neither above nor below, but precisely towards the verse which had been indicated before. The monk who had sought to form conjectures by this, seeing that my action had accorded, without premeditation, with his intentions, came to me a few days after, and told me what he had done, and how wondrously my first movement had coincided with his own."

Thomas Cantipratensis relates how that Cardinal Conrad, Archbishop of Paris, was in doubt as to what reception he should give to the Order of Preachers, some members of which had lately entered the city. He hesitated as to their having been legitimately constituted, and questioned their value. Whereupon he betook himself to prayer; and then going to the altar opened the Missal at the words, "Laudare, benedicere, et predicare," whereupon his scruples vanished, and he extended to them the right hand of fellowship.

"I know a religious man who had designed to serve God in the secular life," writes Paciuchelli (In Jonam, vol. i. p. 9); "he once poured forth his prayers to God, and asked that he might be permitted, if it were His will, to fulfil some desire or other that he had. Having asked the opinion of certain persons of authority, he was recommended, after the most sacred service, to open the Missal and to take note of what should first arrest his attention. He followed this advice, and lo! the first words which presented themselves to him were those of our Lord to the sons of Zebedee, in St. Matt. xx. 23, 'Ye know not what ye ask'; from which he gathered clearly that were his wishes to be gratified, his eternal welfare would be imperilled."

I have heard of a young man in doubt as to his vocation for holy orders, when he found his desire strongly opposed by his parents, inquiring of his Bible in a similar spirit and manner, and reading, "He that loveth father or mother more than me is not worthy of me." I have been told of another man in somewhat parallel circumstances, having lately awakened to religious convictions after a life of great laxity, who sought guidance in the same manner, and read, "Go home to thy friends, and tell them how great things the Lord hath done for thee, and hath had compassion on thee."

A story of the baleful effects of this practice among Scotch Presbyterians appeared in a collection of Legends of Edinburgh by a recent writer. The story related how a designing mother persuaded her reluctant daughter into a marriage with a wealthy but dissipated youth, the son of their employer, towards whom the girl felt great repugnance, by manipulating the Sortes Sacræ so as to make the girl read, "Behold, Rebekah is before thee, take her, and go, and let her be thy master's son's wife, as the Lord hath spoken." As the name of the young woman was Rebekah, the sentence seemed to her to be a message from heaven.

Gregory of Tours mentions a couple of instances of omens taken from Scripture. The one was that of Chramm, who had revolted against his father Clothaire, and who marched to Dijon, where he consulted the Sacred Oracles, by placing on the altar three books, the Prophets, the Acts, and the Evangelists. In like manner, according to Gregory, Merovius, flying from the wrath of his father Chilperic, and Fredigunda, placed on the tomb of St. Martin three books, to wit, the Psalter, the Kings, and the Gospels, and kept vigil through the night, praying the blessed confessor to discover to him what was to happen to him. He fasted three days and continued incessantly in prayer; then he opened the books, one after another, and was so dismayed at the replies which he found, that he wept bitterly beside the tomb, and then sadly left the basilica.

In 1115, differences having arisen touching the elevation of Hugh de Montaigu to the Bishopric of Auxerre, the case was brought before Pope Pascal II., who decided in favour of his consecration, and ordained him himself. It was urged by his friends in his favour, that on the opening of the book above his head, during the ceremony, these words stood out at the head of the page, "Ave Maria! graciâ plena!" and this was regarded as a token of his chastity, humility, and exemplary piety, and of the favour in which he was held by the Blessed Virgin.

According to the use of the ancient church of Terouanne, on the reception of a new canon, it was customary to open at random the Psalter, after that the volume had been sprinkled by the dean with holy water, and the paragraph at the head of the page was transcribed in the letters patent of the new canon. The same custom was in force, as late as last century, in the cathedral of Boulogne, and the bishop, De Langle, tried in vain in 1722 to abolish it.

The Bollandists relate that St. Petrock of Cornwall, when in doubt whether to undertake a pilgrimage to the Holy Land or not, was decided by opening his Bible at the passage in Isaiah, "Et erit sepulchrum ejus gloriosum." A similar story is told of St. Poppo, a Belgian saint of the eleventh century.

The anecdote is well known of King Charles and Lord Falkland consulting the Sortes Virgilianæ in the library at Oxford. The lines they met with and which were so singularly verified afterwards, are marked with their initials in the book, which is still preserved.

Rabelais refers to the Sortes Virgilianæ when he makes Panurge consult them on the subject of his marriage.

Gregory of Tours, sad at heart because of the desolation produced by the ravages of Count Leudaste in and around the city, entered his oratory; "and," as he tells us himself, "full of trouble, I took up the Psalms of David, in hopes of finding, when I opened the book, some verse which might bring me consolation. And I found this: 'He brought them out safely, that they should not fear; and overwhelmed their enemies with the sea.'"

Gregory relates another story akin to the subject. Clovis, at the moment when he was marching against Alaric, king of the Visigoths, sent his deputies to the Church of St. Martin, at Tours, saying to them, "Go, and maybe, in the holy temple you will find some presage of victory." After having given them presents for the sacred place, he added: "O Lord God! if Thou art on my side, if Thou art determined to deliver into my hands this unbelieving nation, hostile to Thy name, grant that I may see Thy favour, or the entry of my servants into the basilica of St. Martin, that I may know if Thou deignest to be favourable to Thy suppliant."

The envoys having hastened to Tours, entered the cathedral at the moment when the Precentor gave out the Antiphon: "Thou hast girded me with strength unto the battle: thou shalt throw down mine enemies under me. Thou hast made mine enemies also to turn their backs upon me: and I shall destroy them that hate me" (Ps. xviii. 37, 40).

Hearing this, they gave thanks to God, presented their offerings, and returned with joy to announce the omen to their king.

Divination by Scripture has been forbidden by several national councils, probably on account of the superstitious use made of it. The sixteenth canon of the Council of Vannes, held in 465, forbids clerks under pain of excommunication, consulting the Sortes Sacræ. This prohibition was extended to the laity by the forty-second canon of the Council of Agde, in 506. "Aliquanti clerici sive laici student auguriis, et sub nomine fictœ religionis, per eas, quas sanctorum sortes vocant, diviniationis scientiam profitentur, aut quarumcunque scripturorum inspectione futura promittunt." It was also forbidden by the Council of Orleans in 511; again by that of Auxerre in 595; by that of Selingstadt in 1022; by that of Enham, in 1009; and by a capitulary of Charlemagne, in 789.

Related to Sortes Sacræ are those messages which are supposed to be conveyed by the chance hearing or reading of a passage of Scripture. These are not, however, to be regarded in the light of superstition, and it is quite possible, and indeed probable, that certain texts accidentally met with may influence for good or bad those who are in a disposition of mind to be so affected.

The well-known story of St. Augustine's conversion is to the point. He relates himself how sitting in a garden-house, in great trouble of mind, he heard a voice say, "Tolle, lege"; whereupon he took up the sacred Scriptures and read, "Not in chambering and wantonness, not in strife and envying; but put ye on the Lord Jesus Christ, and make not provision for the flesh, to fulfil the lusts thereof" (Rom. xiii. 13, 14).

St. Anthony was moved to the assumption of the religious life by accidentally hearing—"If thou wilt be perfect, go and sell that thou hast, and give to the poor, and thou shalt have treasure in heaven: and come and follow me" (St. Matt, xix. 21).

St. Louis when trying a murderer was much inclined by his natural tenderness of disposition to pardon the man; but his resolution to let justice take her course was strengthened by opening his Psalter at the words, "Feci judicium et justitiam."

But, to conclude, the true use of Holy Scripture is best learned from our English Collect, which asks that we may read, mark, learn, and inwardly digest its glorious lessons, taken as a whole, and not wring disjointed directions for conduct from stray passages.

CHIAPA CHOCOLATE

Gage, the Dominican, a great admirer of chocolate, a man who combated with all his energy the objections which medical men of the seventeenth century made to its use, derived its name from atte, the Mexican word for water, and the sound it makes when poured out,—choco, choco, choco, choco!

O Professor Max Müller! what do you say to this? Whatever the derivation of the name may be, the composition of the beverage is well known. Cacao, sugar, long-pepper, vanilla, cinnamon, cloves, almonds, mace, aniseed, are the main constituents, and the cake-chocolate used in Britain is believed to be made of about one-half genuine cacao, the remainder of flour or Castile soap.

We are not going any further into the mysteries of its composition, which may be ascertained from any encyclopædia, for our business is with a circumstance in connection with its history probably known to few.

And first for our authority—the afore-mentioned Dominican. Thomas Gage was born of a good family in England; his elder brother was Governor of Oxford in 1645, when King Charles retreated thither during the Great Rebellion. Whilst still young, Thomas had been sent to Spain for education, and had entered the Dominican order, and having been, like so many Spanish ecclesiastics, fired with missionary zeal, he embarked at Cadiz for Vera Cruz, whence he betook himself to Mexico, near which town he made a retreat, previous to devoting himself to a life of toil in the Philippines.

However, the accounts he received of these islands were so discouraging, and the monastic life in Mexico was so inviting, that he postponed his expedition indefinitely. But Gage had no intention of spending his life in ease: he hurried over the different districts of Mexico and Guatemala, making himself acquainted with the languages spoken wherever he went, and he laboured indefatigably as priest to several parishes of great extent.

Gage's account of the cultivation of the cacao and the manufacture of chocolate is interesting, his treatise on its medical properties—conceived in the taste and spirit of his day—curious, and his personal narrative lively and amusing.

One little statement must not be passed over. Chocolate, it seems, is useful as a cosmetic; Creole ladies eat it to deepen their skin tint, just on the same principle, observes Gage, as English ladies devour whitewash from the walls to clarify their complexion.

Chiapa was a central point for Gage's labours during a considerable period. At that time it was a small cathedral town, containing 400 Spanish families, and 100 Mexican houses in a faubourg by itself.

The cathedral served as parish church to the inhabitants: one Dominican and one Franciscan monastery, besides a poverty-stricken nunnery, supplied the religious requirements of the diocesan city. No Jesuits there! quoth Gage, with a little rancour. Those good men seldom leave rich and opulent towns; and when you learn the fact that there are no Jesuits at Chiapa, you may draw the immediate inference that the town is poor, and the inhabitants not liberally disposed.

Liberally disposed! The high and stately Creole Dons, who claimed descent from half the noble families of Spain; the grand representatives of the De Solis, Cortez, De Velasco, De Toledo, De Zerna, De Mendoza, who lived by cattle-jobbing and by pasturing droves of mules on their farms, and who gave themselves the airs of dukes, and were as ignorant and not so well behaved as the donkeys they reared; who ate a dinner of salt and kidney-beans in five minutes, and spent an hour at their doors picking their teeth, wiping their moustaches, and boasting of the fricasees and fricandoes they had been tasting—these men liberally disposed!

They contributed nothing to the treasury of the Church, but gave the clergy considerable trouble. These Creoles particularly disliked and resented any allusion to their duty of almsgiving, and a request for charity was by them regarded as a personal affront.

Gage was soon intimate with the bishop, Dom Bernard de Salazar, a very worthy prelate, perhaps a little wee bit too fond of the good things of this present life, but otherwise most exemplary, very energetic, and as bold as a saint in reforming abuses which had crept into the Church.

Talk of abuses, and you may be sure that woman is at the bottom of them! A certain czar, whenever he heard of a misfortune, at once asked, "Who was she?" knowing that some woman had originated it. The same view may perhaps be taken of abuses and corruptions in the Church.

Dom Bernard de Salazar had the misfortune to live in a perpetual state of contest with the ladies of his flock, and the subject of dispute was chocolate. It was a brave struggle—bravely fought on both sides.

The prelate fulminated all the censures at his disposal in his ecclesiastical armoury; the ladies, on their side, made use of all the devices and intrigues stored in their little heads, and gained the day—of course.

Now the great subject of altercation was as follows. The ladies of Chiapa were so addicted to the use of chocolate, that they would neither hear Low Mass, much less High Mass, or a sermon, without drinking cups of steaming chocolate, and eating preserves, brought in on trays by servants, during the performance of divine service; so that the voice of the preacher, or the chant of the priest, was drowned in the continual clatter of cups and clink of spoons; besides, the floor, after service, was strewn with bon-bon papers, and stained with splashes of the spilled beverage.

How could that be devotion which was broken in upon by the tray of delicacies? How could a preacher warm with his subject whilst his audience were passing to each other sponge-cake and cracknels?

Bishop Salazar's predecessor had seen this abuse grow to a head without attempting to correct it, believing such a task to be hopeless. The new prelate was of better metal. He commenced by recommending his clergy, in their private ministrations, to urge its abandonment. The priests entreated in vain. "Very well," said the bishop, "then I shall preach about it." And so he did. At first his discourse was tender and persuasive, but his voice was drowned in the clicker of cups and saucers. Then he waxed indignant. "What! have ye not houses to eat and to drink in? or despise ye the church of God, and shame them that have not? What shall I say to you?" The ladies looked up at the pulpit with unimpassioned eyes, while sipping their chocolate, then wiped their lips, and put out their hands for some comfits.

The bishop's voice thrilled shriller and louder—he looked like an apostle in his godly indignation. Crash!—down went a tray at the cathedral door, and every one looked round to see whose cups were broken.

"What was the subject of the sermon?" asked masters of their apprentices every Sunday for the next month, and the ready answer came, "Oh! chocolate again!"

After a course on the guilt of church desecration, the bishop found that the ladies were only confirmed in their evil habits.

Reluctantly, the bishop had recourse to the only method open to him, an excommunication, which was accordingly affixed to the cathedral gates. By this he decreed that all persons showing wilful disobedience to his injunctions, by drinking or eating during the celebration of divine service, whether of Mass (high or low), litanies, benediction, or vespers, should be ipso facto excommunicate, be deprived of participation in the sacraments of the Church, and should be denied the rite of burial, if dying in a state of impenitence. This was felt to be a severe stroke, and the ladies sent a deputation

147

to Gage and the prior of the Dominican monastery of St. James, entreating them to use their utmost endeavours to bring about a reconciliation, and effect a compromise, a compromise which was to consist in Monseignor's revoking his interdict, and in their—continuing to drink chocolate.

Gage and the prior undertook the delicate office, and sought the bishop.

Salazar received them with dignity, and listened calmly to their entreaties. They urged that this was an established custom, that ladies required humouring, that they were obstinate—the prelate nodded his head—that their digestions were delicate, and required that they should continually be imbibing nourishment; that they had taken a violent prejudice against him, which could only be overcome by his yielding to their whims; that if he persisted, seditions would arise which would endanger the cause of true religion; and, finally, the prelate's life was menaced in a way rather hinted at than expressed.

"Enough, my sons!" said the bishop, with composure; "the souls under my jurisdiction must be in a perilous condition when they have forgotten that there must be obedience in little matters as well as in great. Whether I am assaulting an established custom, or a new abuse, matters little. It is a bad habit; it is sapping the foundations of reverence and morality. God's house was built for worship, and for that alone. My children must come to His temple either to learn or to pray. Learn they will not, for they have forgotten how to pray: prayer they are unused to, for the highest act of adoration the Church can offer is only regarded by them as an opportunity for the gratification of their appetites. You recommend me to yield to their vagaries. A strange shepherd would he be, who let his sheep lead him; a wondrous captain, who was dictated to by his soldiers! As for the cause of true religion being endangered, I judge differently. Religion is endangered; but it is by children's disobedience to their spiritual legislators, and by their own perversity. I am sorry for you, my sons, that you should have undertaken a fruitless office; but you may believe me, that nothing shall induce me to swerve from the course which I deem advisable. My personal safety, you hint, is endangered; my life, I answer, is in my Master's hands, and I value it but as it may advance His glory."

When the ladies heard that their request had been refused, they treated the excommunication with the greatest contempt, scoffing at it publicly, and imbibing chocolate in church, "on principle," more than ever; "Just," says Gage, "drinking in church as a fish drinks in water."

Some of the canons and priests were then stationed at the

cathedral doors to stop the ingress of the servants with cups and chocolate-pots. They had received injunctions to remove the drinking and eating vessels, and suffer the servants to come empty-handed to church. A violent struggle ensued in the porch, and all the ladies within rushed in a body to the doors, to assist their domestics. The poor clerks were utterly routed and thrown in confusion down the steps, whilst, with that odious well-known clink, clink, the trays came in as before.

Another move was requisite, and, on the following Sunday, when the ladies came to church, they found a band of soldiers drawn up outside, ready to barricade the way against any inroad of chocolate; a stern determination was depicted on the faces of the military—that if cups and saucers did enter the sacred edifice, it should be over their corpses.

The foremost damsels halted, the matrons stood still, the crowd thickened, but not one of the pretty angels would set foot within the cathedral precincts: a busy whisper circulated, then a hush ensued, and with one accord the ladies trooped off to the monastery churches, and there was no congregation that day at the minster.

The brethren of St. Dominic and of St. Francis were nothing loath to see their chapels crowded with all the rank and fashion of Chiapa; for, with the ladies came money-offerings, and they blinked at the chocolate cups for—a consideration. This was allowed to continue a few Sundays only. Our friend the bishop was not going to be shelved thus, and a new manifesto appeared, inhibiting the friars from admitting parishioners to their chapels, and ordering the latter to frequent their cathedral.

The regulars were forced to obey; not so the ladies—they would go when they pleased, quotha! and for a month and more, not one of them went to church at all. The prelate was in sore trouble: he hoped that his froward charge would eventually return to the path of duty, but he hoped on from Sunday to Sunday in vain.

Would that the story ended as stories of strife and bitterness always should end; so that we might tell how the ladies yielded at length, how that rejoicings were held and a general reconciliation effected:—but the historian may not pervert facts, to suit his or his readers' gratification.

On Saturday evening the old bishop was more than usually anxious; he paced up and down his library, meditating on the sermon he purposed preaching on the following morning—a fruitless task, for he knew that no one would be there but a few poor Mexicans. Sick at heart, he all but wished that he had yielded for peace sake, but conscience told him that such a course would have

149

been wrong; and the great feature in Salazar's character was his rigid sense of duty. He leaned on his elbows and looked out of a window which opened on a lane between the palace and the cathedral.

"Silly boy!" muttered the prelate. "Luis is always prattling with that girl. I thought better of the fair sex till of late." He spoke these words as his eyes caught his page, chattering at the door with a dark-eyed Creole servant-maid of the De Solis family. Presently the bishop clapped his hands, and a domestic entered. "Send Luis to me."

When the page came up, the old man greeted him with a half-smile.

"Well, my son, I wish my chocolate to be brought me; I could not think of breaking off that long tête-à-tête with Dolores, but this is past the proper time."

"Your Holiness will pardon me," said the lad; "Dolores brought you a present from the Donna de Solis; the lady sends her humble respects to your Holiness, and requests your acceptance of a large packet of very beautiful chocolate."

"I am much obliged to her," said the bishop; "did you express to the maiden my thanks?"

Luis bowed.

"Then, child, you may prepare me a cup of this chocolate, and bring it me at once."

"The Donna de Solis's chocolate?"

"Yes, my son, yes!"

When the boy had left the room, the old man clasped his hands with an expression of thankfulness.

"They are going to yield! This is a sign that they are desiring reconciliation."

Next day the cathedral was thronged with ladies. The service proceeded as usual, but the bishop was not present.

"How is the bishop?" was whispered from one lady to another, with conscious glances; till the query reached the ears of one of the canons who was at the door.

"His Holiness is very ill," he answered. "He has retired to the monastery of St. James."

"What is the matter with him?"

"He is suffering from severe pains internally."

"Has he seen a doctor?"

"Physicians have been sent for."

For eight days the good old prelate lingered in great suffering.

"Tell me," he asked very feebly; "tell me truly, what is my complaint?"

150

"Your Holiness has been poisoned," replied the physician.

The bishop turned his face to the wall. Some one whispered that he was dead, when he had been thus for some while. The dying man turned his face round, and said:

"Hush! I am praying for my poor sheep! May God pardon them." Then, after a pause: "I forgive them for having caused my death, most heartily. Poor sheep!"

And he died.

Since then there has been a proverb prevalent in Mexico: "Beware of tasting Chiapa chocolate."

Gage, the Dominican, did not remain long in Chiapa after the death of his patron: he seldom touched chocolate in that town unless quite certain of the friendship of those who offered it to him; and when he did leave, it was from fear of a fate like the bishop's,— he having incurred the anger of some of the ladies.

The cathedral presented the same scene as before; the prelate had laboured in vain, and chocolate was copiously drunk at his funeral.

THE PHILOSOPHER'S STONE

"There are many ways," says Del Rio, "in which the Philosopher's Stone is made. Writers contest with each other which is the right way. Pauladamus opposes the opinion of Brachescus; Villanosanus will have none of the mode of Trevisanus. So one assails another, and all call each other foolish and ignorant." But however they may have disputed how to make it, no one succeeded in finding the right way, for no one knew where to look for it; and yet the Philosopher's Stone was before all their eyes to be enjoyed by all alike, but to be appropriated by none. This precious stone, which went by various names, the "Universal Elixir," the "Elixir of Life," the "Water of the Sun," was thought to procure to its happy discoverer and possessor riches innumerable, perpetual health, a life exempt from all maladies and cares and pains, and even in the opinion of some—immortality. It transmuted lead into gold, glass into diamonds, it opened locks, it penetrated everywhere; it was the sovereign remedy to all disease, it was luminous in the darkest night. To fashion it—so the alchemists said—gold and lead, iron, antimony, vitriol, sulphur, mercury, arsenic, water, fire, earth, and air were needed; to these must be added the egg of a cock, and the spittle of doves. Really, said one shrewd and satiric writer, it only wanted oil, vinegar, and salt, to make of it a salad.

Now the curious thing is—as we shall see in the sequel—the alchemists were not far out in their opinion. All these ingredients, or rather most of them—the cock's egg and the dove's spittle only excepted—are to be found combined in the Philosopher's Stone, and only recent science has established this fact.

As the possessor of this stone was sure to be the most glorious, powerful, rich, and happy of mortals, as he could at will convert anything into gold, and enjoy all the pleasures of life, it is not surprising that the Philosopher's Stone was sought with eagerness. It was sought, but, as already said, never found, because the alchemists looked for it in just the place where it was not to be found, in their crucibles. Medals were struck on which were inscribed "Per Sal, Sulphur, Mercurium, Fit Lapis Philosophorum," which was a simplification of the receipt. On the reverse stood, "Thou Alpha and Omega of Life, Hope and Resurrection after Death." It was identified with Solomon's seal; it was called Orphanus, the One and Only. It was thought at one time that the Emperor had it in his crown, this Orphanus, and that it blazed like the sun at night; but the German emperors enjoyed so little prosperity that philosophers came to the conclusion that the stone in the imperial crown was something quite different; it brought ill-luck rather than good-fortune.

Zosimus, who lived in the beginning of the fifth century, is one of the first in Europe to describe the powers of this stone, and its capacity for making gold and silver. The alchemists pretended to derive their science from Shem, or Chem, the son of Noah, and that thence came the name alchemy, and chemistry. All writers upon alchemy triumphantly cite the story of the golden calf in the thirty-second chapter of Exodus, to prove that Moses was an adept, and could make or unmake gold at his pleasure. It is recorded that Moses was so wroth with the Israelites for their idolatry, "that he took the calf which they had made and burned it in the fire, and ground it to powder, and strewed it upon the water, and made the children of Israel drink of it." This, say the alchemists, he never could have done had he not been in possession of the Philosopher's Stone; by no other means could he have made the powder of gold float upon the water.

At Constantinople, in the fourth century, the transmutation of metals was very generally believed in, and many treatises upon the subject appeared. Langlet du Fresnoy, in his History of Hermetic

Philosophy, gives some account of these works. The notion of the Greek writers seems to have been that all metals were composed of two ingredients, the one metallic matter, the other a red inflammable matter which they called sulphur. The pure union of these substances formed gold; but other metals were mixed with and contaminated by various foreign ingredients. The object of the Philosopher's Stone was to dissolve and expel these base ingredients, and so to liberate the two original constituents whose marriage produced gold.

For several centuries after this the pursuit flagged or slept in Europe, but it reappeared in the eighth century among the Arabians, and from them re-extended to Europe. We are not going to trace the history of alchemy downwards, and see one student after another wreck his genius and time on this rock, nor see what use was made of the belief in it by impostors to enrich themselves at the expense of the credulous—we will follow the superstition upwards, and track the stone to the spring of the belief in its supernatural powers. The search for the stone will take us through strange country, give us many scrambles; but, if the reader will condescend to accompany me, I believe I shall be able to bring him to the very real and original stone itself.

The following story I give as it was told to me by some Yorkshire mill lasses, in their own delightful vernacular. I forewarn the reader that the golden ball in the story is the same as the Philosopher's Stone, as we shall hear presently:

"There were two lasses, daughters of one mother, and as they came home from t' fair, they saw a right bonny young man stand i' t' house-door before them. He had gold on t' cap, gold on t' finger, gold on t' neck, a red gold watch-chain—eh! but he had brass. He had a golden ball in each hand.[24] He gave a ball to each lass, and she was to keep it, and if she lost it, she was to be hanged. One o' t' lasses, 'twas t' youngest, lost her ball. She was by a park-paling, and she tossed the ball, and it went up, up, and up, till it went over t' paling, and when she climbed to look, t' ball ran along green grass, and it went raite forward to t' door of t' house, and t' ball went in, and she saw 't no more.

"So she was taken away to be hanged by t' neck till she were dead, acause she'd lost her ball.

["But she had a sweetheart, and he said he would get the ball. So he went to t' park-gate, but 'twas shut; so he climbed hedge, and

---

[24] In another version one ball was gold, the other silver. I sent this story to Mr. Henderson, and it is included in the first edition of his Folklore of the Northern Counties, but omitted in the second.

when he got to t' top of hedge, an old woman rose up out o' t' dyke afore him, and said, if he would get ball, he must sleep three nights i' t' house. He said he would.

"Then he went into t' house, and looked for t' ball, but couldna find it. Night came on, and he heard spirits move i' t' courtyard; so he looked out o' t' window, and t' yard was full of them, like maggots i' rotten meat.

"Presently he heard steps coming upstairs. He hid behind t' door, and was still as a mouse. Then in came a big giant five times as tall as he, and t' giant looked round, but did not see t' lad, so he went to t' window and bowed to look out; and as he bowed on his elbows to see spirits i' t' yard, t' lad stepped behind him, and wi' one blow of his sword he cut him in twain, so that the top part of him fell in t' yard, and t' bottom part stood looking out o' t' window.

"There was a great cry from t' spirits when they saw half t' giant tumbling down to them, and they called out, 'There comes half our master, give us t' other half.'

"So the lad said, 'It's no use of thee, thou pair o' legs, standing aloan at window, so go join thy brother'; and he cast the bottom part of t' giant after top part. Now when t' spirits had gotten all t' giant they was quiet.

"Next night t' lad was at the house again, and saw a second giant come in at door, and as he came in, t' lad cut him in twain; but the legs walked on to t' chimney and went up it. 'Go, get thee after thy legs,' said t' lad to t' head, and he cast t' head up chimney too.

"The third night t' lad got into bed, and he heard spirits stirring under t' bed; and they had t' ball there, and they was casting it to and fro.

"Now one of them had his leg thrussen out from under bed, so t' lad brings his sword down and cuts it off. Then another thrusts his arm out at t' other side of t' bed, and t' lad cuts that off. So at last he had maimed them all, and they all went crying and wailing off, and forgot t' ball, and let it lig there, under t' bed; and the lad took it and went to seek his true love.[25]

"Now t' lass was taken to York to be hanged; she was brought out on t' scaffold, and t' hangman said, 'Now, lass, tha' must hang by thy neck till tha' be'st dead.' But she cried out:

'Stop, stop, I think I see my mother coming!
O mother! hast brought my golden ball

---

[25] The portion within brackets I got from a different informant. The first version was incomplete; the girls had forgotten how the ball was recovered. They forgot also what happened with the second ball.

And come to set me free?'

'I've neither brought thy golden ball
Nor come to set thee free,
But I have come to see thee hung
Upon this gallows tree.'

"Then the hangman said, 'Now, lass, say thy prayers, for tha' must dee.' But she said:

'Stop, stop, I think I see my father coming!
O father! hast brought my golden ball
And come to set me free?'

'I've neither brought thy golden ball
Nor come to set thee free,
But I have come to see thee hung
Upon this gallows tree.'

"Then the hangman said, 'Hast thee done thy prayers? Now, lass, put thy head into t' noose.'

"But she answered, 'Stop, stop, I think I see my brother coming,' etc. After which she excused herself because she thought she saw her sister coming, and her uncle, then her aunt, then her cousin, each of which was related in full; after which the hangman said, 'I wee-nt stop no longer, tha's making gam o' me.' But now she saw her sweetheart coming through the crowd, and he held overhead i' t' air her own golden ball; so she said—

'Stop, stop, I see my sweetheart coming!
Sweetheart, hast brought my golden ball
And come to set me free?'

'Ay, I have brought thy golden ball
And come to set thee free;
I have not come to see thee hung
Upon this gallows tree.'"

In this very curious story, the portion within brackets reminds one of the German story of "Fearless John," in Grimm (K. M. 4), of which I remember obtaining an English variant in a chap-book in Exeter when I was a child—alas! now lost. It is also found in Iceland,[26] and is indeed a widely-spread tale. The verses are like

---

[26] Powel and Magnusson, Legends of Iceland (1864), p. 161.

others found in Essex in connection with the child's game of "Mary Brown," and those of the Swedish "Fair Gundela." But these points we must pass over. Our interest attaches specially to the golden ball. The story is almost certainly the remains of an old religious myth. The golden ball which one sister has is the sun, the silver ball of the other sister is the moon. The sun is lost; it sets, and the trolls, the spirits of darkness, play with it under the bed, that is, in the house of night, beneath the earth.

But the sun is not only a golden ball, but it is also a shining stone; and here at the outset we tell our secret: the sun is the true Philosopher's Stone, that turns all to gold, that gives health, that fills with joy.

In primeval times, our rude forefathers were puzzled how to explain the nature of sun and moon and stars, and they thought they had hit on the interpretation of the phenomenon when they said that the stars were diamonds stuck in the heavenly vault, and that the sun was a luminous stone, a carbuncle; and the moon a pearl or silver disk. Even the classic writers had not shaken off this notion. Anaxagoras, Democritus, Metrodorus, all speak of the sun as a glowing stone,[27] and Orpheus[28] calls the opal the sunstone, because of its analogy to that shining ball. So Pliny also.[29] The old Norse spoke of the stars as the "gemstones of heaven," so did the Anglo-Saxons.[30]

But perhaps the clearest idea we can have of the old cosmogony is from the pictures preserved to us of the world of the dwarfs. When a superior conception of the universe was general, then the old heathen idea sank, and what had been told of the world of men was referred to the underground world, peopled by the dwarfs, who were the representatives of the early race conquered by the Britons, and by Norse and Teuton, a race probably of Turanian origin. Our British and Anglo-Saxon and Scandinavian forefathers knew of the cosmogony of the conquered race, and came to suppose that they inhabited another world to them, a world of which the vault that overarched it was set with precious stones; and as the aboriginal inhabitants were driven to live in caves, or in huts heaped over with turf so as to be like mounds, they regarded them as a subterranean people, and their world to be underground. In a multitude of stories the trolls or dwarfs are said to live in tumuli or cairns. This is nothing more than that their hovels were made of

---

[27] Cf. Xenoph. Memor. IV. vii. 7.
[28] The apocryphal Lith. 289.
[29] "Solis gemma candida est, et ad speciem sideris in orbem fulgentes spargit radios" (Hist. Nat. xxxvi. 10, 67.)
[30] Grimm, D. M. p. 665.

sticks stuck in the ground, gathered together in the middle and turfed over. The Lapp hut, even the Icelandic farmhouse, look like grass mounds. In many tales we hear of human children carried off by the dwarfs, and when these children are recovered they tell of a world in which they have been where the light is given by diamonds and a great carbuncle set in a stony black vault.

William of Newburgh[31] says that at Woolpit (Wolf-pits), near Stowmarket in Suffolk, were some very ancient trenches. Out of these trenches there once came, in harvest-time, two children, a boy and a girl, whose bodies were of a green colour, and who wore dresses of some unknown stuff. They were caught and taken to the village, where for many months they would eat nothing but beans. They gradually lost their green colour. The boy soon died. The girl survived, and was married to a man of Lynn. At first they could speak no English; but when they were able to do so they said that they belonged to the land of St. Martin, an unknown country, where, as they were once watching their father's sheep, they heard a loud noise, like the ringing of the bells of St. Edmund's Monastery. And then, all at once, they found themselves among the reapers at Woolpit. Their country was a Christian land and had churches. There was no sun there, only a faint twilight; but beyond a broad river there lay a land of light. Giraldus Cambrensis in his Itinerary of Wales tells another queer story of the underground world, and notices that some of the words used in it are closely related to the British tongue.[32] But in neither story are the sun and stars spoken of as stones incrusting the vault.

The underground Rose-garden of Laurin the Dwarf, by Botzen, is, however, illumined by one great carbuncle.[33] The same sun-stone—a white, marvellous stone—reappears in the "Grail Story," which is from beginning to end a Christianised Keltic myth. In it the Grail is originally not invariably a basin or goblet, but a stone. It is so in Wolfran von Eschenbach's Parzival. In that there is no thought of it as a chalice: it is a stone which feeds and delights all who surround, cherish, and venerate it.

> Whatsoever the earth produces, whatsoever exhales,
> Whatever is good, and sweet, in drink and meat,
> That yields the precious stone, that never fails.

---

[31] Hist. Anglic. i. 27. See also Gervase of Tilbury, cxlv., for an account of the subterranean world reached by the cave in the Peak of Derby.
[32] Itin. Camb. i. 8.
[33] See for account of the gem-lighted underworld, Mannhardt, Germ. Mythol. (1858), p. 447.

In the Elder Edda, in the Fiölvinnsmal, Svipdagr is represented as climbing to the golden halls of heaven, and when he comes there he asks who reigns in that place. The answer given him is:—

> Menglöd is her name ...
> She here holds sway,
> And has power over
> These lands and glorious halls.

Now Menglöd means she who rejoices in the Men, the Precious Stone,[34] that is, the sun. She is the holder of the sun, as in the Yorkshire story the lass holds the golden ball.

Matthew Paris says that King Richard Cœur de Lion was wont to tell the following story:—"A rich and miserly Venetian, whose name was Vitalis, was wandering in a forest in quest of game for his table, as he was about to give his daughter in marriage. He fell into a pit that had been prepared for wild beasts, and on reaching the bottom found there a lion and a serpent. They did not injure him. By chance a charcoal-burner came that way and heard the lamentations of those in the pit. Moved with pity, he fetched a rope and ladder and released all three. The lion, full of gratitude, brought the collier meat. The serpent brought him a precious stone. The Venetian thanked him and promised him a reward if he would come to his house. The poor man did so, when Vitalis refused to acknowledge any debt, and threw the collier into prison. However, he escaped, and went with the lion and serpent before the magistrates and told them the tale, and showed them the jewel given him by the serpent. The magistrates thereupon ordered Vitalis to pay to the collier a reasonable reward. The poor man also sold the jewel for a very large sum."[35]

Richard must have heard this story in the East; there are no lions in Venetian territory. Moreover the story is incomplete. We have the same story in a fuller form in the Gesta Romanorum.

A seneschal rode through a wood and fell into a pit, in which were an ape, a lion, and a serpent. A woodcutter saved them all. Next day the woodcutter went to the castle for the promised reward, but received instead a cudgelling. The following day the lion drove to him ten laden asses, and he had them and the treasure they bore. Next day, as he was collecting wood and had no axe, the ape brought

---

[34] Egilson, Lex. poet. linguæ Sept. Men = monile, thesaurus, saxum, lapis.
[35] Roger of Wendover's Flowers of Hist., s.a. 1196. The story is an addition made to the original by Matthew Paris.

him boughs with which to lade his ass. On the third day the serpent brought him a stone of three colours, by the virtue of which he won all hearts, and came to such honour that he was appointed general-in-command of the emperor's armies. But when the emperor heard of the stone he bought it of the woodcutter. However, the stone always returned to the original owner, however often he parted with it.

The same story occurs in Gower's Confessio Amantis. The story spread throughout Europe, and is found in most collections of household tales. It occurs in Grimm's Kinder Märchen (No. 24), and in Basili's book of Neapolitan tales, the Pentamerone (No. 37).

All these were derived from the East, and were brought to Europe by the Crusaders. The story occurs in various Oriental collections. The Pâli tale is as follows:—

In a time of drought, a dog, a serpent, and a man fell into a pit together. An inhabitant of Benares draws them up in a basket, and they all promise him tokens of gratitude. The man of Benares falls into great poverty; the dog thereupon steals the king's crown whilst he is bathing, and brings it to his preserver. The man who had been helped by the other betrays him, and the preserver is imprisoned. The poor man is about to be impaled when the serpent bites the queen; and the king learns that she can only be cured by the man who is on his way to execution. So the poor fellow is brought before the prince and the whole story comes out.[36] In this version the stone does not appear; nor does it in the Sanskrit Pantschatantra.[37] But in the Mongol Siddhi-kür (No. 13) we have the stone again. A Brahmin delivers a mouse from children who teased it, then an ape, and lastly a bear. He falls into trouble and is put in a wooden box and thrown into the sea. The mouse comes and nibbles a hole in the box, through which he can breathe, the ape raises the lid, and the bear tears it off. Then the ape gives him a wondrous stone, which gives to him who has it power to do and have all he wishes. With this he wishes himself on land, then builds a palace, and surrounds himself with servants. A caravan passes and the leader is amazed to see the new palace, buys the stone of the man, and at once with it goes all the luck and splendour, and the Brahmin is where he was at first. Again the thankful beasts come to his aid. The mouse creeps into the palace of the new owner of the stone and discovers where he hides it, and with the aid of the bear and ape it is again recovered. Here we have the serpent omitted, which is the principal animal to be considered, for really the serpent is the owner of the stone that

---

[36] Spiegel, Anecdota Pâlica (1845), p. 53.
[37] Benfy, Pantschatantra (1859), ii. p. 128.

grows in its head. This idea is very general—that the carbuncle is to be found in a serpent's head. Pliny has this notion; indeed it is found everywhere.[38] The origin of this myth is that the great serpent is the heaven-god—and on the gnostic seals we have the Demiurge so represented as a crowned or nimbed serpent. In the head of this great heaven-god is the sun, the glorious stone that gives life and light and gladness and plenty. In the West the story was told that the Emperor Theodosius hung in his palace a bell, and all who needed his help were to ring the bell. One day a snake came and pulled the bell. The emperor, who was blind, came out to inquire who needed him; then he learned that a toad had invaded the nest of the serpent. So he ordered the toad to be removed. Next day the grateful serpent brought the emperor a costly stone, and bade him lay it on his eyes. When he did this he recovered his sight.

The same story is told of Charlemagne. He was summoned to judge between a toad and a serpent, and decided for the latter. In gratitude the snake brought the Emperor a precious stone. Charles gave it, set in a ring, to his wife Fastrada. It had the power to attract love. Thenceforth he was inseparable from Fastrada, and when she died he would not leave her body, but carried it about with him for eighteen years. Then a courtier removed the jewel and flung it into a hot spring at Aix-la-Chapelle. Thenceforth the emperor loved Aix above every spot in the world, and would never leave it.

In the story of Eraclius, the hero finds a stone that has the power of preserving the bearer from injury by water. Eraclius, armed with this stone, lies at the bottom of the Tiber, as one asleep, and is not drowned. In Barlaam and Josaphat the hermit undertakes to give his pupil a stone which will afford light to the blind, wisdom to fools, hearing to the deaf, and speech to the dumb.

There is a strange story in the Talmud[39] of a serpent that has a stone which gives life. A man goes in quest of it. The serpent tries to swallow the ship in which he sails. Then comes a raven and bites off the serpent's head and the sea is made red with its blood. A dragon catches the falling stone and touches the dead serpent with it; it revives and again attacks the ship. Then another bird kills the creature, and this time the man catches the stone. The power of the stone was so great that it revived salted birds that lay on the table ready to be eaten, and they flew away.

In Buddhist stories, the original signification of the marvellous stone is completely lost, as completely as in the European mediæval stories. The Indian Buddhists remembered that

---

[38] Cf. Benfy, op. cit. i. p. 214.
[39] Bababathra, 74, 6.

there was a wondrous stone of which strange stories had been told, and which possessed the most surprising powers, and they made use of the idea to illustrate their doctrine—the stone was no other than the secret of Buddha. He who attained to that was rich, happy, serene. It is called the "Tschinta-mani," that is, the Wishing-stone, because he who has it has everything that can be desired.

In the Buddhist collection of stories entitled The Wise Man and the Fool is the tale of the king's son, Gedon, who, grieved at the misery there is in the world, goes in quest of the "Tschinta-mani." He takes with him his brother Digdon. They reach a castle, where he is warned to strike at the door with a diamond bat. Then five hundred goddesses will come forth, each bearing a precious stone, but only one of these is the Wishing-stone. He must select the stone without speaking. He does so, and chooses the right one. On his way home, on board ship, a storm arises, and he is wrecked; but, as he bears the precious stone, he is not drowned, and he saves his brother. Digdon, envious, steals the stone, and puts out his brother's eyes, and goes home. Gedon follows, forgives his brother, recovers the stone and his sight.

Elsewhere the Wishing-stone is described as giving light by night as well as by day, as far as one hundred and twenty voices could be heard calling, the one catching and repeating to another; and by this light could be seen the seven kinds of treasures falling from heaven like a rain, which are offered to all.

The idea of the marvellous, luminous, enriching, health-giving stone remains, its original significance absolutely lost, and is given a new spell of life, in that it is used as a symbol of the teaching of Buddha.

In Europe, also, the idea of the marvellous stone remains; it is not used allegorically, except in the Grail myth, but it haunts men's minds; they believe in it, they suppose it must be found, and they try to manufacture it out of all kinds of ingredients.[40]

Neither Arab nor European alchemist, nor Buddhist recluse, dreamed that the stone that gave light, that nourished, that rejoiced, that enriched, was the sun shining above their heads. The conception of the sun as a stone was so old, so rolled and rubbed down, that they had no notion whence it came. The idea remained, and influenced their minds strangely; but it never occurred to them to ask whence the idea was derived.

---

[40] I said at the beginning of this article that the alchemists were right in believing the Philosopher's Stone to be complex, made up of many metals. We know now that the germ idea of the stone is the sun, and the spectroscope allows us to analyse the sun's light and discover in the solar atmosphere a multitude of metals and ingredients, in fusion.

There is something pitiful in looking at the wasted lives of those old seekers, bowed over their crucibles, inhaling noxious vapours, wearing out the nights in fruitless experiment; but, like all history, that of the alchemists teaches us a lesson—to look up instead of looking down—a lesson to seek happiness, wealth, contentment, in the simple and not the complex, in light instead of in darkness.

I believe that this is the only one of my articles in which I have drawn a moral, but the moral is so obvious that it would have been inexcusable had I passed it over. But I know that as a child I resented the applications in Æsop's Fables, and perhaps my reader will feel a like objection to having a moral appended to this essay. That I may dismiss him with a smile instead of a frown, I will close with a copy of verses extracted by me some thirty and more years ago, from—I think—a Cambridge University undergraduates' magazine, verses probably new to my readers; but as they enforce the same moral in a perfectly fresh and charming manner, and as they deserve to be rescued from oblivion, I conclude with them:

I was just five years old, that December,
And a fine little promising boy,
So my grandmother said, I remember,
And gave me a strange-looking toy:

In its shape it was lengthy and rounded,
It was papered with yellow and blue,
One end with a glass top was bounded,
At the other, a hole to look through.

'Dear Granny, what's this?' I came, crying,
'A box for my pencils? but see,
I can't open it hard though I'm trying,
O what is it? what can it be?'

'Why, my dear, if you only look through it,
And stand with your face to the light;
Turn it gently (that's just how to do it!),
And you'll see a remarkable sight.'

'O how beautiful!' cried I, delighted,
As I saw each fantastic device,
The bright fragments now closely united,
All falling apart in a trice.

Times have passed, and new years will now find me,
Each birthday, no longer a boy,
Yet methinks that their turns may remind me
Of the turns of my grandmother's toy.

For in all this world, with its beauties,
Its pictures so bright and so fair,
You may vary the pleasures and duties
But still, the same pieces are there.

From the time that the earth was first founded,
There has never been anything new—
The same thoughts, the same things, have redounded
Till the colours have pall'd on the view.

But—though all that is old is returning,
There is yet in this sameness a change;
And new truths are the wise ever learning,
For the patterns must always be strange.

Shall we say that our days are all weary?
All labour, and sorrow, and care,
That its pleasures and joys are but dreary,
Mere phantoms that vanish in air?

Ah, no! there are some darker pieces,
And others transparent and bright;
But this, surely, the beauty increases,—
Only—stand with your face to the light.

And the treasures for which we are yearning,
Those joys, now succeeded by pain—
Are but spangles, just hid in the turning;
They will come to the surface again.

B.

So the old ideas, old myths, are turned and turned about, and form new combinations, and are ever evolving fresh beauties, and teaching fresh truths. Perhaps in the consideration of these ancient myths, and seeing their progressive modifications, their breaking up, their coalitions, we may find the fresh application of the old saw, that there is nothing new under the sun.

THE END